THE LONG-SHINING WATERS

Also by Danielle Sosin

Garden Primitives

THE

LONG-SHINING

WATERS

DANIELLE SOSIN

milkweed
editions

© 2011, by Danielle Sosin
All rights reserved. Except for brief quotations in critical articles or reviews, no part of this book may be reproduced in any manner without prior written permission from the publisher: Milkweed Editions, 1011 Washington Avenue South, Suite 300, Minneapolis, Minnesota 55415.
(800) 520-6455
www.milkweed.org

Published 2011 by Milkweed Editions
Printed in Canada
Cover design by Christian Fuenfhausen
Author photo by Ken Bloom
Interior design by Rachel Holscher
The text of this book is set in Warnock Pro.
11 12 13 14 15   5 4 3 2 1
First Edition

Please turn to the back of this book for a list of the sustaining funders of Milkweed Editions.

Library of Congress Cataloging-in-Publication Data

Sosin, Danielle, 1959–
    The long-shining waters / Danielle Sosin. — 1st ed.
        p.   cm.
    ISBN 978-1-57131-083-5
    1. Superior, Lake—Fiction.   I. Title.
    PS3569.O714L66 2011
    813'.6—dc22

                                        2011002077

This book is printed on acid-free paper.

For
Lucien Orsoni . . . "for the cry-eye"

and for

My father, Henry Sosin . . . for always

The eagle, the eagle
Patient like him
From the rocks on high
You will perceive a lake . . .

From an Ojibwe hunting song

THE LONG-SHINING WATERS

1622

The cold wind off the lake sets the pines in motion, sets their needled tops drawing circles in the sky. It cuts through boughs and they rise and fall, dropping snow that pits the white surface below. The hardened leaves rattle and sail, and the limbs of the paper birch sway, holding the sky in heavy wedges.

The dark bundle, like the nest of a squirrel. Dark bundle, tiny corpse, lurching with the branches against the sky as the big water, Gichigami, slings against the shore. Spray over ice-covered rocks.

In long dark lines, the waves advance, crowding together as they near the shore, mounting and breaking over themselves, leaping at the rocks like wolves. The wind keens, causing branches to knock and deadfall to creak in the frozen forks of trees. The dark bundle rocks on its limb, in the dark sky, above trackless snow.

The waves like wolves leap over each other, toss sea foam from their open mouths. They hit the rocks and fall back again, only to rise howling and leaping, hitting and falling back again, until one after another they paw over the rocks, escape from the churning water, pads icing up in the snow, yellow eyes and patches of grey fur blowing.

Surging, they leap into the woods, dark lips curled over bared white teeth, toward the tree where the bundle churns in the sky. Yellow eyes and blowing grey fur, cracking branches, cold dry wind in their teeth.

Her hand. The woven mat. Night Cloud's sleeping back. Dreaming. Another dream. Grey Rabbit's eyes dart like tiny fish as crouched wolves shift shape around her, expanding in edgeless and rolling shadows. The wigwam is full of the heavy sounds of sleep: her two sons, her husband, his mother.

Grey Rabbit blows at the fire, causing the embers to sparkle orange and ash to lift like feathers from the coals. Again, and the new wood crackles into flame. Her family lies undisturbed, their feet pointing toward the warmth. The air is close. Night Cloud's low snore. All the bodies softly rising and falling as if she were rocking in a sea of breath. Breath and shadow moving the bark walls. The fire whistles, but no one stirs.

Since the first snow of winter she's seen children in her dreams. In danger and in death they come to her, taking the place of rest and worrying her days. She crouches near her two sleeping boys. Standing Bird looks strong and defiant, the jut of his chin set toward manhood even as his spirit journeys. But Little Cedar, limbs askew beneath the furs, looks vulnerable and warm cheeked. His eyelids flutter and then stop moving. She searches his face for traces of hunger. Again, Night Cloud returned without game.

The corpse, abandoned, sways on a limb. The heavy sky. The sharp-toothed wolves.

She won't speak of the things she's shown at night. She won't tell anyone about the children of her dreams. She smoothes the hair off Little Cedar's forehead. Her family needs her, especially now, with the food cache dwindling and no fresh meat to replace what they take. She'll walk steady as the sun for them, even as the specters of winter sweep down.

Quietly, Grey Rabbit feels through her pouch, clasps for a moment the banded red agate that Little Cedar gave her. She draws a heavy fur around her shoulders and ducks out into the darkness.

Bullhead rolls over to see the door flap close, feels the cold air sweeping in. Again, her son's wife leaves in the night.

Grey Rabbit stands motionless until the fire pit emerges, and then the first ring of pines with their high jagged tops that point like arrows to the sky. Her path cuts through low spruce, then rises along the birch-covered slope that protects their camp from the north's killing winds. She tries to make her way in silence, to draw no attention in her direction, but her skins swish against the snow as she moves through the vertical weave of white trunks.

The ridge is home to massive old pines. She can feel their reaching boughs above her, feel the thinness of her skin. The grove possesses a frightful strength, yet she has always sensed goodness in its spirit. She rests a moment against the rough trunk of a tree, her heart drumming in her ears, then makes her way to the windswept ledge.

The shore below is ice locked and still, strewn with boulders cleaved from the cliff. The last time she'd come, Gichigami was raging. She'd made her offering despite her fear, there, in the presence of the underwater spirits and the one who churned the waters with his serpentine tail. The waves were smashing against the rocks, wild like hair, swirling white, whipping strands, and the water leapt and pounded, shattering the moon.

Grey Rabbit kneels and digs down through the snow. She places tobacco on the cold rock and a birch-bark dish that holds a small bit of the good berry. She opens herself to Gichi-Manitou, the Great Mystery, as the wind blows cold against her face, and her nose stiffens with the smell of frozen waves. She asks for favor for her family, and that Little Cedar be protected. She asks to understand her dreams.

The ice cracks and pings down the shoreline, echoing off the high cliff. There's no moon on the water, just shadows of ice. Just sharp cold air against her forehead, and clouds of breath in front of her face.

2000

Nora reaches for the nail that holds the Christmas lights, her breath fogging against the mirror behind the bar, when something from her dream takes form, a feeling almost as much as an image, causing an empty swirling inside. She kneels on the bar stool and closes her eyes, hoping her mind might retrieve a scrap. But no. Nothing. It is usually like that, just a little sliver of something when she's awake that had been part of something bigger. She moves her stool against the double-door cooler, bumping the new calendar that slides down on its magnet. January, again, already. The string of Christmas lights sags low—green, pink, yellow, blue—doubled and swinging in the barroom mirror as she lowers them from the nail.

There. She tugs her sweater down, her mood deflating at the sight of the mirror without the lights. They add a bright touch to the Schooner's atmosphere, given the cold short days of a northern Wisconsin winter. Nora stands before the mirror, winding the string of lights. Her roots are starting to show again. She's going to stick with the new copper color. It gives her more oomph than the brownish red. Reaching for her cigarette, she finds just a long piece of ash in the ashtray. It seems to always go like that, light one and get distracted or stuck at the other end of the bar. The clock reads 3:40 AM, bar time. Len won't come to clean for a couple more hours.

There's something about taking down Christmas decorations that always makes her feel empty. It's like after the movies when the lights come on, the story's done, and there she is, sitting with her coat in her lap. Sometimes she even gets the feeling at home in the silence of her apartment, after the TV twangs off.

Two by two Nora pulls bottles off the back bar to get at the strings of lights taped to the riser. The idea for the riser lights came years before, when her mirror swag fell in the middle of a rush. At the time, she was too busy to care, so she kept on working with the lights back in the bottles, and she grew to like the way they shone through. Pink in the vodka. A warm glow behind the brandy.

Well, it can't be Christmas all the time, and cleaning's the best way she knows to start over. The sharp smell of vinegar rises as it mixes with the steaming tap water. Nora pours herself a vodka, and with timing that is second nature, rights the bottle and reaches back, turning off the faucet.

Footsteps cross overhead, followed by the sound of a bench scraping across the floor. She smiles as she wrings the rag, then wipes the riser with long strokes, her attention on the ceiling, listening. Rose's piano music drops down through the floor, slightly muffled and otherworldly. Angelic—the firm piano chords and the tinkly upper notes. The softest, sweetest sounds come from that tough old girl.

Nora hums and eyes the ornaments as she wipes the bottles and stands them back in place. The ornaments are everywhere— hooked into the netting that drapes from the ceiling with the glass floats and corks and the life preservers, hung from the rigging of the model schooner that's displayed on its own shelf by the pool table. All around her, pieces of her history are dangling from thin threads. Nora swishes her rag in the bucket of water, wrings it, and wipes down the bottle of Crown.

The Indian girl with the papoose was a gift from Delilah, their best cook in the boom days, before the mines shut down. Those years were nearly fatal for the towns on the Iron Range. Superior got plenty bruised as well, with its railroad and shipping industry. But she's not complaining, she's been luckier than most. The last things to belly up in any town are its bars; well, its churches, too. She dumps the old water into the sink.

A waltz. The piano music feels just right as Nora pushes a chair around the floor, climbing up and down to get the ornaments from the nets. She unhooks the log cabin that Ralph, her late husband, made entirely of whittled sticks. Together for seven years, married for three. The cabin twirls in a circle from an old piece of leather. That's twenty-four years she's run the bar on her own.

She climbs down and sets the ornaments on a table. The silver angels holding hands like paper dolls. The elf on the pinecone from her sister Joannie in California, reminding her that she needs to mail a birthday gift. The old rusty red caboose. She'll wrap them each in tissue paper and tuck them snugly in a box, like little children off to sleep.

Nora slides the chair up against the jukebox to get at the ornaments hung from the old bowsprit. The glass bird looks like it swallowed the pink jukebox light. It came in on a salty all the way from Greece. She smoothes the bird's feathered tail between her fingers, then unhooks her daughter's plaster handprint, painted green and red but only on one side. She'd thought about having her granddaughter make one so Janelle could hang them side by side on their tree. She'd even thought of making one herself, a trio going three generations. It was a good idea, but she never made it happen. They were barely in town long enough to open gifts as it was.

The music stops abruptly. The bench scrapes out.

Nora climbs down from the chair, holding the Santa straddling an ore boat that John Mack gave her. It's been two years now, and the bar is still absorbing his death. When in port, he was a fixture—last stool on the left—always trying to start up his debate: Lake Superior, is it a sea or a lake? Telling his sailing stories to anyone who'd listen: sudden storms coupled with poorly loaded freight, nasty tricks played on green deckhands. She wraps the freighter in a piece of crumpled tissue paper, seeing his speckled blue eyes, how they'd draw people in as he spun his tales. Landforms changing shape. Strange sounds from the horizon. It's still unbelievable that after years on those freighters, he fell out of his fishing boat and died of hypothermia. They found his body the morning of her fifty-fifth birthday.

The sky through the window is tinted orange from the glow of the neon Leinenkugel's sign. Nora opens the door to the empty street and the steely smell of winter coming in from the ore docks. Lake Superior may bring in her business, but it's heartless; you wouldn't catch her on it for anything.

It's snowing again, tiny flakes like salt, dropping through the streetlight halos. There's not even a car to be seen, not a single black track on the street's white surface. The tiny flakes drop down from the blankness, landing on her sweater and the toes of her shoes. The chimney on the VFW is a silhouette against the sky. There was something in her dream. She's carried it all day.

Nora feels the cold air reach her lungs, feels the particular time of night where it seems like she's the only one awake, the only witness to the snowy street, to the air blowing in from the frozen harbor, and the small falling flakes that are touching everything.

1902

Snow sweeps past the window on a northwest wind coming down from the hills toward the lake. Berit feels like her cabin is a rock in a river, the way the wind rushes past on either side, full of snow and icy crystals. She turns from the back window by the bed to the front one that looks over the water. The snow is flying nearly horizontal, blowing out over their frozen cove, reaching the open water in dark strips of agitation that chase, one after another, toward a vague grey horizon.

Down at the fish house the window is blank. Gunnar hasn't lit his lamp. He is bent, she is sure, over his task, straining his eyes and leaning in some posture that she will have to rub out of him later. Sometimes she wishes he'd slow down. Everything in sight, he built single handedly. The fish house is a beauty—two stories, and now the new net reel standing beside it to replace the one that the gale took last year. Extra things, too, that he makes just to please her, like the bench out at the end of the point, where she can lean back against the old pine. "You can sit there and watch your lake," he teases. But it's true in a sense, the lake is hers. First, she lived on Michigan's Keweenaw Peninsula, then Duluth, now Minnesota's North Shore.

A gust of wind hits the cabin so hard that Berit feels like she's been shoved. The hill is in full whip and bend, the pine boughs winding back and forth as if hurling invisible stones, and the birch she'd admired just that morning, sweeping down the slope like a wedding veil, have completely turned in temperament. They lurch, bend, and jostle together, knock and stir like an army of skeletons. She holds her hand to the chinking between the logs to feel for any biting lines of cold. Wedding veils to skeletons. Her thoughts do grow strange.

The smell of bread is a comfort with the storm coming down, and she's glad it's baking day as she wipes the spilled flour from the tabletop, strip by strip bringing back the wood planks, the wet wood making her think of spring, as most anything does these days. It will be a relief when the steamship starts running again. Steady mail and fresh supplies. She swishes her rag in the tepid wash water. Four years they've been up the shore. She thought the isolation would get easier. She pauses, frowns. She thought there would be children.

Again, she finds herself stationed at the window, her damp fingers touching the cold glass. Soon the steamship will dare venture out. Just knowing she'll pass by regularly makes everything easier, marks those days apart from the others, even if it's just Gunnar rowing his fish out, to be transported back to Duluth. She closes her eyes—the boat's heavy bow plying the icy water of the lake. She can almost hear the low drub of her engine, the way it bounces off the rocks.

Her fingers leave small marks on the windowpane and she touches their cold tips against her cheek. She must stop indulging this way. It only makes it worse and the boat slower in coming, but her mind is as reinable as the wind on the water, and her thoughts rush out one after the next. News from her family on the Keweenaw. Fresh coffee beans. A sweet squirting orange.

A stream of snow is blowing off the roof of the fish house,

where finally, the lamp is lit. She'll bring down a piece of fresh bread on her way to fetch water. Berit surveys her cooling loaves, smelling the deep rye and yeast. She'd love to plunge her hands right in, wear a loaf around like a fancy muff. She'll cut a thick piece from the best-shaped one and bring it to Gunnar still warm.

Gunnar glances up from his net seam to see Berit in her dark coat, making her way down the snowy path, buckets in one hand, a dark bundle in the other, walking with her crooked limp that he loves. His Mrs. with something good for him, braving the wind to make a delivery. Already his mouth is watering, thinking of all the baking she'd done. The door opens with a wave of cold air, and there she is stamping her feet, a long strand of hair flung across her red cheeks, her grey eyes blinking away the snow.

"It's blowing," she says, nudging the cat from her leg.

"Yah, it sure came down quick." He flexes his fingers and then cracks them loudly, which doesn't get the usual rise out of her. "Something smells good in here."

Berit hands him the warm bundle, which he makes a ceremony out of opening. "Now, this is surely a piece of heaven." He holds the bread under his nose, then smiles as if she'd given him spring's first strawberries. He takes a bite and sets the bread on his workbench. "Heaven. But I smell earthly paradise nearby." He grabs hold of her coat and still chewing, slowly draws her near.

Berit jerks her coat away. "I'm sure you'll make do with your bit of heaven."

She scoffs as she opens the door, but Gunnar can see that her eyes are shining. The warm rye nearly dissolves in his mouth. What a figure she cuts as she heads down the path, dangling buckets in the fading light. He raps on the windowpane with a lead, just to get her to turn around.

Berit's cheeks are flushed, but not from the wind. She hears the tap tapping beneath the blowing, but she's not going to look back. Thoughts of their morning give her stabs of pleasure. The things between them these days, she just doesn't know. She'd never imagined this new hunger that has taken hold, that rises like heat and falls like good rain. To experience this now after all they'd been through, all the sorrow, disappointment, and anger, just all of it. Betrayed by her body, that's how the loss felt. And then that sad year of distance.

Now those times seem long ago, though it was only last autumn when everything changed. She still puzzles about the suddenness, and how it seems to point to the day when Gunnar was so late from picking his nets. She recalls the strange pauses in his work rhythm, and the way he kept glancing back out to the water. She can still see clearly the look in his eyes as he took the fish shovel from her hands, so full, and brimming with such a grave gentleness. "It's time," he'd said. "We have each other. That's blessing in plenty." Those were his words, and then he'd kissed her.

Since then he'd been a man determined, wooing her back slowly and sweetly. Now there are whole other worlds they share, places they go that are almost like dreaming. She just isn't certain what's proper sometimes. Good Lord, when she thinks of Nellie and Hans down the shore, or in the other direction the Torgeson brood. Well, she just can't picture it.

The little light that's left is fading fast, but the wind has yet to die down, making the snowfall nearly invisible, though she feels it like tiny needles against her skin. Berit steps onto the ice. Covered with wavering lines of old snow, it looks like a floor of grey marble. She's smiling at how Gunnar had tugged on her coat when a gust of wind catches her buckets and she slips, banging her knee on the ice.

With a foot in one bucket to keep it from rolling, she lowers the other into the water hole, paying attention to her task now. In the dim light, the water hole is black and foreboding. It sets her insides against themselves, causing her to feel strangely cautious, as if she might pull the bucket from the lake and find it filled not with water, but with some horror instead. She hauls the rope up, and there it is, a pail of water with a small piece of ice, but its harmlessness doesn't ease her feeling, so she works with haste and turns back toward land and the light from Gunnar's window, lying yellow across the snow.

From below, the surf churns grey and white. It billows like the bottoms of clouds, creates a sound like rolling barrels, or the distant muffled stampede of hooves.

What prickling sensation at the precipitous drops—one hundred feet, two hundred feet, and more—where the slow-growing fish feed. The herring and the whitefish I once sought. The rising siscowet and the trout. Suspended overhead like long dark shoes. Like deeds left undone. The shape of regret.

On the lake bed the sediment rests in layers. Grey matter from the north. Red from the south. One era's story deposited over the next.

And my own story, to which I cling.

Yet all this, too, is somehow mine.

I see the relic surfaces bearing the scour marks of ice. The fine, flowing patterns etched in the rock are as my own fingerprints.

Dimpled silt. The solitary burbot swims.

Ringed vibrations surge and rebound.

And rivers of mud waves lie in long troughs. Each red clay canyon has its own dark sounding. Each cave, a pulsating entrance.

The roaming currents carry the whisper of words. Bimitigweyaa. Bon voyage. I try to understand.

2000

The long blue door of Nora's Buick creaks. Creaks when she opens it and creaks when she shuts it. She tightens the scarf around her neck. Even though she'd started the car earlier, the darned heater is still blowing cold air. The streets are icy and driving is slow with the grey sky pressing down on the buildings, making everything look so squat and dingy that in comparison, the traffic light is dazzling. Bright red, it hangs over the intersection, shining like a perfect maraschino cherry.

The Schooner's pretty quiet, just a few second-shifters, though it won't be long until business picks up. The locks are open again, and the ice cutters are out. Once the ships can pass, the railroad, everything, will start swinging into gear. Still, winter is hardly over.

Nora shoves the door to the bar open, causing the green shamrocks she'd hung from the netting to twirl and glint in the low light. Willard waves from the kitchen at the end of the bar, where he's dropping a basket into the fryer.

"It's freezing." Nora hangs her coat.

"No lie. Listen, do you mind if I split? Cheryl is sick, so with the kids getting home. . . . I haven't restocked the longboy yet."

Nora lights her first cigarette of the shift. "How was the day?"

Willard shrugs.

"I hope she doesn't have that stomach flu. Len had it, he said it was killer."

"Yeah, but short. She's just wiped out."

"Did Finn come by about the stove? He was supposed to show up around ten."

"Nope." Willard slides his arm into his jacket.

"Did he call?"

"Nope. I'll see you tomorrow. You're the best. Hey," he says, turning from the door, "the fries are for the guy shooting pool."

Nora raises the metal basket and shakes off the hot grease, then dumps the fries into a hotel pan lined with paper towels. She puts out ketchup and a napkin dispenser. "Fries," she calls toward the back of the bar.

She'll have to try and reach Finn again. Jesus. That's twice he hasn't showed. It's bad enough not to come when you say you will, but it's plain disrespectful to not even call.

A tall boy straddles a stool and leans his pool cue against the bar. "Did you know the table is crooked back there?" He shakes salt and then pepper over the basket.

"There's nothing wrong with my table, it's the floor that's crooked." How's she supposed to handle a rush on burgers when half the grill won't heat?

"They're adjustable, you know. All you have to do is screw them up or down from the legs."

Seriously, she's not in the mood. He looks like a college kid, with pale hair that falls in an *I could care less* sort of way. "You can? My God, you're a regular genius." She leans in with a tone of voice honed glass-sharp over the years. "I can't imagine how I ever got by before you set yourself on that stool."

"Schooner." Nora clamps the phone between her ear and shoulder. "He's not here, Bev. I know, hon, try the 22."

"Excuse me."

It's the kid again, flush cheeked and looking sheepish. "Excuse me, but could I please have some mustard?"

Nora sets a fresh squeeze bottle on the bar.

"Thanks," he says, and then, "I'm sorry." His words come out in a near-whisper.

She wasn't expecting an apology. With the kids, it's mostly know-it-all attitude.

"Forget it." She puts a little sweetness in her voice, but now the boy won't meet her eye. Nora watches him in the mirror, his chin propped in one hand while his long arm moves like a crane, lifting and dropping to the basket for fries. "That table's been trouble for years," she offers. Still, he won't look up at her.

Nora opens the longboy to check her stock, jotting a quick list on an order pad. In the back room, she makes up a mixed case. Finn's the one she'd like to have words with. She really is trying to watch herself. She knows how people can react so differently. Some are like frying pans where everything slides off, some are like mirrors—back at you in a flash, but some are like water—touch them anywhere and you're in.

The boy is halfway through the basket already. Nora sets the case of beer on the floor behind the bar. "If you want to try and fix the table, I'll take care of your tab. I don't have a level, but you can eyeball it with a water pitcher. The footing slips back, though. It won't last long."

"Really?" the boy lifts his head.

"I'm Nora Truneau." She extends her hand.

The boy wipes his fingers across a napkin, takes her hand and gives a bow with his head. "Deets."

"Well, Deets, welcome to the Schooner."

There's the sound of footsteps down the back stair, then a crack of blue dusk and a shot of icy air. Nora pours a Manhattan, double cherries, and places it in front of Rose's stool, where she lands like a bird on a limb, her hair dark and wiry with streaks of white, her bony shoulders settling in.

"How are things?" Nora asks.

Rose just nods and looks at her with those large, brown, ever-startling eyes. They dominate her face, but it's not just their size. It's the way they contrast with the rest of her body—small, rickety, almost brittle—but then those big eyes, always liquid and swimming, like two dark dams barely holding.

"Rose, this is Deets."

"Pleased." Rose nods, lifting her hand in front of her mouth.

"Did you lose your bridge again?" Nora asks, shoving the warm bottles to the back of the cooler, feeling the sliver of protectiveness that has worked its way under her skin in the years since Rose became her tenant.

"It's not lost," Rose says, skimming her lowball in its wet spot on the bar as if it were circling in its own private skating rink. "It's somewhere up there." She lifts her chin toward the ceiling.

How she can keep track of anything, Nora doesn't know. Not that her place is messy, it's just full. She has all of Buck's stuff still around—his accordion on the chair, his guitars and drum, even his shaving brush on the shelf in the bathroom.

The beer-after-work folks are starting to drift in, and Nora's glad to be picking up the pace. She turns the news on over the bar, catching bits of it as she works. A train derailed near Ashland, groundwater toxic waste, Native American treaty rights, then clips of the lake in a year-ago storm, the waves crashing over the shipping channel walls. "You ready for another?" she calls to Deets, who is on his knees in back, examining the pool table.

Rose reaches up and bats at a shamrock, setting it spinning in the TV light. "He'll never get that leg to stick."

Nora shrugs. "Yeah, I know."

"Do you remember that Irish commercial with all the green fields? That's what these make me think of. What was it for?"

"Soap. Irish Spring." Nora knocks a cigarette from her pack, and a lighter appears in front of her. "Thanks," she says to Deets, who seems fully recovered.

"Wouldn't spring in Ireland smell like sheep shit?" he says.

Nora lets out a smoke-choked laugh.

"Aye, lassie." He feigns a thick brogue and leans toward Rose. "Ya smell as ripe as my field boots, ya do."

It's Nora's big laugh this time, coming right from the gut. "What do they have now, comedy majors at the college?"

That one gets a cackle out of Rose.

"I don't know. I've been out for ages."

Nora is a bit surprised. She's usually on the money with people's age. "What are you doing still in town?"

"I'm not. I just moved here. I came for the lake." He flashes her a knowing smile.

"The lake?" Nora wets a rag in the sink. "You moved here for the lake?"

"I've always wanted to live here. My uncle has a cabin on the Canadian border. I used to spend half the summer up there. You know, hunting for agates, scouting for boats. Oh man, the night sky on that beach. The black sea of stars. That's what my uncle calls it. It felt more like home than my real home."

"That lake's an ass-cracker," Rose says into her lowball.

"I can't explain it, but I've always known I'd live here. I might learn to dive and try timber retrieval. There's wood on the bottom from the logging days."

"Old-growth trees." Rose sips her drink. "I saw it on TV. Rich people want the wood for building, and people who make instruments, too. I wonder how an old-growth piano would sound."

"My real dream is to work on a freighter. But I have to find out what it takes to do it."

"I can tell you what it takes to work the ships." Nora points to the pool table. "Either balls bigger than those, or else a very small brain. Don't you know people die out there? You've got half an hour in that water if you're lucky."

"I'm a good swimmer."

"It's not about swimming. It's about hypothermia. Why not live somewhere warm, like California? I've got a sister out there, and it's all palm trees and sunshine. When I talked to her this morning she was drinking coffee on her patio. Really." Nora wipes the bar. "If I were your age I'd turn tail and head west."

"I recall your tail turning plenty at his age." Rose stubs out her cigarette.

"Don't you believe a word she says."

"How about that infamous night down at Tony's?"

"All right. Fine. You two can reminisce. I've got work to do."

Nora gathers empties from the floor, stopping to chat with Ed and his crew, who are occupying the long table in front, then cleaning the mess left by Jimmy D., who can't drink a bottle of beer without peeling off the label bit by bit and rolling the paper into little balls. She sets the empties on the bar. She likes to get to them early on, before the beery film dries inside.

"Schooner." Nora has the phone on her shoulder while she scrubs a pair of glasses on the brushes.

"Listen, don't get mad, okay? I know we're supposed to come down on Friday, but it looks like it's not going to work out."

Nora dunks the glasses into the rinse tub, then sets them on the drying rack.

"Mom?"

"Janelle, I already did the shopping. And I promised Nikki a trip to the bowling alley."

"Yeah, she told me about it. Do they have special times that are kid-appropriate?"

"It's bowling. There aren't any special times, except during leagues." The silence on the other end of the line is loud. "Is there a problem with bowling?"

"It's just not going to work, Mom. We've got a lot going on. It'll be better for everyone if we make it another time."

"Well, that depends how you define *everyone*." Nora puts two more glasses on the brushes. She had a feeling this was going to happen again. "Where's my Bun? Does she like her purple rabbit?"

"Nikki loves everything that comes from you, Mom."

"Put her on."

"She's away on a playdate. I already told her the weekend is cancelled. You could come here. I'm not the only one with a car."

Nora stops scrubbing. "I work Saturday night," she says in a measured tone. "I always work on Saturday night." She places the glasses on the rack and takes on another pair of dirties. Again, there's nothing but silence on the line. Nora keeps her eyes on the brushes as she works.

"Look, I'm busy," she says finally. "I really can't talk now."

"I can hear you washing glasses. You can't be that busy."

Nora looks blankly around the bar, catches Rose giving her a sympathetic look. The water sloshes in the stainless steel sink. There's the sound of quarters being pumped into the cigarette machine, then the rod being pulled and the metallic thwack back, followed by a soft thud.

1622

Grey Rabbit struggles to get to the surface, where patches of light undulate and swaths of color twirl in icy clouds. The pressure in her chest is a frozen boulder. She works her arms to push herself upward, kicking her legs with all her strength, but it's slow, slow, the water's thick as wind and she has to fight to move through it. Her chest feels like it will burst apart. She is nearly there. She kicks and flails, at last propelling herself up and free.

But no, there is no relief. And there, above her, the taunting surface, twirling and swaying clear and ice blue, and then a child splashes in. The girl's face wavers, growing huge and then small. Her eyes closed, her mouth a blue pucker. Grey Rabbit beats at the water like a frantic bird, trying to rise up and reach the child with her arms, but there is pressure against them, something holding her down, no, pulling, now lifting her upward, nearer and nearer to the sloshing light. Her face breaks the surface, and she gasps for air, mouths the dry brown emptiness around her. The child. She sees the tawny brown roof of her wigwam, then Bullhead's broad back, turning away.

She's no longer underwater; her spirit is in her body. The sky through the smoke hole is purple. Her stomach tightens. Food. They need food. Bullhead is making a soft clicking noise with her mouth. "There's fresh snow," she says. "The tracking will be good. Night Cloud will take Standing Bird along." She stirs the fire and disappears out the door flap.

The girl's round face, her lips a blue pucker. The image propels Grey Rabbit upright. Across the fire, her sons lay curled and sleeping. From outside come the sounds of Bullhead laying wood. Her words were neither reproachful nor angry, though Grey Rabbit sensed something between them meant for her. She drops her head as shame moves through her, quick as fire in dry grass. She should have been up and tending to her work, but instead she has let all the weight fall on Bullhead.

At the log on the slope above their camp, Grey Rabbit loosens her clothing and squats, her sleep-warmed skin meeting the cold air. The smell of wood smoke lifts through the trees. Around her, the pines hold dots of snow in their bark, and everything is purple and newly rounded—the wigwam like an overturned bowl, the spruce boughs splayed like thick dark hands. Below, mist rises from Gichigami, veiled and shifting, growing thicker with the light. Soon the water will be entirely hidden, transformed into a vast land of cloud.

Grey Rabbit pushes snow over the hole her urine carved, feels the new sharpness of her hip bones and a slight dizziness as she stands.

Slowly she descends, apart, watching, her sons sitting near the fire, Night Cloud returning from the direction of the river. His path leaves a dark line in the snow.

Night Cloud looks up to see his wife moving gingerly down the slope. Thinning. And quiet as a winter tree. He must make a sizable kill. He had placed another offering at the river cave. He finds tracks, scat, and bedding places, but the animals will not show themselves.

He raises a hand in greeting as she nears. Her moods, too, are a growing concern. But then she has good reason to be dissatisfied with him. "New snow." He musters a hopeful tone as they meet. She nods and only half smiles. "The day feels good," he says cheerfully.

"You made another offering?"

Night Cloud places a reassuring hand on her shoulder and tries to hold her eyes with his own, but her gaze slips away from him. She gestures toward Little Cedar, who sits near the fire, poking sluggishly at the snow with a stick.

"In the last new snow, he romped like an otter," she says. "He's not old enough to fast."

"He is often slow to wake."

"Yes, but still. . . ."

"He's strong," says Night Cloud, pushing aside her words, as they approach the boys at the fire. "It's a good depth for tracking." He nods at them, and sweeps his arm over the snow.

"How soon will we leave? I brought the pull-sled." Standing Bird assumes a tall posture, hoping that his father will notice the things he's already gathered for the hunt, and the skillful way he's begun to pack.

"Be patient. We will start soon enough. Come, Little Cedar," Night Cloud beckons to his youngest. "I'll fashion a target for you in the woods. You can practice with your bow while I am gone."

Standing Bird turns away, hands on his hips, as Little Cedar hops off his stump, poking him in the back with his stick as he passes.

The early morning veil has lifted, leaving the afternoon sharply defined. The white plains of snow, the clear sky, the big water ruffled like the wing of a dark blue bird.

Grey Rabbit sits sewing a rabbit-fur hat, though her mind has wandered back to the morning, to the pride she'd felt watching Standing Bird pack the pull-sled. Part man, he is, but still part boy. Part mink the way he changes color to match his father. "Listen well," she'd warned as they set out. "Stay within hearing distance of your father." And though disquiet had lodged like a burr in her skin, she'd made an effort to join the joking and the rain of banter as Night Cloud and Standing Bird walked north into the hills. They left behind the long tracks of their snow-shoes, now grey vines in the bright white snow.

Grey Rabbit turns the hat over in her hands and runs her fingers through the soft white fur. It will be warm and cover Standing Bird's ears well. She glances at Bullhead across the fire, at work on the seam of a birch-bark container. Little Cedar is in the near woods aiming his small bow at the piece of hide his father had fastened to a tree trunk. He misses his mark, puts his hands on his hips, then plods through the snow to re-trieve his arrow.

"Do you think they will find game?" Grey Rabbit breaks the silence. Bullhead doesn't reply. The unanswerable question is left echoing in her mind as she pets the soft fur and stares up at the ridge.

Bullhead watches Grey Rabbit worry the hat's fur, her eyes on the ridge, but her eyes unseeing. The girl has always been one to wander far, but this is not a time to indulge. Bullhead runs a length of a fiber between her fingers and tests its strength before working it through the hole in the birch bark. More than once, she has awakened to find Grey Rabbit gone, or hovering over the boys as they sleep. And then, come morning, the girl won't wake. Bullhead takes a deep breath, trying to quell her irrita-tion. Something's not right. She mulls over their circumstances, but there seems little to interpret. The cold has not been un-relenting. The snow has not grown too deep to hunt. Could it be that the spirits are unhappy with her son? If they are, they all have much to fear. For its power, she had given him her nugget of pink copper, tied in a piece of soft skin. She'd slipped it into his hand as he left.

Out beyond the frozen shallows, the light plays on the deep blue water like tossed handfuls of tiny suns. Bullhead works her fiber slowly along the seam, each stitch a question, another worry. Has hunger set upon the others, those camped back in the hills, or at hunting grounds along the shore? And what of her sister, Three Winds? She'd been weak with illness at the end of the fall ricing. She sees her sister's party as they pad-dled away, grew small, then rounded the point, out of sight. If their hunts have been fruitless, too. . . . She stops her mind from weaving the thoughts. At Sugarbush she'll hear all the news. She won't weave a web for herself from which she will be unable to escape. No. She pictures Three Winds tending a fire, roasting an enormous moose flank, which crackles and drips. Bullhead swallows. Her stomach knots.

Tonight, over the fire, she'll tell a Nana'b'oozoo story. One where despite his spirit powers, his human side lands him in a bundle of trouble. A romping tale of summer mischief, which will make everyone laugh out loud. And if the spirits allow, it will come with such vividness they'll hear the sweet birdsong, smell pine pitch and frogs. But now it is she who stares into the air while Grey Rabbit works steadily on the hat.

"Look," shouts Little Cedar.

Grey Rabbit is on her feet, Bullhead behind her in the snow.

"What is it?" Grey Rabbit calls, but Little Cedar only jumps and gestures, nodding toward the big water.

There's something large and white on the horizon, much larger than the patches of light around it. It's not blinking, but shining steadily.

Grey Rabbit's dream comes flooding back. The child's wavering face, its awful blue lips. Dead. She's sure. The child was dead. She grabs hold of Little Cedar's clothes.

The strange light lingers on the horizon, and the great horned serpent swims through her thoughts. He could have easily held her underwater, helpless to reach the floating child. She tugs Little Cedar closer. "Did it speak to you? Do you hear anything?"

Little Cedar shakes his head, and sidles up flush against her leg.

Grey Rabbit searches the horizon, then the open water near shore. She turns to Bullhead, her eyes dark with fear.

"A big sheet of ice, shining in the sun," says Bullhead, nodding as if in agreement with herself. She has seen something similar before. She gives Little Cedar's hat a playful pat. "Why don't you come back to the fire with us, Little No Eyes," she says, using his pet name, given for the way his eyes close when he laughs. "There's plenty of work you can help with. Come. Don't forget your bow."

Little Cedar puts his hand in the snow, where the arced shape had cut its way down. He pulls out his bow and aims toward Gichigami.

"It's gone," he squeals, and they turn back to the water where the horizon, once again, is an unbroken line.

"Come, both of you. It's cold here," says Bullhead.

Little Cedar protests, but only in word. He walks between them, a seed to their shell. Grey Rabbit keeps a tight hand on his shoulder and a wary eye turned toward the shining big water.

1902

The white-maned waves rise and fall, cascading toward shore in carousel lines. Rumbling spray and muffled thunder. Knuckled legs churning and watery hooves, kicking up whorls of sand. Every edge rough washed. Every sharpness worked smooth. Rock. Wood. Bone. Glass. Frothing necks riding blue water breach and then sink back again, plunging headlong into roundness.

A cove of smooth grey stones, soft and flat and sun warmed against her cheek. They press into her ribs in hard sickles. Ear to rock, she can hear their hoofbeats, can feel the vibration in her bones. Warmed hair, frigid spray from the lake, cool wind, and the gulls flying stiff winged.

They cascade toward shore in carousel lines.

Cool on her arm. Cold. Her arm's cold. Berit draws it under the quilts and holds it between her legs. No more wild wind, no hoof-driven waves. She rises to her elbow and stretches. The air smells of ash. The fire has dwindled. Out the window is a wide, pale winter morning. With Gunnar at the lumber camp, the fire is solely her duty. Again, she has slept past stoking time. She throws the quilt over her head, warm in her dark cocoon.

Another week and he should be back. She slaps the quilt

down and jumps to the floor, icy on the soles of her feet. The coals are still hot so the new logs flare. She adjusts the flue and is back in bed, pulling the warm covers around her. The crackling wood is a friendly presence, a certain kind of company.

Her sketchbook lies on the chair where she left it. If she'd propped it up when she fed the stove, she'd be able to see it from the bed. She's working on a sketch of bears, trying to do it from memory. The new wood whistles and pops. Drawing is the one thing that saves her, it has since she was a girl. She'd have come unhinged without it, eleven years old and bedridden for months.

She'd been cobbing for rock on the dump heap near the mine, drawn by the hope of finding missed copper. And though a feeling in her stomach had warned her, she ignored it and kept on climbing. The rest still remains a blur—the sliding and twisting, the ripping pain. There were two round clouds in the sky as she lay there, and the sound . . . bam . . . bam . . . bam . . . rhythmic and forever, of the stamp mill on the hill.

She filled the first sketchbook she was given, front to back, both sides of each page, and the cardboard cover as well. She drew pictures of everything around her: a wilting daisy in a tin cup on the bed stand; her leg, twice broken, propped on a folded quilt; the dark pine woods of the Keweenaw out the window.

If Gunnar could see her lolling like this. But the salt beef is in the lake and it's time to haul it out. He would have his say about her cooking it when there's still a bit of moose hanging in the cool-shed. She recalls the animal's wary brown eye as she'd stood at the door, the bull in her sights, waiting for it to move from the garden, not wanting to drop it in her potatoes. It was her last, biggest, and easiest kill of the fall. Gunnar will squawk, but she's saving the last of the moose for his return. In three leaping bounds Berit reaches her clothes, which she'd left to warm by the stove. She dresses quickly, last, her black skirt, which tents the warmth around her legs.

The snow is dropping straight, no wind, as she walks down the path with her buckets and auger. There are fox tracks on the lake that weren't there the day before. They skirt the shoreline, cross over her rope, and climb the rocks just short of the point. The snowfall creates a leaden hush, and now and then floating slabs of ice clack together in the water. The skin of ice on the hole shatters with a swift poke. The weighty meat twirls at the end of the rope as she pulls it from the cold water.

Now the snow's coming down in big fleecy clumps, and she's shifting the weight of her load as she walks up the path, thinking about when she wants to start the beef boiling now that it won't be too salty to eat, and then whether to have it ready for dinner or supper. It doesn't seem to matter much when Gunner's away. The ripped net in the fish house still needs mending, but there's something about horses on the edge of her mind, and she lifts her eyes as if in search of them through the cottony curtain of falling snow where a man is standing, and fear combs up the back of her neck, and her feet slide out, and the buckets fall.

John Runninghorse stands over her with a startled expression, his head cocked, his black hair catching snow, holding dead snowshoe rabbits that dangle along the length of his leg. "For the love of God," Berit blurts out. He lays down his stringer and offers her a hand, but she's already scrambling to her feet, flustered and brushing snow from her coat. "Gunnar's not here," she says breathlessly.

He nods and moves past her on the path, gathering her empty buckets as he goes. What in heaven's name is he doing at her place, showing up at this time of year? Berit's heart slows to a dull knock, and she circles her wrist, which is going to be sore. The snared rabbits lay stretched at her feet, fat clumps of snow gathering in their white fur. Fresh. She can tell as she lifts them, still pliable and swinging as she continues up the hill.

Again, she is startled when she sees the large snowshoes leaning against the cabin. It's rare to see anything that she doesn't know by heart, or that she didn't set in place with her own two hands. She leaves the rabbits hanging from a nail by the door. Oh, what a stew she could make of them. Through the window, John's a boulder crouched on the lake, a lattice of snow falling around him. She feeds the fire to get coffee started, then ties her good apron around her waist—not one of her everydays that she makes from flour sacks. It is hard to imagine why he's come. It's obviously not time to help set the anchor rocks. There isn't even a pudding to serve. Just yesterday's soup. That's the best she can do. At least the sugar bowl is full.

Gunnar would want the best for John. He thinks the man is some sort of prince, though she has never understood why. Not that there's anything wrong with him, it's just that she feels uncomfortable in his presence. And it's not because he's Indian; she's known Indians all her life, having grown up near them on the Keweenaw. She's not like those women, the newly comeover, who are afraid they'll be murdered in their sleep, their children stolen, and all manner of things.

"He knows more about this land than I could ever hope to." That's the kind of thing Gunnar says when he's been around John. Once Gunnar told her that John knew a hundred different plants in the woods. "What they're good for. When to get them. Sure, but he doesn't think anything of it. In fact, he seems embarrassed about it. He says that in his grandmother's time, everyone knew twice as many." It's hard for Berit to imagine these conversations, since John will barely meet her eye, much less talk, and Gunnar is shy with most anyone but her. The lid of the kettle starts to rattle, and now John's coming up through the snow. He's got the auger balanced over his shoulder, and her piece of salt beef cradled in his arm.

Berit raps on the window and holds up a coffee cup, but John passes without looking in. Before she knows it, he's in the doorway, standing there in his heavy wool coat, mitts to his elbows, boots to his knees. Filling it. Though he's not that tall. He's broad, but that's not it either. He's one of those people that just seems bigger.

"Please come in. Sit down. Do forgive me. I just didn't see you standing there . . . Of course, I wasn't expecting anyone . . ." Her voice is babbling like a stream.

John nods and scrapes a chair from the table. She's glad he chose the one facing the window, so she can stand behind him near the stove. She pours him coffee and offers sugar and a spoon, feeling the cold coming off of his clothes.

"What brings you?" She retreats back to heat the soup, a false cheerfulness in her voice. Here she'd been pining for someone to talk to and now she can't seem to manage.

John tastes the coffee, nods, adds sugar.

Lord, the bed is still unmade. "I hope you like pea soup," she says, moving the pot to the center of the heat. She'll have to be careful when she ladles it up so as not to scrape the bottom where she burned it yesterday. "It's not much, but I'll get that beef boiling."

When she turns she finds him looking at her drawing on the chair. His head bobs approvingly, and she feels a puff of pride. People have always been complimentary of her pictures. When they lived in Duluth she drew a series of cards in colored ink that some said she could sell if she wanted—deer bedding in the snow, pinecones, tumbling waterfalls. Someday she'll paint. Have a palette of oils and be able to mix any color. She looks at John, then at her lead-drawn bear. John turns away with a funny expression.

"They're black bears," she says, picturing them painted on canvas.

He stirs his coffee.

"Well? What do you think?"

He lifts his cup and nods.

"No, tell me, what do you think?"

"Your bears don't have tails."

"What?"

"No tails."

Berit takes the book from the chair. "Bears don't have tails. I've never seen a bear's tail."

"Maybe you've only seen them from the front."

"What kind of tail?"

"Small. Furry."

She can feel heat rising on her neck. John sits gazing at the tabletop, as if there was something interesting there, a smile, she thinks, playing at the edge of his mouth. She certainly doesn't see what's amusing.

"Well, it's a drawing from memory. I'll have to wait until spring and see for myself. Honestly I can't recall seeing a bear with a tail."

"All the animals in these woods have tails. All the mammals, that is, except you and me."

Berit carries her book to the nightstand, not really sure what she's feeling. Why should she care what he thinks? He probably has never even seen a real painting. She certainly didn't like the reference to her tail, or his, or that she doesn't have one.

The soup is burning. Berit hurries to the stove and lifts the pot off the heat. She can only make the best of it. She ladles the steaming soup into a bowl. "So what brings you this way? You never did say." There's the false cheer again.

"Rabbits."

"Rabbits?" She sets the bowl in front of him.

"That's why I came. I'm delivering them from Gunnar."

"Where? You've seen him?"

"He's at the lumber camp, down by Swing Dingle."

"Yes, I know, but . . . you were there?"

John is looking at the tabletop again. "I did some hunting for the camp and then for him, too." He holds the soup under his chin and starts in, not seeming to mind the heat.

"Well, how is he? What did he say?"

"I agreed to dress the rabbits," he says between spoonfuls.

"I meant for me. Any word for me."

He eats like he hasn't had a meal in days, scraping every bit from the edges of the bowl. Then he rises abruptly and produces a piece of paper that's folded in a tight square.

Berit unfolds it to find a strange hand, neat and uniformly upright. *My Dear, My Mrs.*, the message begins . . .

I'm sending John with some rabbit, as I know they're your favorite.

"I don't understand," she looks up. "This isn't Gunnar's hand. He can barely write."

"It's mine."

"Yours?" She looks at the neat rows of cursive, too late to cover her disbelief.

"Boarding school," he says in a stony voice. But she has gone back to reading . . . *as I know they're your favorite. Be certain that I am thinking of you, my dearest. It is so odd to hear his voice in this way. Things are moving in good time, so I hope to be home as planned. Don't consider saving any rabbit for me. I don't want to find even a morsel left over . . .*

John puts on his hat and draws the knife from his belt. He examines its edge and then slides it back in its sheath, watching

Gunnar's wife as she reads. Her pale skin, her thin frame, her hair the color of dried grass, bundled at the back of her head. He'll dress the rabbits as he'd promised. "Don't let her talk you out of it," Gunnar had said. "She'll go on about how she can do it herself." Well, she's not talking, she's leaning against the cupboard, fully engrossed in the letter, and he needs to get back to his trapline if he's going to make it back to camp and then home, if he's lucky, before the week is out.

John closes the door on the cabin's warmth and the earthy smell of pea soup. He lifts the rabbits from the nail, wondering what, if anything, she knows of the story Gunnar told him at the logging camp.

The telling has stayed strong in his mind, the heaviness in Gunnar's voice, all the stops and starts as he seemed to search for words. They'd sat together in an empty log sleigh. There was a bright moon and the wind stirred the shadows, as the camp's men snored and coughed. No, his wife doesn't know about the dead man in the lake. It was clearly the first time that Gunnar had spoke it out loud.

John lays out one of the rabbits, and with a deft hand puts his knife to its fur. He makes his cut at the rabbit's hind foot, then draws the blade up the inside of its leg. He'll stretch the furs, give Gunnar's wife the meat, and leave the entrails for scavenger birds.

Horse-stinger. Dragonfly. Oboodashkwaanishiinh. Predatory, of the order Odonata, meaning tooth.

They are of the most ancient creatures. Once they flew the skies as big as kites.

I knew them as sudden visitors. They'd alight on a seat plank or gunnel. Stay for a time. Fly off into the blue.

Their first life is in water. Their second in air. I see them transform on the floor of the lake. Each time shedding and growing a new skin. I follow them across the shallows. Try to join as they climb from the water, on a reed, a plank, a plane of rock.

But I know now.

Their path is not mine.

I watch through the wavering blue above as the dragonflies leave their last casings, crawl slowly out through the backs of their heads. Their black skins remain on the shore. Empty and weightless in the breeze.

They mate in winged circles, shining and airborne. Arching their bodies to form a wheel. Curving. The male clasps the female behind the head. This wheel. This ancient flying dance.

There is one who still feels the rhythm of our dance.

The particulars of my life are now hers to hold.

I take myself from these shining bright shallows. In search of something, yet I do not know what.

I move with the rhythm of the dragonflies.

They are here. Aloft in the water currents. The small. And their ancestors, whose long pulsing wings ripple the shadowy images. A luffing sail. A lost crate of lemons. A silver button tumbling to the lake bed.

2000

Nora turns onto the avenue to find smoke billowing into the sky. There's a siren coming in from the east, and all of it feels like a scene in a movie. The street is blocked off, and red lights are streaming across the faces of the buildings.

"Quick hurry Jesus Nora!" Willard was hysterical on the phone.

Nora abandons her car at the blockade, her legs shaking as she moves down the sidewalk. Fire is leaping from the two upstairs windows, like some cartoon building with flaming eyes. She steadies herself against the wall of the drugstore as a sickening sensation turns her stomach.

Thick torrents of water arc from the hoses. "Put it out." Tears spring to her eyes. "Put it out." She weaves through the shiny red trucks, mist from the hoses, fast-moving men.

"Nora. Get back. "

It's Willard shouting. He has her by the arm. She twists away.

"Nora, Jesus." His arm wraps around her waist. "Stop. Are you crazy?"

She beats back with her fists and butts back with her head, but he has her now, and he holds her tight.

"There's nothing you can do," he whispers at her ear.

The flames are leaping through the roof, causing a ruckus

among the firemen. Radio voices and static crackle in the air as the red lights stream around and around and black smoke twists up to the sky.

"Come on, honey." Willard loosens his grip. "Nobody knows what happened. Shit. Come on now, we'll go sit with Rose."

Nora wriggles free. "Oh my God, where's Rose?"

"Don't worry, okay? See, right there."

Nora lets herself be steered across the street to where Rose sits on a low cement wall. She's wearing tennis shoes and her ratty fur coat, and has Buck's accordion strapped across her chest. Willard puts her next to Rose, then sits himself, still holding on.

The ground surrounding her bar is a lake, reflecting flames and jumping with sound, trampled by men in big rubber boots. Nora thinks the heat feels good on her face, thinks that it's strange for her to think that. Her mind is buzzing, it's radio static. She rises, but Willard pulls her back to sitting.

"They got me out the window with a ladder, but I said I wasn't going unless they took the box, too." Rose fingers the pearly buttons of the accordion, then reaches over and gives Nora's hand a squeeze.

Nora can't take her eyes from the flames and the black cloud of smoke rolling over the rooftops.

"Hey."

Jimmy D. stands before her in full gear, sweat beaded on his face. "We've got another truck on the way. But these old wooden buildings . . . well, we're doing what we can."

"I hope so," she manages, "if you ever want another free beer."

A smile passes over Jimmy D.'s face, then fades to an expression that makes Nora feel sick, and she lowers her gaze to his boots.

She can't grasp what's actually happening. She feels like she's not really there, but somewhere deep inside herself, a place that's round, and smooth, and mouthless.

"My piano's up there. My piano's burning," says Rose.

1622

The river splits around a black rock with a white cap of snow before sliding back under the ice and over the little waterfall. Bullhead squats to rest for a moment near the small stretch of open water. There are two bubbling lines streaming out from the rock in a pattern the shape of flying geese.

Walking up from the big water has tired her. She had hacked a hole in the ice at a place that felt right, but there, as in her usual spots, the net had come up dripping and empty. Fish. Her mouth waters. Trout. Salmon. Whitefish. Herring. Cooking on sticks near a crackling fire. She would turn them slowly until they were done just right.

For two days they've eaten soup cooked from pieces of hide, lichen, and the stringy inner layers of bark. Night Cloud snared a rabbit, but it was small and shared mostly with Little Cedar. How proud Bullhead was of Standing Bird as he sat solemnly with his broth, the smell of cooked rabbit thick in the air, cramping her own stomach over and over with a desire more insistent than any passion she'd known.

A wind moves through the pines and they toss and creak, dropping small bits of snow to the ground. Little Cedar grows vulnerable. She has seen it many times before, the slowed response to what usually excites, and the dullness that settles over the eyes, like a snake as it begins to molt. She made a decoction of dried ox-eye root to give strength to the boy's limbs, but its effect was mild. If only she'd had the root newly pulled, not dried. She could've chewed it and spit the softened bits directly onto his arms and legs.

The rock and water make a gurgling music, and the faint light plays in the streaming bubbles. Bullhead can hear Grey Rabbit working in the woods, her bone rasping against the high rock wall as she scrapes lichen to add to the soup. How quickly the soup leaves her stomach feeling empty, without even pumpkin blossom left for thickening.

Bullhead takes in a long weary breath. The air smells of old snow and open water. Across the river a chickadee sits perched on an icy limb. Its feathers are puffed around its body, causing its head to look small. Even the little birds make their own way, not nearly so weak as her kind, who are born without feathers, warm fur, or thick hide. She pulls off her rabbit-skin mitt, looks at her fingers, the mean scar on her thumb. Yes, the Anishinaabeg were given the power to dream. And yet they are so fragile, so dependent, that they must take the very skins of other animals and wear them over their own to stay warm.

The chickadee sits puffed on its limb. The river water is dark, but also light in the places where it carries the color of the clouds. Bullhead follows the movement of the water. It slides in smooth sheets, circles and bends, wrinkling in lines that shrink and expand. Constant, constant. Constantly changing. Always the river, yet never the same. Slowly, the waters claim her, and her thoughts dissolve into the current. Gone is Bullhead, mother of three. Gone daughter, sister, clan member, widow. There is just the swift water as it twirls and glides, moves in smooth sheets that carry her downstream.

The sky lightens for a brief moment, illuminating Grey Rabbit's hands and the patches of lichen, squash-orange and green, and then the light is gone and the rock face goes dull. Grey Rabbit looks to the sky as the long yellow crack in the cloud mantle passes, moving swiftly toward the big water. She must finish her work and get back to Little Cedar. She'd left him lying quietly by the fire, whispering to the cattail warrior in his hand.

Deep into the night she sits with him, willing herself to keep a close watch. But each night sleep overtakes her, and another child appears. The last was a girl, crying in her cradleboard. She disappeared into the woods, carried off by a creature made of ice.

Food. They need food. They had talked of moving on, in hopes of finding the animals in another place. Soon they will have to. Grey Rabbit rubs snow across her scraped knuckles, then wipes clean the long edge of her bone.

Bullhead makes her way toward the rasping sound. Her time at the river has soothed and calmed her, allowing her to see more clearly, to notice the wind-carved snow behind tree trunks, and the soft pink patterns in the bark of the red pines. "Ah, good." She spots a dark vole in the snow, its feet curled and frozen, its head half eaten. She turns the rodent over in her hand, and drops it into the fish basket.

Her son's wife looks small standing before the rock wall that rises from the forest. She has scraped a good amount of lichen already. She works hard every day, focused as a hawk, yet she stays as distant as one, too. Something troubles the girl. Something more than Little Cedar. Bullhead ducks below a snow-laden bough. She has tried sharing a number of stories about hunger, of times when she'd worried over her own children, but none of them have nudged Grey Rabbit to speak. She can only trust that the girl will confide if she needs.

"Don't be so lazy." Bullhead sets her basket on the ground. "Get those, up there." She pouches her lips toward a high spot on the rock. "Those are the good ones. Those taste like beaver tail."

Grey Rabbit smiles at the joke, though her smile fades when she sees what is in the fish basket.

Bullhead takes a scraping bone from Grey Rabbit's bag and chooses a spot of her own to work. It's an ancient rock with a solemn spirit, home to moss and lichen, and two small cedars growing out of a high crack. She places an offering at the base of the rock.

The two work in silence, tending their own thoughts, while their scraping falls into a shared rhythm.

Herring on a stick, slowly crisping near the fire. A line of herring, one more succulent than the next.

Little Cedar crying in his cradleboard, disappearing into the woods.

A bird's call breaks the silence. It echoes off the high rock wall. Bullhead and Grey Rabbit stop scraping, and turn to meet each other's eyes. Again, the bird calls, and they look to the trees, smiling at each other with growing delight. They search the bare limbs and the green pines for the one that cawed, black crow—whose return marks the coming of spring.

1902

Gunnar straps on his skis, then hoists his pack. The warmer days are turning the snow wet and heavy, so the more distance he can cover before the sun rises, the better. He's no stranger to the hour before night gives way to day, as he's up and rowing to his nets as soon as the sky holds enough light to navigate. Sure, it's not exactly the same in the woods. Woods cling to darkness longer than water.

He winds the scarf Berit knit around his face, straps his poles on his wrists, and shoves off. For a time he can follow the cuts of the logging sleighs, its snow-covered width discernable in the dark. The grade is downhill so he uses his edges, slowing to avoid scraps of bark that are large enough to throw him over.

It's likely John got the rabbits to his Mrs. He can feel her on the other end of his journey, and he'd love to let loose and ski at full steam. But he has to keep from working up too much of a sweat. If the temperature drops suddenly it will freeze on him.

The woods are quiet except for the swish of his skis and the wool-to-wool of his pant legs. The lake isn't visible, but its icy smell is in the air. He can feel it below like a sleeping animal, breathing its dark watery breath. It was quite a story that John had told him. A giant, twenty miles long and turned to stone, lying face up in the lake. He couldn't quite follow the whole tale, or tell whether this Nana'b'oozoo was a man or a god. Maybe he was some type of Indian troll. Humanlike. Shape-shifting. In Aunt Dorte's stories back home, trolls often turned to stone. John could have made the yarn up to distract him after his own grim tale, but that didn't seem to be the case. He'd told it like it was true. It would be something to see, this Nana'b'oozoo, a sleeping giant in the lake.

The sleigh cut looks like a grey floor, laid along the bottom of a dark cave. No sign yet of the dawn. Gunnar loosens his scarf, already warming as he poles up an incline. It was good of John to hear out his story, not that he feels much better for the telling, not that it changes what he'd done. He reaches the top of the hill and takes the slope down, gliding past the indiscernible woods, keeping to the grey trail, as that day, indelibly set in his mind, unfolds before him in the darkness.

It was a fresh pine morning with rippling dark breakers, the lake still billowing from a two-day northwester, and he was worried about his catch. The northwesterly wind was still blowing strong enough to keep him from getting back to land. It finally let up late-morning, and so he launched his skiff into the lake. He rowed straight-lined away from shore, practically feeling Berit's thick silence as she watched him through the windowpane. They'd fought. Sure. Well, not exactly. A small quip the night before and no words exchanged come morning. It was a pattern that had grown too familiar. Too many things had grown in place of the children.

The first stiffness left his shoulders as he worked the oars, his course taking him over familiar lake bottom—the basalt table that continues off his cove, with its high spot that he has to skirt, and the group of mammoth boulders, then the scattered few that are visible only when the lake lies flat, at five fathoms, still visible at seven, before the bottom drops away.

The air was crystal and sharp, smelling of pine pitch and rot, and the seagulls were crying loops in the air, following in hope of easy food. He positioned himself first by pine and stone face, then by the shapes of the familiar ridges. As he rowed, the land transformed itself as always from a stagnant footing, solid with home and wife, to an abstraction of shape and texture, a tool for navigation, and a goal that meant safety if the weather were to turn. He was hoping there'd been no damage to his gang, though the herring should be fine if he could get them in soon.

At the top of a swell, he spotted the red cloth fastened to his uphauler, then down he went into a trough, where there was nothing to see but water and sky. The swells were too big to bring her in standing, so he waited for the lake to lift him again, adjusted his course, and rowed on.

The gulls settled on the dark blue water, paddling back and forth, watching him work his ropes. "You best forget about it," he addressed the flock. "I'll not be tossing any storm herring today." One more day of weather and the fish would have been ruined, gone so soft that bones would poke through their flesh when he went to pick them from the nets. Sure he gets tense when he can't get out; he hadn't meant to speak to her so curtly.

He started in at one end of his gang, hauling a section of net to the surface, lifting it across his boat, the cold water running from the ropes. One by one he freed herring from the mesh and dropped them into the bottom of the skiff. They were fine. The catch was fine. Too much time he could spend worrying.

When the section of net was cleared of fish, he pulled himself along below it, bringing a new section up and over, then watching the cleared one fall back to the lake, corks up, leads untangled. Everything was rolling and shining and wet as he rode up and down with the swells, the herring at his feet like sickle moons. He worked methodically, choking the fish in one section of net after another, his eyes moving from his task to the water, to the ridges, to the sky—always watching for weather.

A gull squawked and shit white in the boat as he started in on a new net. But something was wrong. The net resisted him. Its pull was skewed, and it wouldn't come over the gunnel like it should. And sure if that net wasn't one of his best. Not good. Not good at all. He hadn't been able to afford new nets for some time. Maybe if he'd worked more of that year's winter timber. But he couldn't bring himself to leave, not with Berit so low.

He maneuvered himself further along, watching the net as he pulled it from the water, then the cleared side to make sure it sank back right. Could be that the lake had tossed a timber his way. The bulk of the problem was coming right up. There. A couple fathoms below, and it looked like a huge ball of a mess. Almighty. He couldn't afford this. The weight of it was starting to strain, turning him so he was taking the swells at an angle. Then he stopped pulling. It lay below him in the water.

A man.

There was a man tangled in his net.

He rose and fell, rose and fell, and the sun shone and sparkled on the water.

A head and shoulders cocooned in the mesh. Black hair, or else some kind of cap. His thoughts raced nowhere and everywhere at once, like the blue sky and water that was all around him.

There was a man in his net. The fish lay in the bottom of the boat and the gulls bobbed on the water, watched with round eyes. He hauled the net closer to the surface. Something shone white. It was a hand. He felt his breakfast in his throat.

A man. A dead man. Wound in his net. He was wearing dark wool. If it was a uniform he'd never seen it. He pulled the straining net higher, and the body rose up and broke the surface along the skiff.

A white ear was sticking through the mesh. Water lapped at a waxy cheek.

He rose and fell with the body, feeling like he was in a dream. Even the fish at his feet looked unfamiliar. If he could wake and start the day over, open his eyes to Berit's back. But it was no dream, sure as the cold in his fingers. He'd have to get the man into the boat.

The coat's silver buttons were tangled in the net, and his leads were wound up and through. The man's leg was bent at an ugly angle, but he couldn't tell whether it was from his net or sometime before. Cutting him out would be the fastest, but he'd lose the net for certain that way.

He took hold of a cork to get a sense of what was what. The body shifted and the face rolled toward the sky. Black hair growing from a porcelain forehead. A mustache over lips like a bruise. His breakfast surged up again and he turned away. Water drops shed from the ropes, hit the surface in expanding circles.

He couldn't afford to lose the net. He had no choice but to untangle him. He'd let the steamer know at the end of the week. He tried not to look at the face as he worked, unwinding the leads, tugging the net here and there. How long he'd been down was impossible to know, the way the lake holds things as they are, too cold for bloating gases, too cold to rot wood.

The buttons were impossible, so he cut them off the coat and let them sink out of view. A glint of light flashed as the body rolled. It was his other hand, his finger, a gold wedding band.

A gull paddled close, turned its head side to side.

Berit.

He couldn't bring a body home to Berit. Already, she worried too much, feared for him in weather and not.

The white face stared up to the sky, unrelenting in its life-lessness. The most gruesome thing he'd ever seen.

He rode the swells.

She'd never forget it. He couldn't bring the body in.

Would it be so wrong to leave him to the lake? Every man who had ever worked on the water had to come to terms with his own drowning there. There was probably a law, but who was to know. Laws were made for towns, for the problems of people who lived as close as stacked wood. They didn't really apply to him. God's laws were a different matter, but he hadn't killed the man. He was dead when he found him.

He couldn't bring the body home.

Using his knife as sparingly as he could, he worked steadily to release him, trying to block thoughts of the dead man's wife, and focusing on his own instead. If it were he who had drowned in the lake, Berit would want to have his body. "Buried, not out there adrift," she'd say. "Not left with the hope that you'd re-turn." But Berit knew, she knew. The lake's a killer. She'd lived her entire life on its shores. She knew the water temperature didn't bend toward hope.

The dead man's wife was not his concern. He had a live one with enough sorrow as it was. He would not bring the dead man home. God forgive him. He couldn't do it.

The sunlight shone innocently on the water, but the gulls, they were watching him closely. The net was damaged, though not beyond fixing. First, he decided, he'd take care of the body, then after come back and finish picking the nets. He'd tie him to the skiff and tow him further out.

When he reached down to get the rope around the man, he half expected his bones to poke through, but he was as solid as a cold side of meat. Gunnar tied the rope under the man's arms, let out a length, and secured it to the skiff. There was no real reasoning to where he was going, just out deeper, one mile or four, he wasn't sure when he'd stop.

A black head plying the waves. The body turning, showing the white face. Staring at the man was a danger to himself. He should have been watching the sky and the water, but putting himself in danger felt only right. He vowed to the dead man— or to God, he wasn't sure—that from that day forward his life would change. He would coax his Mrs., his marriage, back to life.

Gunnar skis on as the sun lifts from the lake and is swallowed into a bank of clouds. He'd made good on his promise; their life has turned around. But still, he thinks of the man he left out there. His grieving wife. Maybe a passel of children. Not a day goes by when he doesn't come to mind.

When the morning is well established, Gunnar stops to rest. He plants his poles in the snow and slides the pack off his back. He circles his shoulders and pops his neck, looking back toward the ridge he'd helped log, the sheared stumps and the bramble of brush. They'll come through and burn what's left.

Gunnar unscrews the cap to his canteen. As he drinks, the sun pokes out for a moment, causing a patch of water to brighten and then dim. He wipes his mouth across his sleeve, feeling small and fragile.

At fourteen, I crossed the ocean. The unpath'd waters. The deep salt sea. My feet solid on the ship's deck, I imagined beneath the water surface. The fishes. The mammals. The corals. The algae. All the hidden dangers below. My face to the wind, I imagined exotic lands. Tried to grasp the great distances, and the endless horizon.

But the ocean was incomprehensible.

Too vast. Too far. Too deep, my mind said.

I had the luxury of giving up and turning my attention to other things.

As a man I worked the great Gichigami. Lake Superior. The sweet-water sea. I knew its waters touched no exotic lands. That its creatures were few. Dull colored. Benign. Still, like the ocean, its horizon is endless. I grappled as I stood on her shore, as I rode her waves in each morning's light. But always I was left uncertain.

It is a fact that Superior is easily measured. In length. In width. In hundreds of miles.

Superior should be comprehensible.

It is not.

And that discord is readily felt.

The Great Lake is movement at peripheral vision. It is sound at the limit of audible frequency. It is the illusion of the ability to understand.

2000

Nora stands on the blackened threshold, keys in hand. There is no door. It's cold and wet and everything stinks like fire, though it's not the smell of a fireplace. It's the smell of things you're not supposed to burn, vinyl and plastic; the stench is bad. Her heart beats in her ears as she takes a step forward, uncertain whether the floor will hold.

Weak light angles down from a large patch of sky framed in stumps of charred wood. What's left of the bar is largely unrecognizable, mounds of blackened and soggy debris. She lifts a metal pole and pokes through a pile. A broken picture frame. Part of a drawer. It could be her stuff, it could be Rose's—it's hard to tell since there's no floor keeping their things separated.

She always imagined firemen putting out fires as if that were that, but it's impossible to say which caused more damage, the fire itself or their water hoses. She pulls her sweater up over her nose, but it's no match for the acrid smell. She pokes at broken glass and table legs, water soaking through her shoes.

Edging herself behind the bar, she peers into the long mirror. It's broken and sooty. Her face doesn't show.

Nora stands unmoving where she'd stood so many years, as a sensation of heaviness sinks through her body, anchoring her feet to the floor. She should simply get out. She knows it's dangerous.

A plane passes overhead, leaving a vapor trail like a zipper in the sky. She's chilled right through. It looks like a boxcar came down on her pool table. It's Rose's refrigerator. There are dark recesses and unrecognizable shapes, tiny sounds that she can't discern.

Nora lifts one foot just to know that she can, then tries the other but the toe of her shoe is caught. With her pole she uncovers a piece of netting to find it's holding a glass float. Fist sized and bottle green, it's filthy and dripping, but somehow intact. A feeling wells in her chest. She can't even tell whether it's happiness or sadness.

She should walk away.

She doesn't have the strength.

If she leaves, there will be no going back.

She's knows that she's not making sense.

There's a rumbling train, and the metal-on-metal shriek.

She can't leave, and it's starting to scare her.

She doesn't expect a miracle—the cigarette machine to blink on, or the bottles to reconstruct and line up on the riser.

Something else is in the room. She senses its presence in the shadows.

She can't even move her arms.

Slap. She feels the sound in her chest. A pigeon bolts from the kitchen, and Nora flies.

Burt Schnell slips a free fifth of vodka into Nora's bag.

"Thanks," she manages. "That's nice of you." She doesn't realize her fingers are sooty until she holds out her hand for change.

"What a loss," he says, "a crying shame. I remember when we were kids, my dad would bring us in for burgers. Me and my sister used to practically kill each other trying to get the bar stool across from Josephine."

Nora nods and feels her throat tighten. She hadn't thought of Josephine, her carved figurehead behind the bar.

"And the thing is," Burt continues, "the Schooner hadn't changed a bit. It was timeless, you know, like real places are." He shakes his head. "Irreplaceable. So what are you going to do now? It's hard to imagine you anywhere else."

"I know." She slides her bag off the counter. "I can't think that far ahead yet."

Nora puts the liquor in the front seat and drives to the super-market at the other end of the lot.

She's standing in a row of detergents and fabric softeners, flanked by orange and pink plastic bottles. Everything is absurd. The bright swirling labels. The moms wheeling their kids in shopping carts. The "everyday low prices." The bulk peanuts.

Water douses the produce, but no one seems to notice.

1622

"And the birds rose up all together, laughing and talking and congratulating themselves." Bullhead lifts her hands in the air. "And each and every one flew away."

"What happened next?" Little Cedar asks. "What happened to the man?"

Bullhead reaches over and pinches his leg. She laughs and adds a piece of wood to the fire, causing shadows to bounce higher on the wall. "He was flung into the night sky. I'll show him to you at Sugarbush."

The sound of Bullhead's laughter meant more to their survival than Grey Rabbit had realized. Once more, she thanks the animals who had offered their lives to feed her family. At first the meat felt bad in their stomachs, like hard balls of clay slow to dissolve. Now its good effects are evident. Standing Bird stares at the flames, his arrow-sharp focus back. And Little Cedar is playing again.

Warm light wavers on Night Cloud's face. The tightness in his jaw has relaxed as well. He's no longer stony eyed and quick with gruff words. His feelings come through his eyes so strongly. The morning he awakened from the dream where he was shown the echo rock wall in the woods, his eyes were filled with such gratitude and relief that she knew of the gift before he had spoken.

"Are we going to hear another one?" Standing Bird asks his grandmother without looking up from the space between two pieces of wood where the flames appear and disappear, creating an eye, a row of teeth, or two tall twirling dancers. He reaches over and pinches his little brother's knee, and mouths the words, "Windigo, windigo, windigo."

Grey Rabbit silences her oldest with a look as Little Cedar squirms and covers his eyes. She, too, would rather not hear of the windigos, the horrible winter specters with man-eating ways. She puts her arm around Little Cedar, feeling the thinness of his shoulder. She tilts his face and feels his cheeks for warmth, but he twists his head free of her.

Even though they have food enough, the dreams of endangered children have continued. In the last there'd been a lost boy who wandered into a clearing full of bad medicine. Girl or boy and whatever the age—somehow the dreams seem to point to her youngest. She can't explain why this is. She has never been known as a powerful dreamer. She knows she should ask Bullhead to help her interpret, yet each time she means to, she falls silent.

"We'll leave for Sugarbush as soon as the time is right," Night Cloud announces. Grey Rabbit meets Bullhead's eyes across the fire. Most of the preparations are already finished. What's left can't be done until the end.

"And when we get there, we can open the cache," Little Cedar pipes up. "Tell us everything that's buried in it?" he asks, but then he recites the list himself. "Rice, and fish, and beaver, and maple sugar, sugar, sugar." His eyes squint shut with pleasure. Again, Grey Rabbit puts her hand to his cheek.

Bullhead sucks her teeth and then clears her throat with

a short cough. "The time has come for me to tell a story that happened as a small party of canoes were on the way to their Sugarbush."

Bullhead's dark eyes travel around the circle, and everyone settles in to listen.

Despite the mood of caution and the respect that's necessary when journeying on Gichigami, everyone was happy and excited. The winds of winter were growing tired, and soon the fisher would swing up in the night sky, followed by the songbirds winging back to the trees. Everyone was anxious to see friends and relatives, and to hear how the winter had passed for them.

It was a mild grey morning when the party launched their boats, but the day turned cold and bright and Gichigami was rolling beneath their canoes.

Among them was a girl named Hole-in-the-Rain; she was young, only about this high, and cold. She was always cold. It happened that she was one of two, and her tiny sister, who was much weaker, didn't survive the long cold winter of their birth.

Ever since, and even in the summer, Hole-in-the-Rain would wear a fur in order to keep the cold away. She especially didn't like being on the water. Not only were the water spirits frightening, but she wasn't allowed to move around in the boat, and the cold went straight to her bones.

Hole-in-the-Rain tried to amuse herself as the small party paddled across the bays, their boats moving in a line like ants. She peered down into the water, though she couldn't see below the surface. "Stay low and sit still," her mother warned, but the girl kept glancing over the side.

It was at the hollow-rock river, where they had stopped to rest and eat, that Hole-in-the-Rain first heard the voice. It was clear and sweet, and it called her by name. She pulled her fur tight around her, and followed the voice around the rocky point. There she found the very small cove. "Come play with me," called the voice. "I've been waiting for you all morning."

No one was on the beach or back in the trees. Hole-in-the-Rain turned in circles. She looked low to the ground for the little people, but there were none. "Where are you?" she called into the cold clear air.

"Here, here," the voice came again. "Now we can go exploring together." Hole-in-the-Rain looked over the water, and there she saw her between the waves. A watergirl.

She had long dark hair that floated out around her and a beautiful face. But her eyes were strange; completely round like those of a fish.

"I saw you," the girl continued, "looking down at me from your boat. Come on now. We have so much to do." She reached her hand to Hole-in-the-Rain. "There are lots of places I want to show you."

Hole-in-the-Rain could not believe that a girl was swimming in the water when the rocks along the shore were still held in a rim of ice. Even in the summer, Gichigami was freezing. "How can you swim in that cold water? You must be like ice through and through."

"I'm not cold at all. It always feels good here." The girl in the water observed Hole-in-the-Rain closely, looking her up and down with her strange round eyes. "I can see that you don't believe me, but it's true. Come, you'll be fine. I promise. The water will feel like a warm breeze, and there are so many things to see. There are caves to explore, treasures to find."

Hole-in-the-Rain considered the invitation. After all, it would be nicer to play with a new friend than to sit still all day in the cold boat.

"Come along." The beautiful girl held out her hand. "What are you waiting for?"

Hole-in-the-Rain was tempted to go, but she was also afraid. Gichigami was the coldest thing she knew. The last time she'd waded in, the water grabbed her ankles so tight that it hurt. "I'm afraid I'll be cold. I'm always cold."

"Do I look cold to you? The girl reached again for Hole-in-the-Rain. "Look at my arm. Do you see any bumps? Now give me your hand. I'm getting impatient."

It was true, she didn't look cold at all. Hole-in-the-Rain took a step toward the water and was just reaching out her hand when her mother came around the point and saw what was happening. "Get back," she yelled, and quickly scooped up a rock and hurled it at the watergirl. The rock struck her hard on the side of the head, and her round eyes bulged.

"Mother, stop!" screamed Hole-in-the-Rain. Her new friend was bleeding at the temple, but her mother bent for another stone, and again hit the watergirl in the head. The second rock stunned her and she sunk below the surface, where she lay floating motionless.

Hole-in-the-Rain began to cry. "You've killed her, Mother. You've killed my new friend." But just then the beautiful girl came to. She rolled and slapped her tail angrily, then sped away beneath the waves. She had lost her chance to steal Hole-in-the-Rain down to the watery underworld.

Little Cedar is wide eyed. "Would she have died?"

Night Cloud shakes his head. "No. She would have adapted to their world. She would not be dead, but not alive either."

"But how could she breathe underwater?"

"She would learn to breathe as the water creatures do."

"But what about the cold? She would be so cold."

Standing Bird looks up from his flame, which is now flicking like a snake's tongue. "They can't feel hot or cold, Little-Know-Nothing."

Grey Rabbit lets out a long sigh, and both of her sons turn to look at her. She smiles faintly and looks at her hands. She wishes Bullhead had not told that story. Things can happen so easily. Little Cedar would have reached for the watergirl's hand.

They've packed most of their belongings and buried the others, leaving only the bent skeleton of their wigwam standing in the morning light. Grey Rabbit steadies the canoe, neatly loaded with rolls and bundles and everyone in their place. Never has she been so happy to move on.

Tobacco falls from Night Cloud's hand in offering and floats over the water's surface. He nods. Grey Rabbit shoves off and climbs in as the boat glides away from shore. No one speaks as they start their journey, each getting used to the feel of the shifting water, an unsteadying sensation after a long season on land. It's quiet except for the chop of the waves and the sound of Bullhead humming softly beneath her breath.

Grey Rabbit dips her paddle into the clear water, feels its resistance against her stroke, watches the drops fall in a long arc as she lifts the paddle forward again. There are icicles hanging in the mouths of rock caves, where the water thunks with a hollow sound, and a place along shore where the lake has piled ice, one sheet into the next, like giant fish scales in the sun.

Grey Rabbit looks back at their wake as the water closes over the disturbance of their passing. It is possible for things to return to calm. On the cliff near her offering place, the oldest pine stands taller than the rest, its windswept arms, its guardian spirit, bathed in the yellow light of morning.

1902

Gunnar rows away from land, feeling the extra weight—John, the anchor rocks, the buoys, and all the rope—force him low in the water. The water has a blue-black chop, but it's calm enough to get the boulders overboard. He points up the shore with his oar. "It's a new spot, further out. See the cliff face near the double hump? About a mile, a mile and a half."

John lets out a long breath, conscious of the offering he'd made before getting into the boat. He's never been comfortable on the big water, and this time he feels worse than ever. He hasn't seen Gunnar since Swing Dingle, and now, on top of the unpredictable water spirits, he has thoughts of Gunnar's drowned man to contend with. Still, the day of work is worth the salt fish to him, and he trusts Gunnar, and Gunnar trusts the boat. It's a good design, pointed at both ends, and constructed with strong cedar ribs. Not an improvement on the canoe, though it has its similarities. The land slides by—the slanting rock shore and the shaded forest floor where the snow is still holding.

Gunnar angles them toward the horizon, and John feels the growing distance from land like a low vibration throughout his body. It's as clear looking down at the boulders underwater as it is looking up through the air, causing him to feel slightly disoriented about the relative size of things, his place in the world, and which element he is part of.

When the lake bottom drops away, there's only the dark reflection of his head. He rests his feet on the enormous coil of rope. It holds the smell of deep water.

Gunnar appears to not notice whether they're in forty feet of water, or three hundred. But of course he's aware; he's completely alert. John follows his gaze up to the ridge, where rounded cloud shadows darken patches of land. It's admirable, how the oars seem to elongate Gunnar's arms, and the boat becomes an extension of his torso. The man becomes more water strider than human.

"You best not put your feet there," Gunnar warns, looking up at the ridge again.

John takes his feet off the coil of rope. "What's up there?" he finally asks.

"Weather," says Gunnar, noting John's discomfort. "Only keeping watch," he adds. John's used to Gunnar watching the sky, it's just that he seems more vigilant than usual. John shades his eyes and scans the horizon, but reading the sky from so far out in the water is not the same as reading it on land.

"I was hunting last fall when that big storm hit. It felt like the waves could've snatched me from the woods."

"Yeah. That was a big force, for sure. It came bearing down from there," he points with his oar. "But the thing with northeasters is I can see them coming. And even if they blow up faster than I can row, at least they blow me in. It's more likely northwesters this time of year." Gunnar tilts his head toward the ridge. "They give me no notice and blow me out. I could row for hours, giving all of my arms, and not make a bit of headway toward shore."

"Has it happened?"

Gunnar nods and then shrugs.

John listens to the rhythmic work of the oars and waits for him to tell the story.

"I tied myself to the boat. Tied the boat to the nets." He rows without saying anything more.

John watches the water drip from Gunnar's oars. He turns back toward the landscape and the places he knows well, but the animal paths and needle beds, the rivers, ravines, and out-croppings of stone, have all been reduced to vague patches of color. They're far enough out to see the wide, bare notches along the ridge, where the loggers have begun to clear the trees.

"It wasn't too bad," Gunnar starts up, "six, maybe seven hours bailing. No real damage, except to the fish. I couldn't get back out to my nets again before the fish went soft."

"Another storm?"

"Yah, no. I needed some tending. I froze myself right to the boat."

Berit has the fish house warmed up, the barrel stove keeping off the chill that seems to come every year with the thaw, finding its way though the smallest of holes, even the tiny openings in the weave of her sweater. She leans forward in her chair, dips a cedar float in linseed, and then, with a piece of a dress beyond wearing, rubs the oil into the wood. It's a strong smell, slightly rancid, and it mixes with the other smells of the fish house— trailings, preserving salt, sweat, wet wool, and the dense watery smell of the nets in the loft.

She rubs the oil vigorously into the float, repeating to herself once again that it would be good for Gunnar to have a partner. Not only could they work more nets, they could run hook lines for trout in the spring. And, of course, he would be that much safer. She certainly doesn't see a problem with that.

"We barely have enough as it is," he'd said. "Where would he live? Your work would double." He'd shot back words before giving her ideas time.

"He could live in the net loft until he builds his own place." She had thought it through. Her idea was feasible.

Berit sets the float on the drying rack and dips another into the oil, the light cedar wood turning darker on contact.

"Where would we store the nets?"

"Build a temporary shed."

The exchange felt more like a children's game than a real conversation. And then Gunnar stopped talking all together, and turned his back to her in the bed. Come dawn he acted like nothing had ever happened, just launched in, telling her about his dream. The thought of it gets her blood moving. She slaps the float down in her lap. He thinks that because he won't discuss something, it somehow ceases to exist.

The cat is rubbing against her leg, back and forth, her tail up and twitchy. "Go on, Katt-Katt." She nudges her away, but the cat only moves to her other leg. "Go on now, you're as stubborn as he is."

Berit stands at the window. The lake is dark under bulbous white clouds. She can't see the boat, but then she didn't expect to.

She twirls her arms, stiff from splitting wood, and settles back in her chair with a raw float. Soon, she's back at the window again. The dark blue lake. The clouds in the sky. Time barely moves when he's out setting anchors.

2000

"You're sure you're going to be okay?" Nora asks a second time from the threshold of her living room. Rose, sitting in the easy chair, nods without taking her eyes from the TV. She'd been planted in that chair for almost three weeks now, watching science shows or the History Channel. The blouse she'd borrowed hangs across her small shoulders, her body looking lost inside. She reaches to the windowsill where the sun is shining through the amber glass ashtray and taps off her ash without taking her eyes from the program.

Nora runs over her purchases in her mind. She'd bought bourbon, bitters, and sweet vermouth; oatmeal, pancake mix, and the "real maple syrup" Rose had asked for; pickled herring, hot dogs, and toast. The only fruit Rose wanted were bananas and the maraschinos. It's all on the cupboard's bottom shelf, so Rose won't have to climb a chair.

"Well, you're well stocked."

"I know. Thanks."

"The number is on the refrigerator. And don't forget, Willard is coming by."

Nora's suitcase, a bulky hard box, clunks along the stairwell. Joannie always rolls her eyes when it slides down the carousel at the airport, but it's in good shape, hardly used, and Nora likes how easy it is to spot.

She steps into the bright morning. It's just as well to leave town. She had wanted to stay and see Rose's reaction to the Casio piano she'd bought for her, but it had to be ordered in. Stay or go, she couldn't decide. And then, after another harangue with the insurance company, her urge to leave won out over waiting.

Nora slides her suitcase onto the backseat of the car, situates her notebook on the passenger seat, and closes the long creaky door. From the curb, her window in the old brick fourplex reflects the blue sky and the new green buds of the elm on the boulevard.

"Forget something?" Rose asks on a stream of smoke.

"No. Saying good-bye is all. Say, there's a bird on the sidewalk by the stairs. I almost clobbered it with my suitcase. It didn't even move. It might have flown into the windowpane."

Rose nods.

"Well, I'm not sure how long I'll stay, but you know where you can reach me."

Rose fixes her with her watery eyes, points the remote at the TV, and the room goes still. Smoke curls up from the ashtray. The shadow of a gull glides over the carpet. "Nora, listen to me. You're going to be just fine."

The glass float looks like a bottle green baseball, hanging in its netting from the rearview mirror. It swings as Nora rounds the curve off of the bridge, her car now heading through Duluth. It always strikes her the way the lake dominates Duluth, with its hills that angle down to the shore, when in flat Superior all you see of the lake is the shipyards, and the sheltered water of the harbor.

The wooden paddle marked *SS Arnold*. Nora flips her notebook open to the page headed "Pool Area," and, with one eye on the road, adds the paddle to the list. It kills her that she can't remember. At what point had she stopped seeing her surroundings? It's crucial that she get it all written down, to preserve the memory, or at least to know what was lost.

Nora lights a cigarette and cracks the window, tries to settle in to the drive. One good thing about driving—it answers the question of what she should be doing with her time. And Nikki was excited on the phone. "You can sleep in my bed again," she said. "I've already got my sleeping bag rolled out on the floor." Hopefully things will go smoothly with Janelle. Often they are nothing but oil and vinegar. Frankly, she's still miffed at her for not coming down when the bar burned. The Schooner had been a big part of Janelle's growing up, and not all bad the way you'd think to hear her talk. Nora holds her cigarette to the edge of the window, letting the wind take the ash. A little support would have been nice. Of course single parenting is demanding, but still, Janelle should have made the trip.

London Road, with its parade of big houses, is slow going as usual, but the traffic lightens up after the Lester River. Nora turns onto the scenic two-lane instead of the faster highway, so she can buy Janelle the smoked fish she loves. The lake, a stone's throw from her car window, is dark blue swells close to shore, but in the distance it settles to a flat light blue. There's a freighter out there like a long dark shoebox. Strange how graceful they look from far away, when up close they are all steel and grind.

She has only been able to remember a few of the boats in Ralph's framed photographs of sunken ships. Nora pages through her notebook to find the right heading. The *Benjamin Noble*,

Algoma, Aurania, S. R. Kirby, the *Mataafa, Bannockburn*, the lumber hooker *C. F. Curtis*—a mere handful of what was hanging on the wall. He had an obsession for the ships gone missing. Never heard from again. Never found. The ore freighter moves along the horizon. There's a crack in the lake where boats disappear. That's what some people say. A crack in the lake. It's ridiculous. Still, the thought makes her skin crawl.

The French River. Traffic has disappeared. There's only her car and the shadows of trees on the road. Nora wonders what Rose is doing. She pictures her sitting in the easy chair. When she'd first offered Rose the spare room as a temporary place to live, she worried about having constant company. But it's been nice to have someone around. And having Rose in her home isn't really very different than when she was living above the bar. It's not that they do so much talking. It's the fact that they don't have to explain the silence.

Nora flips through the notebook to the page headed "Storeroom." Things kept in storage too long have a way of disappearing from memory, and there were boxes in there that hadn't been opened in years—boxes marked "Ralph's" and "Apartment" in heavy black letters, belongings of Janelle's that she refused to take, but didn't want thrown away either. Her stomach sinks. Her foot lifts off the gas. On the back shelf. The stack of white boxes. Her entire collection of ornaments.

A pile of snow from the winter plowing is shoved into a corner of the fish shack's lot. It's shrunk down, icy, and full of dirt. Nora can feel its cold air as she walks past. The store is part fish and part flea market, everything fairly mixed together. A hundred. Easily. There were that many ornaments. Each from a different time and place. Some from people long-gone. Nora drifts through the jumble of merchandise while the clerk wraps her order of herring. There is a pair of ancient wooden skis on the wall. A faded croquet set, not quite intact. She flips through a leaning stack of pictures—a poster of fur-trading voyageurs paddling in birch-bark canoes, another titled "Superior's thirty-nine," which shows all the lake's lighthouses, stout ones, tall, stripped, and brick. Behind it she finds a painting similar to the one that hung over Rose's couch. Nora lifts the large framed canvas and holds it to the window. It's a scene of the lakeshore, sunset-orange, with a gull in the water, one in flight, and in the distance someone in a tiny boat. The painting is bigger than Rose's, and maybe hers didn't have a boat. For $12.99, she can hardly go wrong.

Buoyed, Nora opens a Santa box, hoping to find it filled with ornaments, but it contains just a string of lights. A stuffed mink stares from a log. A piece of shellacked wood says Welcome to the North Shore, with rocks painted to look like a family glued on. Nora lifts a tray with Norwegian rosemaling. It's pretty, but cracked right down the middle. She unearths a pair of moccasins decorated with plastic blue beads. Too small for Nikki. Nothing else worth getting.

The lake looks different once she's through Two Harbors, striped dark blue and light, grey and white. Looking out, it's hard to tell where the water ends and the sky begins. Nora stubs out her cigarette. Part of the painting is visible in the rearview, a gull crossing an orange sky.

The nautical map between the doors to the johns. It had a boat on high seas, and a serpentlike sea monster looming menacingly in the distance. She writes it in the notebook and sets down her pen, a wave of shock breaking over her again. It's gone. All of it. Just like nothing.

1622

The constant sound of chopping wood is in the air and the sweet smoky smell of boiling sap. Grey Rabbit has chosen a far section of the grove in order to work alone. The reuniting of the families has been a swirling wind—the stories told and reenacted, harsh news, and softer tales of sorrow and relief—but now she wants to think in quiet.

Grey Rabbit kneels under a wide bare maple, the shadows of its branches like dark veins over the snow, and talks to the tree as she touches its bark. She is known to have a gift with the maples, and she wishes to continue to do well with them. She feels the need to prove herself, to stop the concerned glances of Bullhead and Night Cloud. She places an offering at the base of the tree, fingers the spot, and makes her first cut.

She aches for Coming-In Woman, who lost her eldest girl. No one knows what became of her. Some say spirited away, others say she was taken by an animal, most believe she fell through the ice.

Little Cedar is nearby with a group of children. Having finished with their work of setting out containers, they are running and chasing through the trees. It's clear that he's unhappy with her for making him stay in view, but that's the way it must be for now.

If her dreams ended after Little Cedar regained his strength, they would have been a good omen, a warning of the danger he had been in. Grey Rabbit takes a spile from her bag and pounds it into the cut she'd made. But the children of her dreams still come, and always, as before, they're desperate and beyond help. She knows no one who would cast bad medicine on her, nor of any large offense connected with her family. And yet there were no stories told of hunger as bad as what her family suffered. She must approach Bullhead and make an offering, ask her advice about the dreams, but the time never seems to be right. Why that is, she doesn't understand. She needs to be alone, and to listen if she hopes to gain any understanding. Yet once alone she begins to feel severed. And that rift is more frightening then the worst of her dreams. Her mind turns in circles like a wounded fish.

Grey Rabbit stands and breathes the damp air. She can't see Little Cedar, though she hears the playful voices of the children in the woods. She calls his name as she peers through the trees, walks through the snow with its long-veined shadows, calling again, louder and more insistent. She told him not to run off. She won't begin on another tree until she has him in her sight. "Little Cedar," she calls in a harsh tone, and then turns to find him standing close.

He's short of breath and his face is red from running. "What?" he says, his hands on his hips.

I find places devoid of motion or sound. No ping. No fin. No shaft of light. The silt lying undisturbed.

And then suddenly objects like leaves in a wind. A flower vase. A cask of rum.

Laughing boy. Calendar. Broken oar.

And something just ahead. Passing out of view. A dark shadow. The water closing behind it.

I understand that I should follow.

Though it is lost again. Like a fleeting dream.

I traverse clinker trails without understanding. Search the open mouths of caves.

There.

He hovers near the steep rock shoal.

Somehow I always knew.

The man in the dark coat.

I approach.

He scatters like a murder of crows.

2000

"At first everyone was so nice." Nora sits at the table near the picture window where the sky over the lake is streaked with long morning clouds. She swirls the coffee at the bottom of her mug.

"What was that?" Janelle asks from the tiny galley kitchen.

"Everywhere I went people would come up to me and say how sorry they were, and how much they'd miss the place."

"Nikki, get your stuff together." Janelle bags a sandwich and picks an orange from the bowl. "I love this painting, Mom. It almost glows. Rose had the same one?"

"No, it wasn't the same, but it reminds me of hers."

"It's cool, Nanny. She's gonna like it."

"It sure captures the beauty." Janelle squats next to Nikki, where the painting leans against the wall. "We've seen the water like that, out our window."

"Yeah, like a dreamsicle."

"You're a dreamsicle," Nora says from the table.

Janelle tugs on Nikki's shirt. "Go get a sweater, and don't forget your lunch."

"Anyway," Nora says, "I couldn't even walk down to the Milk House without somebody bringing up the fire. Everyone seems to have adjusted, though. Some have gone over to the Boxcar, and some are at the 22."

"Well, Mom, come on, what did you think, they'd stop drinking?"

Nora lifts her eyebrows and looks into her cup.

"Drinking what?" Nikki asks, zipping shut her little red knapsack.

"Nothing, Miss Big Ears. Now go get a sweater. How about your purple one?"

"Your Aunt Joannie thinks I should come out to California."

"That might be a nice break. You always seem to like it."

"No, to live. She wants me to move there."

"You're not serious?"

Nora shrugs and wipes toast crumbs onto her plate. "She thinks it would be good for Mother."

"Grandma Bernie's mind is gone. How could it be good for her?"

"I can't find the purple one." Nikki skips in. "How about this one?" she says with a twirl.

"Oooh. That's a pretty red dragonfly on your pants," says Nora. Nikki twists to see her rear pocket. "Oh yeah, Mom embroidered it." She flips her ponytail as if it were nothing.

"Remember, Nanny's picking you up from school, so don't go getting on the bus."

"Nanny, will you come out and wait with me?"

"Your Nanny doesn't have her shoes on, and you need to get going."

"Of course I will, Bun," Nora says, rising. "Just let me get my purse."

The morning air smells like pine and cold water. Nora walks Nikki down the gravel drive, taking care to avoid the ruts, branches, and soggy leaves that were lying under the snow all winter. Nikki plops down on a little wooden bench enclosed on three sides and topped with a slanting roof.

"This is sort of like my playhouse," she says. "But I don't play in it much 'cause it's too close to the road. Sometimes I count the semi trucks."

"It has a nice view."

Nikki nods, swinging her feet. "I've seen deer over there in the trees."

"Really?"

"Bears, too."

"No."

"Sure. Lots of times. I wasn't even scared."

Nora lights a cigarette.

"Nanny, you shouldn't smoke. It can kill you, you know."

"A lot of things can kill you, Nikki."

"Mom says it's unrespectful to your body. She says it's the worst thing you can do."

Nikki hops off the bench and picks up a pinecone. "Want to see how far I can throw?" Her pinecone hits the far lane and rolls. "Want to bet if a car will run over it?"

Nora waves until the bus rounds the curve out of sight, then goes back to the bench to have a cigarette. It's quiet except for the occasional car, and a squirrel rustling in the brush. It feels like her first real smoke of the day. She inhales, then blows out a long slow stream. A jay is in the pines across the road, and it looks just like a calendar shot, a dab of bright blue against all the green.

"What are you going to do?" Everyone has been asking, even people she hardly knows. As if it isn't a personal question.

"When one door closes, another one opens." Those were

Willard's words. She's not sure it's true, though it's a nice thought. She hasn't seen any open doors.

She stubs out her cigarette and flicks the butt into the trees.

Nora steps to the edge of the driveway as Janelle pulls near and rolls down her window. "Is there anything you want me to bring back?" She's dressed for work in her gold-and-white checkout uniform.

"I'm fine," Nora says, suddenly seeing Duane in Janelle's face. It's her eyes and the way she's looking up. Nikki, too, looks more like her father, with fragile skin and a thin face. Funny how these men found a way to stick around, even though they'd both left. At least her Duane had sent money now and then. And later she had Ralph's help, though Janelle never accepted him. Those were tough years. It was lose-lose trying to build bridges between the two of them.

"Nikki's done at three, I'll be back around five. You going to be all right by yourself?"

A map of Minnesota that Nikki's been coloring lies open on the coffee table, the shirt Janelle's mending drapes over a chair. Nora wanders through the little rooms. The house looks so lived in that the quiet feels heavy. There are three glass butterflies suctioned to Nikki's windowpane—an orange one, a yellow, and a red. The wings glow. The colors look slick and edible, like the stained-glass windows of a church. Her mother cleaned at one for a time. "Joannie. Nora. Let's head over for services," she'd sing-song, as if attending were an employee benefit. Always, Nora would find herself staring up at the windows. There was something in the way the light came through the glass that stole her attention away from the service, and made all the words sink into the background.

The look of the lake out the window has totally changed,

gone from dull grey to rippled and steely. Nora steps over Nikki's sleeping bag on the floor, unbuckles her suitcase, and takes out her notebook. All night long she could hear the waves hitting shore. Janelle calls it soothing, but Nora finds it unsettling, with the house so close to the edge, and the water drumming in her ears.

Nora sits at the table, the notebook open to an empty page. "What Next?" she writes across the top. She sips her coffee, taps the pen on the page. Write anything, she tells herself. She looks at the lake, then back to the page. Her eyes wander over the room.

As Nora rounds the house she hears the sound of wind chimes, the wooden kind that sound hollow when they collide, though she doesn't see where Janelle has hung them. She sets her things at the picnic table and cups her hand around her lighter, her back to the cold wind coming off the lake. "What Next?" it says at the top of the page.

The hollow knocking is coming from the water. Nora sets the pen down and rubs her eyes. She puts her mug on the notebook to keep it from blowing and walks to the edge of the little yard. Out beyond the slanting rock ledge there are chunks of floating ice as big as bathroom mirrors clacking around in a sea of ice chips. They weren't there the day before.

She smokes and watches. The sound is soothing and it's pretty the way the ice is glinting. It looks like a giant grey daiquiri. Further out, a gull floats in the swells, and she wonders that it doesn't freeze to death. Beyond it there's only open water and a long-lined horizon.

"What Next?" The page looks impossibly blank. "Rebuild," she writes, though she already knows that her settlement will come in well below the cost of new construction.

1902

Gunnar can hear it in her breathing, short and shallow. He loves knowing her pleasure, knowing that she is now only sensation. No awareness of the coming day, no chores, no worry on her mind. There's nothing at all between Berit and his tongue.

He starts again, slowly tracing upward, each time reaching a little higher, while his fingers hold the familiar weight of her hips. She's close so he stops, and then starts in again, snaking his tongue in slow circles until she gasps, her back arching off the bed.

The birds are winding down their predawn ruckus, and sure, he should get out of bed. But he's feeling lazy and lulled by Berit's warm skin as his arm rises and falls with her breath. There are two places in the world that he considers home, where he has never questioned belonging. There, with his head close to Berit's, gathering her body into his arms; and then out on the lake, riding the swells, feeling her in the same way. The sky out the window is still black, and he'd like to stay a bit longer, but reluctantly, quietly, he gets out of bed.

There's light enough to see, but it's still before the sun when Gunnar settles into his skiff. He has an anchor setup of smaller twin boulders, split-roped out the first one hundred feet. He figures he can get them over the gunnel in quick succession by himself. It's important that he add another net to his gang. With prices down from three cents a pound to two, he has to increase his catch to stay even.

The lake is high but not steep or cresting, so he undulates easily over the swells. The first rose light is on the horizon, and Gunnar keeps an eye on the brightest spot as he rows. He loves the particulars of first light, and the slow way that it comes around. The morning has clouds like a mountain range to the east, as if a new continent had risen over night. The sun, though still not showing itself, is turning their bases a deep scarlet.

He has a half a dozen gulls in tow, keeping him company as he rows, and on shore the hills are coming clear, with the tallest pines separating from the sky. The sun comes up, an enormous pink ball, lifting slowly out of the lake, turning the backs of the swells pink, and it's going to be another fine morning.

Gunnar rows out a net's length while keeping an eye on his seaward uphauler. It's anchored at about 240 feet. His new rope is plenty long. He stands now while rowing, aligns himself with his buoys. Everything around him has turned to rose: the sky, the water, even the bobbing seagulls.

Squatting low, he gets his strength below an anchor rock and puts it over the gunnel, the rope whipping. Quickly he lifts the second one, and the lake swells underneath the boat, as if coming up to take it from his hands. Gunnar lets the boulder splash into the lake, and he's overboard feet first, ice cold engulfing the crown of his head.

His mouth clamps shut. His arms flail. He's incredulous and reeling with panic as he struggles the knife out of his pocket. The rope is coiled around his leg.

"Stay calm," a voice says from some corner in his head, but

he can't control his panicked movements as the anchor rock pulls him relentlessly downward.

His rib cage is caught in a giant clamp.

He's a comet of bubbles dropping into darkness.

He cuts frantically.

The pressure is going to kill him.

Whether he's sawing at the rope or his leg, he doesn't know.

He can't even feel his grip on the knife.

The darkness closes in around him, tunneling his vision, encircling. He can't believe he could be so stupid. His ribs are going to cave in.

His muscles spasm.

His mouth opens.

The lake flows down his windpipe.

When his blade finally makes it through the rope he feels the pressure slowly leave his chest. Feebly, he moves his arms and begins to swim upward. He's not even cold anymore. Berit will be furious with him for his carelessness.

There's a strong current swirling around him, and a sound like whispered conversation. It's beautiful, hushed, Indian maybe, and the wings of the dragonflies pulse in rhythm. He propels himself upward with his arms and one leg. He must have broken the other or pulled it from its socket. He's looking up through a keyhole at the hull of his boat. It appears like a leaf floating overhead. There's cold light streaming down, and one oar dangling. Leaves have always pleased him most in the autumn, when they sail and twirl down from the trees. He sees a copper flash, and then a scaly muscled wall of black glides directly in front of his face.

2000

"What smells funny in here?" Nikki asks as the car door groans shut.

"I don't know. What do you smell?"

"Eeww, it's this," she touches the netting of the glass float. "It smells weird."

Nora backs out of the parking space. "It was in the fire," she says. "Should we go somewhere?"

"I thought everything got burnt up."

"Yeah, mostly."

Nikki holds the float in front of her eyes. "Oooh, It makes everything green. Underwater world," she sings. "Hey, do you want to go to the agate beach? It's so fun."

Nora drives past the gas station, the last thing in what is considered town. "Are you sure you know how to get there, Bun?"

"Yeah, I've been there a million times. There's a sign for it. It's the beach with the cross. Last year I found the biggest agate ever. Like this," she says, making a C with her hand the size of a half-dollar. "I'll show it to you when we get home. It's an orange one with white and brown rings that make a picture like a cave. Jack tumbled it for me."

Mr. Numerology. Nora rolls her eyes. "Thank God your mother sent him packing."

"Nanny!" Nikki's mouth drops open, but then she giggles. "He was kinda weird."

Nora nods with a cigarette between her lips. "Kinda." She puts the lighter to its end.

"Ick. Peeuw." Nikki makes a face.

"Open your window. There's plenty of air."

Nikki rolls down the window and leans her head over.

"You look like a dog sticking your head out like that."

"I am," she laughs, and starts barking at everything.

The sun, falling toward the ridge, shines on the surface of the lake, but the long arc of beach where they stand is already sunk in shadow. Nora looks out over the grey water. There's no chime-ice anywhere.

"What was that cross about?" she asks. They'd taken a short path to the mouth of a river, where a big cement cross had been erected. But Nikki was anxious to get down to the beach, so they'd just stayed a second and turned around.

"We had to learn about it in school," Nikki says, bent over searching the rocks.

"So, what happened? Is someone buried there?"

"No. It's about this missionary guy." She picks up a rock and examines it, then tosses it disappointedly back to the ground. "You want to know the story?"

"Sure. Tell me."

"Well, you see, there was this missionary." Nikki straightens up and looks at her. "They wore these long black coats," she slices her hand at her ankle. "Anyway, he came here to save the Indians because they didn't believe in God. So once he had to go in a boat to help this one, and he got caught in a big storm. But then, what happened, just when his boat was going to crash into the rocks, it went into that river instead."

"That's it?"

"Yep. It was supposed to be a miracle." She starts searching for agates again.

"That doesn't sound like much of a miracle."

"Hey, a perfect skipper." Nikki beams, holding out a smooth flat stone.

"Don't go so close, Bun," Nora warns, but Nikki runs down to the water and side-arms the rock into the lake. It skips across the surface four times, then drops in and disappears. Nikki raises her arms, victorious, her small body in front of the great grey lake.

In that instant, Nora feels the full force of her love.

"Gorgeous, Bun. Absolutely."

It's after four when Nora glances at her watch. Nikki had been sitting out on the rock ledge, staring at the water for a long time. "It's my special place," she said. All that's visible are her head and shoulders. Nora couldn't begin to guess what's been going through her mind while she sits and stares. The water looks cold, dark, and unwelcoming.

"Can we go somewhere for a snack?" Nikki asks, climbing back down to the stone beach.

"Sure. A quick one. Any ideas?"

"There's a Dairy Queen."

"I don't remember that."

"Well, it's kind of far away. Grand Marais."

"Nikki, we're not driving all the way up there. Think of somewhere between here and home."

"There's nothing good."

"What about that place we passed with the sign for pie?" Nikki pouts.

"Come on, it might be great. Let's find out."

Nora pulls in at the Windigo Resort, wondering if it's even open. There are only two cars and the place looks sleepy. Inside, the dining room is dark and cordoned off. "It's only open weekends this time of year," a teenage boy informs them from behind the front desk.

"Oh, Nanny. I'm so hungry, I'm gonna die."

"You can eat in the bar," the boy offers, "but it's not the full menu."

Nikki climbs onto a bar stool, her eyes widening at the giant moose head that's mounted over the register. There's a young couple watching TV from a booth, a pitcher of beer and a full ashtray between them. No one seems to be tending bar, until the kid from the front desk appears again. He hands them a menu in a plastic sheath. "Something to drink?"

Nora wonders if he's old enough to serve. "What kind of pie do you have?"

"Apple and lemon meringue."

"Yuck." Nikki drops her head to the bar.

"I'll have a vodka rocks." She pats Nikki on the back. "Isn't there anything else that looks good? They have french fries, onion rings, chicken wings."

"Gross."

"How about ice cream. Do you have ice cream?" she asks the boy.

"Vanilla."

Nikki makes a bored face.

"What about a root-beer float?" Nora suggests.

"Yeah." Nikki perks up.

The boy sets Nora's drink on the bar. "Sorry. No root beer."

"Ohhh." Nikki hangs her head.

"Listen, you got a pint glass?" Nora lights a cigarette.

"Sure."

"Three-fourths 7UP, splash of red grenadine, ice cream, whipped cream, and two maraschinos."

Nikki's not entirely convinced, but when the boy adds the grenadine and the drink turns bright red, she's grinning and kicking her feet in anticipation. "Wow, Nanny. What's it called?"

"Well, I used to make them for your mom. I think she called it a cherry jubilee."

"Juuu ba leeee," Nikki sings to the moose.

1902

The world is composed of rose light, its softness held within the walls of the cabin. It lies over the chairs, spreads across the tabletop, surrounds the tall jar of pussy willows. Berit pulls the bedcovers to her chin. It's beautiful, tranquil, and somehow so full. It would be enough to capture even a hint of it in a picture. She could draw the shapes of the furniture, use shadow to create the illusion of depth. But what of the fullness, if that's even the word. None of those things alone are creating it. It's something else, ungraspable. She's seen it accomplished with oil paints. It is something about the layering of the pigment that allows the color itself to emanate light. Berit draws her legs up and wraps her arms around them. Already, the soft pink light is fading.

Usually she rises with Gunnar, but this morning he had left without waking her. Of course he's capable of getting his own breakfast, but he only heats the dregs of the previous night's coffee and then takes whatever is cold and handy instead of sitting to a good hot meal. It never feels right, but he doesn't believe her when she says that she'd rather be awakened. She hadn't meant to fall back to sleep after—well, she had.

There are wolf tracks around the woodpile, though Berit hasn't seen one for a few weeks. She knocks the logs against each other to scare off any spiders. There's no sense bringing more into the house. To make double use of the wood, she's going to cook a pot of beans while she heats the laundry water. With the bacon they now have down in the cool-shed, the beans will be especially good.

Berit stokes the stove to its limit. She has her large pots and kettles arranged, the big tub in the middle of the floor, and the soiled clothes in piles on the chairs. She has a fresh bar of soap that came in on the new steamer. The packet freighter *America*, she's called, and what a vessel. *Stately* is the word they'd decided best described her after listing other possibilities one night after supper. Gunnar had of course been focused on her seaworthiness. "Sixteen to twenty miles per hour," he'd said. What she can't get over is the news about the inside. If they take a trip to Duluth one day, she'll see it for herself. A social salon that has a piano. A grand staircase. She can't wait to stroll down that.

Berit decides on the rest of dinner while she works, the beans, fried trout, and rye rolls to go along. Her cheeks are damp from standing over the steaming tub. A shirt on the surface has an air bubble in the sleeve, and she pushes the shirt to the bottom with her wash-pole. She ought to use the last of the stewed lentils as well. She could add moose and potatoes, that would make a good supper.

Out the front window the sky is blue, and the lake is cobalt and rolling like raw satin. She pauses to listen to it sweep against the shore. She loves the lake in the early spring, when it has tossed off its ice sheets and is free again. Out the back, the birch trees have tiny green leaves, which brings her jars of seed to mind, though it's still much too early to plant. She lifts the water-drenched shirt with the pole. Maybe she'll give the soil in the garden a turn if there's time left in the afternoon.

Berit rifles though dirty clothes, checking the pockets of

Gunnar's trousers, where she's bound to discover a lead or a nest of twine. She lifts a sweater from the pile to find its front speckled with dried fish scales. It doesn't seem to matter how many times she tells him, she still winds up picking fish scales out of newly cleaned clothes. She carries the sweater to the door for a good shake. Was she asking for the world? Good Lord. Is he incapable of brushing them off himself?

Berit replaces the lid of the butter tub, and pushes aside the wedge of wood that she uses to prop open the cool-shed door. She walks down onto their thin strip of rock beach, a dish of butter in her hand. The cold lake air wafts around her skirt hem as she casts her gaze over the water. Gunnar should be rowing in, but she doesn't see his skiff anywhere. She hopes he had an especially good catch, which would certainly put him in a light humor. Better that than he's had some trouble with a net.

Walking up the path, she notes the transition that happens in the short distance from the shore to the house. It grows quieter and warmer, but that's only part of it. It's the feeling of moving across distinct realms. They each have their own, she and the lake. A blue jay is nearby, voicing its call, and the fresh smell of balsam pitch is in the air. She'll hang the clean clothes and hold his dinner. There. She spots it on a high pine bough, a blue dab of color on a field of green.

Berit folds the shoulder of a wet shirt over the line and clamps a wooden pin down over it. There's virtually no wind, so the clothes just hang. The lake undulates and shines; there's nothing daunting about the weather. She pins a dish cloth to the line, her eye moving from the sunlit white to the dark blue water beyond.

The blue water touches the blue sky. Blue over blue where the two seem to meet.

From below, the expanse of water spreads. From above, the clear blue sky curves down.

The thin line is merely sight's limitation.

So much light and air. So much open space. Mesmerizing in its constant stirring.

In the blue, I once found reason to clutch or to let go.

To justify equally action or inaction.

I flung my deepest feelings out into it. The spit and drain of fear. Of desire. Trickled harmlessly. Joined unnoticed. Its muteness a comfort. Its muteness defeat.

I am beginning to know its tendency to absorb everything.

My poor. My Mrs.

At the blue line of the long horizon.

Birds and boats disappear.

1622

Large logs of green wood bracket the fire and the moose-hide vat is swollen with sap, turning the air thick inside the lodge. Three Winds bends to feed the fire and keep it at the right height, while Bullhead stands over her taming the froth. The sisters have been together constantly, though their talk, once as persistent as buzzing flies, has calmed to a satisfied silence.

Grey Rabbit sits along the wall, examining a straining mat. They'll need it in the morning, when the boil is done. She runs her fingers over the narrow strips of basswood, testing the weave for weak spots.

"You should rest now," Bullhead says to her. "You've been tree to tree like a woodpecker all day. I'll wake you when it's your turn to work."

Grey Rabbit feels tired, though she'd rather not give herself over to dreaming. "I'll go see that Standing Bird and Little Cedar are settled."

"You rest," Bullhead more than suggests.

Three Winds backs up her sister. "With hot coals and sap that scalds to the touch, you'll be in no shape to help if you don't sleep now."

To say anything more would be disrespectful, so Grey Rabbit sets the mat aside and spreads her sleeping roll against the wall.

She lies with her head resting on her arm as a slow trail of people carry in wood and the last of the day's sap. Her eyes half open, she watches the sisters work, one broad, one thin, but both similar in gesture and in the rising and falling patterns of their speech. It's lulling, the soft sound of their voices, punctuated by the snapping fire, and her arms are sore from the day's work cutting, and her stomach is full of squirrel, and the weight and warmth of the furs press down on her, and the fire-smoke rises through the hole in the roof.

Bullhead is over her, touching her arm.

Grey Rabbit groggily steps outside to find clouds covering the stars, cocooning their camp in darkness and night woods. Below her the black water pounds against the shore. She bends and scoops up a handful of snow, touching it to her cheeks and neck, holding it for a moment over each eye, her skin waking with the cold. Her nose waking. Her hair smells of sweet sap. The water pounds a rhythm against the rocks, and though she can't see it, she feels each wave sending vibrations up her legs. The giver. The taker. Gichigami.

When Grey Rabbit returns to the lodge, she sees a flash of disapproval in Three Wind's eyes. She'd looked in on her sons, but she'd hurried back. It's warm inside and bright from the fire, the air hanging smoky sweet.

Bullhead is already asleep near the wall, so Grey Rabbit takes her place at the vat. Three Winds hands her the long stick with a spruce branch lashed to it, which she is to dip across the froth whenever the sap starts to bubble too much. The two work together without speaking; there's only the fire and the sleeping sounds from along the wall.

"Long ago, when Bullhead and I were girls learning to do quillwork, an awful thing happened."

Grey Rabbit keeps her head down and her eyes on the spruce bough. Already her legs are hot and itching from the fire's heat.

Three Winds describes how she was jealous of Bullhead's superior skill, and the clean pattern she accomplished. And then, when everyone was asleep, how she laid it in the fire and watched it burn. She told of Bullhead's misery over its disappearance, and of her own, which she concluded was much worse because she never told anyone.

Grey Rabbit turns the story over in her mind, wondering at its telling and what in it was meant for her. She wonders what Three Winds has heard. She must speak with Bullhead soon. The longer she keeps silent, the harder speaking becomes. In the morning, then. After the pour. She balances the dripping spruce bough on the edge of the vat, bends down and squints as she rolls a smoky log.

1902

Berit stands on the point and scans the horizon. "Enough," she tries to hush a red squirrel that natters from a thin spruce. The sun has passed its high point by a hand, and she hasn't seen any sign of Gunnar. Arms crossed, she sits on the bench, but she can't keep her leg from jiggling. Maybe he rowed up to see Hans, or all the way down to Torgeson's to borrow something, though she can't think of what he'd need. She'd heard tell that Torgeson keeps a regular bottle. If Gunnar rowed down and didn't inform her he was going, he'll hear about it for some time.

Berit forces the tip of the shovel with her foot, lifts and turns the winter-packed soil. Lift and turn. Lift and turn. The sun angles back toward the ridge, where a hawk glides silently above the green spires. When she gets to the end of the row, she'll allow herself to look out to the lake. She forces the shovel in, lifts and turns, scrapes caked dirt from the sole of her boot. Four more shovels-full and she'll turn to see him. Three. Two. One.

The water and the sky form an unbroken line.

The sun has slid behind the ridge, leaving the cove in shadow but the lake still in sunlight. Berit paces in her long coat, back and forth along the length of the point. There's a gnawing sensation in her stomach. "Oh," she scoffs. "Oh, if ever . . ." Her face clamps tight, and she blinks back hot tears.

The light is draining from the birch-covered slope and the lake has turned soft pastel blue. It's hardly rolling at all anymore, just rising and falling peacefully. Berit sits on the bench and listens as the lake rises over the stone beach, then slides back to itself with a long hush. She tries to match her breathing with the sound, and to keep the worst thoughts from getting in. Something happened, he's hurt and unable to row. The waves, though not strong, would push him in, deposit him somewhere along the shore. He could be walking home through the woods at this very moment. If he'd been down to Torgeson's all this time, he'd be headed back now while there's enough light to navigate. The lake glubs in a hollow beneath her.

Berit pulls the blanket tight around her shoulders and legs, her feet drawn up on the wooden bench. The brightest stars are already out, and she feels as if she is in a horrible dream. She rocks herself, a short pulsing back and forth, going over the day in her mind. Just this morning they'd lain in bed, the familiar weight of his arm across her waist. Just this morning the cabin was full of pink light. How did she get to this awful place, and what can she do to turn things back.

"Good God." She launches herself off the bench. He'll get his comeuppance when he gets home.

It's dark. There's no denying it anymore. It's dark enough that she should have brought a lantern. A lantern. Lord, how could she be so daft? She rushes up the path toward the cabin. She'll light every lantern she can find. If he's out there the light will help guide him in.

It's black on black, the sky dizzy with stars that twirl and reflect on the lake. Berit sits bundled on the bench, listening harder than she knew she could. The lake fans against the shore. There are indiscernible rustles and scratchings, and somewhere in the woods, an owl. There are other sounds as well, faint and unnamable, that could as easily be coming from the lantern at her feet as from the million stars. She peers back at the windows all ablaze. They look warm and homey, as if there were nothing at all wrong, as if she could go up and find him sitting at the table. It seems likely even that both of them are there, comfortable behind the warm yellow panes, talking, their feet on a chair near the stove.

Berit has snuffed her lantern wick, finding she can see further into the night without it. A distant wolf howls a long drawn out call, and her heart rises like dough in her chest. She listens for the dip of oars. She waits for the skiff to take shape among the stars lying on the black surface of the lake. Again, the wolf howls and she feels the ache of it in her chest, stretching the thin skin of her heart.

2000

"Hi Mom." Nikki kicks off her boots.

"There you are." Janelle turns from the stove, where she's frying ham.

"Look what we got. It's all horses." Nikki holds up the plastic bag from the drugstore, with the coloring book inside. "And a whole box of new markers, too."

"That was nice of your Nanny. Come give me a hug. I was starting to worry about you guys."

Nora turns from the coat rack to see Janelle sniffing the top of Nikki's head. "You smell like smoke."

"I had cherry jubilee."

"Where?"

"At the Windigo."

Janelle glares at Nora across the room, and turns Nikki around by the shoulders.

"You go and turn the bath on, young lady."

"But it's not bath time."

"Now. And I want you to shampoo your hair."

"What were you thinking," Janelle says through tight lips, her neck turning red and blotchy. "You want to raise my kid in a bar, too?"

At dinner, no one talks and the silence is loud. Nora looks at their reflection in the window: Janelle's blurred profile and Nikki's little face hanging sullenly over her plate.

"I'm not very hungry, Mom." Nikki rests her chin on her hand.

"You can finish your ham."

"Am I being punished?"

"Of course not. Your mommy and Nanny just had a disagreement."

Nora is in the bathroom when Nikki knocks. "Nanny, the phone's for you. Do you want me to hand it in?" Nora sets down her tweezers and opens the door.

"Hello?" she says, but there's no reply. "Hello?" She's about to hang up when she hears music coming over the line. It's Rose playing a waltz on her new Casio. She'd know her playing anywhere. Nora sits on the edge of the bathtub and cradles the phone against her ear.

When Nora rounds the house she can't see the picnic table, or even where the yard ends. A wave dashes against the rocks below the ledge. The spray leaps and showers back. Then a moment of silence. No moon. No stars. The sky and the lake are a wall of blackness. Another wave hits and showers. Nora edges back to the rectangle of light cast on the lawn by the picture window. The sidelights of a freighter are visible in the distance. It looks like a long string of diamonds, and it's heading toward the Twin Ports. Home.

Behind the big glass pane, Janelle is gesturing to someone on the phone. Nora taps a cigarette from her pack. Who knows who she's talking to. What she's saying isn't hard to guess. It's amazing, the cruelty in her lightning-bolt temper, and then her thunder can roll on for days.

A wave strikes. Nora can feel the vibration in her feet. Up and down the shoreline it's darker than dark. And yet she doesn't want to go inside and explain again about Nikki's hunger and the closed restaurant.

The shoreline is pitch black.

Nikki is already asleep on the floor, her mouth open, breathing in rushes of air. Nora lies back on the small bed. It's not even ten o'clock. She reaches down and smoothes Nikki's soft hair behind her ear. It's dark. No streetlight shining in. It is darker than any darkness she's used to, but she doesn't want to wake Nikki with the lamplight. The lake out the window hits the ledge and falls back, and Nikki's breath sounds in and out.

1902

There's a low hum, a faint song. And a warm wind playing at the hem of Berit's skirt. It lifts the loosened hair at her temples. The song, low-throated, is in her ears. Its muscled underbeat inside her ribs. The wind presses her skirt against her calves, gusts hot in her face. Her eyelids flutter. The singing grows louder. The air churns. The hot wind pushing her. Roiling currents overhead. The song. The rhythmic stroking. The sharp smell of sweat. The hot vortex of wind pulling her from the bench, upward toward the tumult in the air, working at her grip, prying her away. Lifting her upright, awake and gasping.

Her hands are cold and stiff, and her bad leg aches. The lake is dim and the stars fading, and then the flooding nightmare of where she is, and why. She'd slept. How could she, for even one moment? She stands. Sits. Stands again. She can't have this. She won't. The cabin windows no longer glow, but look flat and tepid in the grey light. Maybe he's there, sick, wounded, not knowing where she'd gone. Berit races up the path, and flings open the cabin door. The bed is empty, the room is still, the bean pot sitting on the stove. She sinks into a chair, the stove blurring through her tears. Pushing at the table, she's up again. No. She won't have it. She stomps out the door.

An edge of orange sun is lifting out of the lake, and the air holds the first hint of a quickening breeze. She walks behind the house and into the woods, climbing up the birch-covered slope, the orange light on their white trunks. She looks over her shoulder as she climbs, her breath hard, her feet determined.

Berit stands panting on top of the ridge, the long empty horizon before her. Water. Sunlight. The small crescent of their cove. There's no sign of Gunnar anywhere.

What of a heart within a chest. Beat. Beat. Perpetually beating. Never smelled. Never seen or touched. A small tenacious drum. Preceding breath. Enduring throughout every minute, month, year.

But still, the heart.

Fragile fist.

What of this place of timeless eddies. These keepsake waters. Where I am. I am not. This slow dissolve of my every quirk and feature. Yet the stilled beat still echoes.

The silky cold's caress is its own fierce intimacy.

This place of holding. The common waters.

This place of circling.

The shores perceived.

My vision expands with every dark fathom.

I strain toward the rumble. The thin-skinned pulse.

1622

The last of the sap is on its final fire and still looking good enough to be grained in the troughs. It ran well, and there's sugar in plenty, and syrup hardening in birch-bark cones.

Little Cedar stands at the open end of the lodge, watching the wind whirl the leaves in circles as it chases the last of winter away. The lodge is a flurry of preparation for the last pour and the cleanup, the women brushing past him, coming and going like swallows.

"Stay to the side." Three Winds shoos him from the entrance.

Grey Rabbit observes Three Winds's scowl, then adds another piece of tallow to the boil. Let the others gossip behind their hands, or hint subtly that the boil is no place for young children. She smiles at Little Cedar, who stands sullenly against the wall. She had no choice but to keep him with her, though even Night Cloud had been of a different mind. "He should watch as we lay the beaver traps," he said. Of course this was true, but after her terrifying dream—she can still see the one-eyed giant on the cliff, tossing handfuls of children to the big water—and then the owl that had followed her in the woods, she felt most fiercely that he shouldn't go.

Grey Rabbit beckons to Little Cedar with a sooty hand. "Stay here by me, and don't stray." She gives him some gum sugar cradled in bark.

It's hot standing so near the fire, and the smell of burnt sugar is in his nose. Little Cedar can see the places where the sap has spilled over and burned to black in the hot coals. He bites off a small piece of the gum sugar, and holds the rest closed in his fist.

"Make sure you scrub everything out entirely." He listens as Three Winds instructs the girls for the washing. "If they're not cleaned well enough, next year's sugar will be off color. If anything needs repair, set it aside. If it's beyond use, it can be burned."

Little Cedar rolls the sweet gum in his mouth, and pushes it along the back of his teeth. He likes to let it dissolve slowly, not chew and swallow fast like Standing Bird. His shins are too hot where his leggings touch against them, and the black smoke is getting in his eyes.

The call goes out and the lodge swings into motion. A line of women forms to fill their containers and whisk them quickly out to the troughs where others wait, paddles in hand, ready for the fast work of graining.

The smoke is going right in his face. Little Cedar tries breathing through his mouth, and looking through his lashes with his eyes half closed. His legs are too hot and his eyes sting. He squeezes them shut and twists away, stumbling into the current of women.

Everything stops at the sound of his scream, with no one even seeing exactly what happened, or whose container the scalding sap sloshed out of when Little Cedar got tangled in all the legs.

2000

Nora tamps a pack of cigarettes against the dash, and opens the cellophane with her teeth. The lake is breaking hard, spray flinging in the air, looking about how she feels inside. So she'd brought enough clothes to last two weeks and only stayed a couple of days. Even as a little girl, Janelle had a way of acting as if she were the one in charge, approving or disapproving of her actions.

Everything out the windshield looks cold, the birch trees and the dark rock they'd blasted through to build the road. Nora, driving slowly, edges over to let an encroaching car pass. She lights a cigarette off the glowing orange coil. If there's anything she'd learned in her years behind the bar, it's that there's never only one way to look at something; there's always the other side to hear, and even that may not be the whole of it. She raps the lighter against the ashtray. What cuts deepest is the accusation that she's a danger to her own granddaughter.

The Caribou River. The sign for the Manitou. It swirls and tumbles toward the lake. Manitou, she considers the word. Manitou, Caribou, possibly related.

"Nanny, it's not fair that you're leaving." Nikki sat sullenly as they waited for the bus. "We hardly got to do anything, or go anywhere, or even color the horses." That part too, she feels terrible about. Nora steers onto the shoulder of the road to avoid a large black flap of truck-tire rubber. She slows and stops, turns the car off, stares at the rubber in her rearview mirror. Wind rocks her car and the tall pines circle. She'd dreamt about a dead crow.

She's on a residential street after a rain. There's the sound of rushing water under the sewer grates, and raindrops blowing down from the trees. It's her street, but it's not really her street. She steps over a puddle on the sidewalk. There are lots of puddles and the grass is wet, though she's not wet, not even her shoes. She stops when she sees it ahead on the sidewalk: a large piece of black rubber, or a black plastic bag. A crow with a twig in its beak stands near the dark shape. It lays the twig beside it on the sidewalk, caws and flies to the tree on the boulevard. She walks closer and another bird lands. The tree on the boulevard has huge black leaves. Not leaves, there are hundreds of crows in its branches. The shape on the ground is also a crow. It's dead, she sees this, and it's enormous, nearly covering the sidewalk square.

No one on the street seems to notice, not the boys down the block tossing a football, or the people passing by in cars. But there's a dog sitting close in the grass. It looks at her and then back to the birds. It's watching like she is, just she and the dog.

She's on a porch, in an old painted chair. The crows leave the tree to lay twigs on the sidewalk. They caw and then fly up again. There's a window screen with rain caught in its squares. There's a damp sky, and puffs of wind on the puddles. The dog is lying across her feet; she feels its warm furry weight. It sighs. Its breath rises and falls. She reaches down to pet its soft fur. And just at that moment she feels its heart break.

Her car takes another gust of wind and the sign she just passed for Split Rock Lighthouse shutters. She has an image of the lighthouse in her mind—perched high on a cliff, the water below—but it must be from postcards and photographs; she doesn't recall ever being there. She could drive in and take a look. She has time. If nothing else, she has that. Nora starts her engine and pulls off the shoulder, her glass float swinging as she makes a U-turn.

The size of the lighthouse operation is surprising. There's a sleek information center with a gift shop, exhibits, even a small movie theater. She'd expected only the lighthouse and a historic plaque. She has no idea where all the people came from, though it feels good being in the midst of something, so when a loud-speaker announces the start of a tour, Nora joins the rear of a group that's already gathered at the door.

The guide, a young scrubbed-faced blonde, leads them to the guardrail at the top of the cliff. "A hundred and thirty feet down," she shouts, as the wind beats everyone's hair around. "The ore in these cliffs reeked havoc with ship's compasses, spinning them off of magnetic north. It wasn't until after the gale of 1905, in which twenty-nine ships were damaged, that Congress appropriated money for the light. Two of those ships foundered right out here," she sweeps her arm along the shore.

"Wasn't it the steamship companies who pushed through the legislation after having lost so many ships?" asks a man with thick glasses and a battered red jacket. Nora rolls her eyes. He's telling, not asking. She holds fast to the guardrail and looks down. The cliff is splotched with orange lichen, and the lake below is crashing against it. Her heart flutters, but it's not falling she fears; it's the welling urge to attempt flight.

A man in a navy blue uniform greets them at the steps to the lighthouse. He has grey wisps of hair sticking out of his cap, and he's acting as if he were back in time, and actually the real lighthouse keeper. He ushers them into the sudden stillness and warmth, where they wait like school children for the group to assemble. It never occurred to her, though now it makes sense, that no two lighthouses would be built the same shape, and that each would have its own flashing sequence to help lost boats figure out where they are. Nora wonders if Ralph ever toured the lighthouse. He must have. He'd love it. She can't recall.

The group whittles to single file as they mount the circular staircase to the light. Nora peers down at the whitecap-flecked lake each time the spiral staircase brings her past a skinny window. Her stomach feels sour and her head full of air. Already, they were on top of a cliff, and now they're climbing even higher. She's higher than the careening gulls. Nora keeps her hand on the banister. She can hear the exclamations of the people ahead of her, who have already made it to the top of the tower.

"This lens was shipped from Paris, France," the guide says, as Nora steps in to join the group. "A bivalve frenzel . . ." But Nora has stopped listening. She's standing before a giant eyeball made of concentric crystal rings. Immediately, she wants to touch it.

"It's floating on liquid mercury," he explains, "despite the fact that it weighs four tons."

All of its edges hold sunlight and rainbows. It's an enormous jewel. The world's biggest diamond. She tilts her head and the rainbows shift.

"It's 169 feet from the focus of the light to the mean water level. Much of my work is its care and cleaning."

Nora imagines a bright beam of light emanating from the crystal eye, sweeping out over the water to find a storm-struck sailor. How relieved he'd be to spot the light, and to have something to set a course toward. The idea of being on Superior in weather is about the most terrifying thing she can imagine. The old schooners didn't even have electricity. Nora scans the horizon for boats. Even in the daylight there are dangerous shoals, engine troubles, human mistakes. Most sailors swear that fog is the worst.

A huge, round, gorgeous crystal eye. Nora wants to walk all the way around it, or just sit near it for a while, but already people are stepping around her as the man herds them back down the stairs.

Gooseberry River. Castle Danger. Then, the tunnel through Lafayette Bluff. Her stomach feels lousy, worse than before. The sturgeon. It appears in her mind, ugly and menacing with its prehistoric plates of armor. It hung in the nets over the back exit. Nora leans over and writes it in the notebook. Her thoughts slide back to the giant lens, then the serious look on the guide's face when he told them that a foghorn blast could move across the water like a skipping stone. She sees a ship captain blinded in a fog, and then the loud as hell sound that's supposed to save him hitting the water and bouncing over his boat. The car goes dark in the Silver Creek Cliff Tunnel, then zooms out the other side into sunlight.

Half an hour or so, and she'll be back home.

Nora turns into a small unpaved lot on the final stretch of the old scenic highway. The water's still rough, but the wind has died, so she gets out and leans against the hood. The outline of the Twin Ports is visible—the hills of the North Shore meeting the flatter land of the south. She can make out the shapes of the grain elevators and ore docks, but it's like she's looking through different eyes. The Twin Ports are business as usual, and she doesn't belong, has no part in it anymore. Nora pushes gravel side to side with her foot, making a small fan shape in the rocks. Her stomach is really rolling around. She needs to get a grip. Maybe Joannie is right, a big change would do her good.

On London Road, an old woman is walking her dog, and everyone is going about their business, stopping for gas, pulling in at the market, driving with cell phones held to their ears. Nora feels like her car is invisible. She passes the lift bridge as it's rising for a Coast Guard cutter, passes the aquarium, the line of billboards, and then exits for the high bridge to Wisconsin. The road takes her out on the spit of land that's all railroad and industry, passes the Goodwill, then lifts onto the bridge, and she's up in the sky with the water below, the ironwork flashing shadows in the car.

Her stomach is twisted up like a pretzel. Nora lifts her foot from the gas as the bridge descends. She could unpack her things, surprise Rose with the painting, maybe go to the 22 and see who's around. The bridge empties onto Hammond Avenue. But instead of heading home, she finds herself veering onto the truck route that runs behind the grain elevators, passing the shipyard and then Barker's Island. She keeps on going through the east end, then Allouez. Her car heading out of town.

1902

Berit lays askew in the bed, her body curled into itself, aware for a moment only of warmth in the soft, brief rise from sleep. One moment of warmth and then the next, a wave that lifts and breaks over her back. There, the bureau drawer hanging open. She pulls the pile of Gunnar's clothes against her stomach as a sound oozes from her mouth. Her body rocks from side to side, propelled by a force she can't control. Dear Lord. Make the nightmare stop. The feeling brings her to all fours and pitches her forward, rocking violently, yowling and bucking as if to throw it off.

Numb, Berit sits at the table, wearing Gunnar's big green sweater, her hair in tangles, her face puffy. Out the window, the clothes hang on the line, going bright and then dull as clouds move over the sun. She pinches off a corner of bread, but it sits in her mouth like a piece of cloth and she has to pick it from her tongue. The lake drums against the shore. She drops her head into the crook of her elbow as again, the whole thing comes cascading down.

Berit sprinkles water on a dish towel and pushes the hot iron across it, the crumpled terrain of the fabric flattening. She noses the iron into a corner, tears dripping off her chin. Ironing. She is ironing clothes, the basket of whites sits at her feet. The last time she saw him they were in bed, his face so close that he had a third eye. Now she can't even conjure his face, just the shape of his head, vague and featureless.

The iron trembles in her hand, and she drops it onto the stove top. What other face has she ever known better? She closes her eyes and wills it to appear, sees his eyes, his chin, but the whole won't compose. She has lost his face. She goes to the window. The fish house stands stone quiet. This has to stop now, Berit reels. This can not be. She breaks at the knees.

The fire is nearly out, but she can't rise from the chair or light the lantern though night has come down. She sits unmoving at the table, her hand resting on two overturned photographs. In one, Gunnar stands with his uncle, their luggage behind them, and the passenger ship. He's squinting into the sun, his weight on one leg, his hands deep in his coat pockets. The other, inside a cardboard frame, is the portrait taken when they married. They sit side by side on a small settee. Gunnar, in a dark suit, looks straight ahead, his face still and serious. She'd dug frantically through the trunk for the pictures, but now she fears looking at them any longer. She fears that those two images of his face will be all she will ever have. Two moments frozen in time, two expressions replacing all the rest.

The morning's rain has blown over, leaving a fine mist in the air and water clinging to the windowpane. Berit puts her arms in her long dark coat, shoves her feet in boots, and opens the door. The pot of beans that she'd thrown in anger sits upright on the ground, nearly clean. She'd heard the bear come for it in the middle of the night, snort and bang the pot around.

She walks down through the mist carrying her bucket, the grasses wetting the hem of her coat. Warm sweetened water is all she can manage, tiny sips that she leaves on her tongue. She doesn't care. Why should she have food if Gunnar can't.

Berit lowers the bucket from the rock ledge. Beast. Betrayer. This lake that she'd loved. She can see down through its clear water, the large boulder, the bed of stones. She's hauling in the rope, feeling the water's weight, when she hears the dip and splash of oars. Her heart leaps. She freezes. Listens. Drops everything and rushes to the end of the point, bursting into tears and waving her arms. He's out there in the mist, rowing toward her. She runs back to land and across the beach to the boat slide, everything blurring as she cries out to the water, the skiff angling in toward shore.

He stills his oars and turns his head. "Mrs. Kleiven. I came over to see that everything was all right here."

Berit stares at the pocked face of Hans Nelson, unable to utter a word.

"Captain Shephard was asking. He said that Gunnar hadn't been out with his fish. I rowed over and found his nets untended. The otters have had a day with them, so I thought I'd better come see if he were ill . . ."

Berit can't hear what he's saying, but she can see the change drop over his face, his expression turning from neighborly to grave.

No. She won't go back with him. No. She doesn't want him to send Nellie. Berit backs away, shaking her head. If they come the next day like he insists, she'll hide in the woods. They'll never find her.

Berit sits on the ridge, her back against the rough bark of a pine. The water and sky are a milky agate, banded with lines of grey and white. If they're coming, it will be anytime now. He'd have his fish in, and dinner would be over. A white-throated sparrow sings its song, the question and the answer repeating over and over. She wipes her eyes and leans her head against the bark, the sickening images rising again. Gunnar, floating faceup in the lake. Facedown, swaying on frigid night waves. Berit wipes the endless water from her face.

Sure enough, she sees a boat coming. Good Lord. He has Gunnar's skiff in tow.

I hear voices. Over thick distance. Cold. Dark. But the sound has no source.

A glimmering image. Color and light from the blackness. Fragments coalesce. Waver. Disappear.

A French chorus rings. Around the silence. Red-headed paddles flash in time. Plunge and pull. Plunge and pull.

The voyageurs come on a dark wall of water.

Ten men to a boat, laden with furs bound for Europe.

A calloused hand. Red wool. A wind-burnt cheek.

Faces stunned. By the beauty. By the cold.

They paddle to the perfect rhythm of their songs.

Alouette.

Gentille alouette.

Currents whirl as the wall of water nears.

Keep to the shore. To the shore. The shore.

Red-headed paddles plunge and pull.

Rile the heavy, slick, black water.

I search among the paddlers for the man in the dark coat.

But the wall curves.

Darts away like a startled fish.

2000

A neon beer sign with a moving waterfall casts a cold bluish light over the surface of Nora's vodka. She rattles the ice cubes and the light breaks apart.

"You're looking rested," Jerry says.

"Thanks," replies Nora, looking at him dead-on, an unspoken acknowledgement hanging between them. His kindness the day before had saved her.

When she'd headed out of Superior without a shred of a plan, she'd driven south into Wisconsin, but the further she drove the worse she felt. After nearly an hour, she turned around and backtracked to the T in the road. She sat at the stop sign a good long time, looking at her options, west or east, staring at the glass float as if it were a crystal ball that might direct her—toward home or away. Finally, a semi came up behind her, its grill filling the rearview mirror, and she had to move.

She ended up on the scenic road east, following the shore of the lake. As she drove, she felt a little bit calmer. Finally, she landed at the Breakers. After sizing her up, Jerry gave her exactly what she needed, room and just enough conversation. He told her which motel to stay at, and where to get a good meal.

Mostly, he made himself a solid presence, his eyes softening kindly when he spoke to her.

"So you're going to stay on then?" Jerry asks, opening a bag of pour spouts with his teeth. He dumps them in a highball and sets them below the bar.

"I might, who knows." Nora lifts her glass in a toast. "I guess I'm fancy free and on vacation."

"To the first of the tourists, then." Jerry lifts his coffee cup.

"Thanks a lot."

"I was kidding," he says. "We don't actually get many tourists. We're more of a drive-though, day-trip town, which is good and bad as I see it. Most of the folks who come through are fine, but a lot of them have a real city attitude. It drives my wife absolutely crazy. She jokes about tattooing 'educated' across her forehead."

"I don't get much in the way of tourists. Mine is more of a working crowd. Though I do have some college kids this year, and they're their own brand of annoying." Nora stops herself. Have. Had. She's talking as if the Schooner still exists. The light from the beer sign slides across her hand and the shiny surface of the bar.

"You okay?"

Nora manages a smile.

"Why don't you stick around for the music. I've got folk-singers coming in, a husband and wife duo, but their music gets kind of jazzy if that makes any sense. He plays guitar and she plays fiddle. They usually draw a decent crowd. Did you book music at your bar?"

"I couldn't manage it. Didn't have the room." Couldn't. Didn't. "I had a cook once who had a lot of talent. He was a first-rate songwriter. He'd set up by the jukebox with a couple of other guys, but that was pretty occasional."

The door swings open and Nora feels the lake air.

"Hey, Frank, it's been a while."

Nora jiggles her drink. She had Rose's piano in the middle of the night, of course, but that was different, and too personal to say.

"Frank Basset, this is Nora . . ."

"Truneau," she says, holding out her hand.

"What brings you through?" Jerry asks Frank, then turns to Nora to explain. "Frank's on the pollution control agency's gravy train. They send him around the region to drink the water and sniff the air."

"Something like that," Frank says, sliding onto a stool a couple over from Nora's.

"Nora's on a little explore," Jerry winks. "Seeking new lives and new civilizations."

"Boldly going." She lifts her glass, feeling the warmth of his generosity again.

"To where no man has ever gone before?" Frank swivels toward her, and lifts an eyebrow.

He has close-cropped hair, more salt than anything, stout hands, a crooked smile. Obviously, a streak of bad boy. She can see it in the ease of his posture, and the way he'd lifted just the one eyebrow.

All the tables near the stage are full, and there are more in the back by the pinball machines. "Another place you should go is Pictured Rocks, on the Michigan coast. It's a spectacular shoreline, crazy caves and rock formations." Frank's writing a list on a napkin for her, but Nora is turned toward the stage. She especially likes the woman's fiddle playing, the way her hair falls in a yellow curtain when she leans forward, and her bow blurs when she plays the fast parts.

"They call them *pictured* because the minerals in the cliffs form striations of color. It's gorgeous. Worth the trip."

Jerry pours them a fresh round. "You two kids going to eat anything?"

"You choose something, Frank," Nora says, tapping her foot in time with the song. "I told you, I'm not making any decisions right now."

"Okay. Chicken wings."

Nora makes a face.

Frank stubs his cigarette in the ashtray they've been sharing. "I thought you said it was up to me."

Nora shrugs.

"I see how you are." He bobs his head as if he has a real case on his hands. "Okay, we're getting onion rings." He slides the menu caddy back on the bar, and looks at Nora sideways to see her reaction.

She smiles and blows out a stream of smoke.

"She's impossible," Frank says to Jerry.

Nora reaches back to the bar for her drink. The whole place has a simmering energy that's lifting right through her. It's good, the buzz and the blur of conversations, Jerry, and the woman playing the fiddle, Frank beside her lighting her cigarettes, and the blue light from the beer sign rhythmically crossing the bar, like luck or a lighthouse flashing home.

1622

"For three days she has hardly eaten." Night Cloud looks up through the bare trees, where heavy drops of water hang from the branches, silver in the weak spring sun. "She draws back like a crayfish when I try to speak with her."

Bullhead carries a walking stick, which she taps along the forest floor mottled with brown and yellow leaves, wet with the thaw and smelling of dirt. Her son is right to be concerned. She has felt Grey Rabbit's distance for some time.

The moist air is a salve to her cheeks as she plants her stick near a tree root in the path and they begin their ascent to the bald rock. Her poor Little No Eyes, she can see him as she climbs, lifting herself higher, planting her stick again, his face half covered in the white poultice. Yet she is happy for the strength of Three Winds's horsemint. The mixture is working to take out the fire, and it seems to be lessening the blistering. His cheek and his neck will surely scar, and his eye, well, it's too early to know.

The bald rock is damp and spotted with bird droppings. Bullhead, breathing heavily, noses her stick against a splotch of brown lichen, thankful she doesn't have to eat it. Gichigami stretches to the horizon, the shallows tawny from the streams high with snowmelt, the deep water changing abruptly to grey.

Night Cloud and Bullhead stand in silence as their eyes follow the sliding water and soft light.

"Its mood is peaceful, somehow watchful," muses Night Cloud.

Bullhead smiles faintly. He has always been the most receptive of her children. Even in his cradleboard he was different than the others. She recalls the playthings she'd hung for him, the stick man and the tiny bow, which he'd bat around. But he wouldn't play roughly with the dried mink skull. Instead, his face would grow still and thoughtful, as if there were an understanding between them.

A raven calls from deep in the forest.

Gichigami laps.

The surface water slides.

"It would be good for her to talk with someone," says Night Cloud.

Bullhead raises her eyebrows and sighs.

1902

Berit walks down to the cove for water, to find the boat slide, which is normally submerged, angling down to dry stones, and the lake receded to well beyond the point. She steps off the stone crescent of beach and, buckets in hand, walks toward the water. It's interesting to stand in the center of the cove and to see all the rocks uncovered. Her point, no longer halved by the water surface, looms twice its usual size. She doesn't remember ever seeing this. Certainly she'd remember walking into the cove. There are seagulls sitting in the stones, their white bodies dotting the lake bed, and further out, small stands of water glare like mirrors in the sun.

Berit trudges out across the lake bed, but the water retreats in step with her progress. She pauses, and looks back toward land. The cabin stands ever so high above her, up the rock slope and then up the hill of land.

The white seagulls sit in the stones. The lake lies perfectly flat and blinding like a sheet of tin under the sun. A faint sound is coming from the horizon, a whine like the quickening steam of a teakettle, and she's scrambling down hot rock ledges, their cracks and crevices stuffed with rumpled clothes.

She's desperate now to reach the water, but it won't let her draw near. Behind her the cabin is no longer visible, just steep rock cliffs and dry stone. The whine rises in pitch. The lake glares. Berit takes a tentative step forward. The lake doesn't move; it lies flat and still. Buckets in hand, she runs toward it, the whine reverberating off the rocks. She's closing the distance; the lake doesn't move. One leg splashes in, cold to the calf, and then the other plunges through, and the water pulls back revealing the crack, and she's falling and falling, screaming wind in her ears.

Berit jerks awake in the corner of the net loft.

Wind keens through a crack in the eaves and buffets the window she's curled against. The afternoon is dense and coal grey, and the lake wild and hurling against the shore. Berit drops her head to her knees and reaches down for the cat, which is curled against her leg in the pile of blankets and quilts she'd dragged up. The shock of the breakers vibrates the walls and the wind whistles through the cracked wood. She pulls a blanket around her shoulders and watches the savage water from inside herself, from a tiny spot shrunk back from the raw edges of her body. She runs a hand over her hair, finds a sticky clump that smells like pine sap on her fingers.

She'd evaded Hans and Nellie twice, running to the woods to hide. They'd left food. A cake. Of all things, a cake. And last time a burlap bundle tagged *S. Vulgarus/Lilac*. The note explained that the shrub had boarded the *America* in Duluth, marked paid in full by G. Kleiven. Captain Shephard had left it in Hans's care. A lilac bush. They'd never discussed it. A lilac for her yard. Her birthday gift. The letter went on with worry and condolences, then mentioned the new church down the shore. It ended with the suggestion that a service be held. But it's unthinkable. She can't imagine gathering with other people, practically strangers, most of them. No. She wants to be left alone.

She'd put the cake out for the animals, then wrote a reply

in her most practiced hand. She thanked them for their kindness, and explained that she'd made arrangements to travel to Duluth and spend time with family members. She'd placed the folded paper on Nellie's cake plate. Stowed some things, moved others to the fish house. It seems to have worked. She hasn't been bothered since. Mostly, she stays in the net loft now.

1622

Grey Rabbit enters to find Bullhead at the fire, a calm but serious look on her face. "Sit with me," is all she says, her eyes expanding as if beckoning her in.

Bullhead unfolds the square of birch-bark on which she has just started a new design. She examines the beginning pattern of her teeth marks in the firelight, then folds the bark into a square.

There is a long period of no words, only the crackling fire between them as Bullhead works calmly, grinding the soft inner bark between her teeth.

At first Grey Rabbit's words barely come, and those that do are only air around the thing itself.

Bullhead nods, unfolding the bark, patiently keeping track of her work.

Then the words, like swarming bees. The dreams. The dreams. She should have spoken. She thought they'd warned of hunger, but the hunger had passed. Still the dreams. She had thought it was clear that Little Cedar must be protected. She had thought she was protecting him. She had never been known as a powerful dreamer. She can't explain why she didn't speak.

A long silence. The crackling fire.

"Maybe you did protect the boy," offers Bullhead.

"But his face."

"Worse might have happened had he gone to the traps. Dreams have many sides. One can only interpret."

The fire smoke lifts in the air between them as Grey Rabbit tries to let that truth in.

Bullhead chews on the soft bark. "Well, it has ended. Now we go on."

"No," whispers Grey Rabbit, looking down at her hands. "The children still come."

Bullhead adds another piece of wood to the fire and tiny sparks rise into the air. She unfolds the design. Folds it again. "There is no one here who is known for interpreting. Not that I trust. At Bawating, yes." She hands Grey Rabbit the opened piece of birch-bark, a beautiful circle of four turtles. "I'll discuss it with Three Winds." She stands and walks out.

2000

A frame of light shines around a bulky drape, and Nora hears running water. It sounds like it's dropping through the wall behind her head. Slowly the pieces connect: Rucker's motel, the bar and the music, then strolling back late with Frank, who has a room somewhere on the other end of the parking lot. She'd had a night, a great time.

She'll walk back to the Breakers for her car, then drive over to the café. Hopefully they'll still be serving breakfast because there is nothing like eggs, hash browns, and a Coke on ice after drinking like she did last night. She ought to call someone. Rose. Janelle. Nobody knows where she is.

Nora opens the door to the sound of surf and the motel parking lot flooded with sunlight. The light's bouncing off chrome and the painted lines, and making the lake back between the trees look like a flashing marquee.

It doesn't take long out on the road before she needs to turn up the collar of her coat. There's a wind off the lake that the sun is no match for. She pulls her sleeves down and balls her hands inside them. The road is a narrow two-lane with soft gravel shoulders, so she walks on the blacktop and checks back for cars. Not a one in either direction, just a pair of small white butterflies tumbling in circles out in front of her. The lake blazes blindingly through the trees, and the birch trunks couldn't be any whiter. She remembers last call, and walking back with Frank. She remembers him teasing her about her shoes, saying something about her not being in the city anymore. Well, she's never been much of an outside walker; she's on her feet enough at work.

The butterflies land on the gravel shoulder, their small wings quaking in the wind. Nora glances at them as she hurries past, then realizes that she's hurrying. When she rounds the bend the Breakers is right there, and thank God, her old Buick is parked in the lot, and not the burned out shell of a car.

The Breakers looks sound asleep, the windows pale, the neon turned off. She has always appreciated the brazenness of bars, the way they sleep shamelessly during the day and only come alive at night. A folded square of paper is tucked under her windshield wiper. It's a note from Frank, saying he'll be free around three o'clock, if she hasn't left for another galaxy and wants to meet him back at the motel. Perfect. Her day has a shape.

The bright sky of morning is now streaked with clouds, the water rolling in toward shore. Nora stands on a sandy beach in her coat with a scarf tied around her head.

"I can see you're not very impressed," says Frank. "There aren't too many people I've shown this place to. I found two of my best agates here."

Nora watches a boat on the horizon. "Well, my granddaughter likes to look for them." She turns to Frank. "I've never given them much thought."

"Granddaughter? You must have started young."

Frank seems different in the daylight, a little too practiced, smoother, more closed. How many women in how many ports, Nora wonders. Not that she's judging, she's just curious.

"Humor me. I don't get to do this very often. We won't stay long. Come on, help me look." Frank guides her by the elbow. The sand, still packed and hardened from winter, barely moves beneath her feet. They amble slowly near a long swath of rocks that parallels the shoreline.

"What exactly am I looking for?" asks Nora.

"Agates."

She jabs him with her elbow.

"Like this." Frank bends over and picks up a rock.

"You found one already?"

"The small fry are everywhere. I told you it's a good beach." He holds a red rock the size of a nickel to the sky. "They're translucent. See how the light comes through? That's one way to tell. Also, they have this banded striping inside."

"Yeah, I know what agates look like. Like the rings of a tree, I always thought."

"I suppose some do. But they're crystallized, not organic. You can't count the bands and know the rock's age. That's kind of an interesting thought, though." He squeezes her arm. "The bands would have formed one at a time, from the outer edge toward the middle, but there wouldn't be a band for each year of growth, like you find with tree rings." Frank turns the rock over in his hand. "There could be hundreds, maybe thousands of years between each band. I don't know if anyone has ever done the research. And time would be the opposite of tree rings. Time would move this way." He runs his finger from the edge of the rock inward. "As opposed to a tree, where time is seen moving in the other direction." He jiggles the agate in his palm. "Regardless, this little rock is ancient. It was formed in a gas hole in molten rock. We're talking millions and millions, tens of millions of years ago."

Nora's mind blanks at the gargantuan time span. She turns

her back to the wind and lights a cigarette. "My question is, how do you go about picking them out so easily? I mean, really." She sweeps her arm down the path of stones.

"Look for the translucent glow," he says, and drops the agate into her purse. "This is the best time, with the sun at an angle."

A light but cold wind blows against Nora's face. Frank keeps stooping for rocks, but throws most everything back. Too small. Not pretty enough.

"Is this one?" Nora asks. "How about this?"

"Quartz. Nope, quartz again."

"Well, they glow," she says, a little exasperated. She'd rather be warm and working a crossword.

"I thought you grew up around here." Frank lifts an eyebrow.

"I'm not much of a water person," Nora says, looking out to the lake. She stoops, pushing her cigarette butt into the sand, and comes up with a cream-colored rock that has a raised pattern in it, like half of a grapefruit.

"What's this?"

"Hey, wow," says Frank, taking the rock from her hand. "It's a fossil. Good find. It could be some sort of sea sponge, or coral." Nora looks at him like he's nuts. "It is," he says. "There was ocean here once. I mean loooong, long, long before the lake was formed."

Nora examines the grapefruit design. "Whatever you say, Mr. Science."

Frank shakes his head and digs his hands in his pockets. "You are a real piece of work."

"Aren't I? Now listen," she counsels, "if you want to find fossils from the loooong-ago ocean, just look for the white ones with the raised designs." She drops the fossil into her purse, feeling encouraged about the hunting now. She recalls how she and Joannie used to walk the railroad tracks, looking for stuff that had fallen off the trains. She doesn't remember finding much of anything other than spikes, chunks of ore, and empty bottles. It was the feeling of anticipation that she liked.

"I've found a lot of great stuff out here," says Frank, taking her arm again.

"Sunken treasure? Message in a bottle?"

"Tackle, floats, handmade fishing leads from the old days. I even find stuff when I'm in a city."

"Like what?"

"I don't know. Rings. Beads. Marbles. Money. I notice anything that shines." He winks at her.

"Yeah, right. And what's the most valuable thing you ever found?"

Frank stops walking, and looks out at the water. "I'd have to say, a good divorce lawyer."

Children play on the ice overhead. They run in clusters with vibrating footsteps. Chase a stone as it skims across the ice. A school of fish flees the one running fastest. Running beyond the bounds of the game.

Without warning, I hear a quick crack of ice. Feet first, the girl crosses through. Her moccasins are decorated in porcupine quills. Her arms spin in frantic circles.

The children on the ice see her disappear. Shrieking, they run out. But only so far. Close enough to see her mitted hand find the shelf of ice, then disappear again.

She can no longer hear her name being shouted. She is a breathless creature. A thrashing bird with numb wings.

When calm settles and spreads through her body, she searches for the hole. For the way back. She finds a place where the light penetrates. A slippery wet cloud of grey. But now she has no sense of why she would care. The girl searches for the lost stone. She feels the slithering black current approach.

She sits here, cross-legged, where the water is still. Holding the game stone in her lap. Fine silt lines her fingers. Her mouth is as dark as blueberry skins.

1902

The sky is visible through the top two windowpanes, the water through the two on the bottom. Clouds drift by. Gulls in flight. The rare boat slips past like a thought, like a year. Sky in the top two panes, water in the bottom, like four separate paintings in flux, now bright blue over dark, then white to grey-green, and later yet, the evening's pink. Some days striped with color, wavy, silver, rippled, popping white caps, rollers, wash of orange. Berit absentmindedly pets the cat, her fingers in its soft fur. The cat purrs, yawns, and stretches.

She should crawl down the ladder and put another log in the stove. It's warm out, she knows, only cold inside, but the bright sun and the sparrows and the grass and water seem best tempered by wall and window.

A gull streams past the upper panes, followed by the clear sound of the cabin door opening. Berit lies absolutely still, wondering if she'd forgot to latch it the last time she was up. She rolls slowly off her pallet of blankets and puts her face to the glass, but there's no skiff in the cove. She stays near the window, crouched and listening. She can hear a fly buzz against the window down at Gunnar's workbench, and the faint whistle of air flowing past the stovepipe. She can hear the loud ring of quiet, but no growl or grunt, no footsteps. The floorboards creak under her weight as she moves gingerly around the nets toward the top of the ladder. She keeps the gun there.

Berit loads a shell and puts a handful in her skirt pocket, then backs carefully down the ladder. The door opens, spilling sunlight, and she wheels around, lifts the gun, and a figure hits the floor.

The man at her feet stares wide eyed, his large open hands in the air. He's wearing trousers and a shirt, his hat fallen beside him. It's John Runninghorse. The big palms of his hands. A flash of fear, and then his dark eyes assessing her. Strange to see him lying there.

"I heard," he says, keeping his eyes steady on hers. Then with a slow hand he pushes the gun barrel to the side.

John stands next to the ladder, watching Gunnar's wife across the room. She sits looking into the bright day—like a mole unearthed, he thinks, or a pale insect. Her hair is in tangles, her face frail. John looks down at the floor between them, where the light from the open door splits the room. He's had his own wrestle with grief; he's no stranger to its grip. And he's seen what can happen when one can't find any gain.

When his grandmother passed over, leaving his grandfather behind, most of him followed her, never to return.

"You're living here?" he says, breaking the silence.

She nods at her hands in her lap.

"Up there?" his gaze moves to the loft.

"Don't go up there," she says.

He didn't expect to find her in this state. He came with condolences, and out of respect. He'd assumed there would be people around to help her. Now he's not sure what to do. He feels pity for Gunnar's wife. Pity, but also anger; there's a small stone of it in his throat. He needs to think about the situation.

John turns his hat over in his hand. Everything is always more complicated with white people. He nods to Berit, and walks out the door.

Berit can hear him walking along the rocks on the shore. It's strange that he's come. She doesn't really care. His footsteps recede, and her quiet returns. He's harmless. Surely he won't beg on about services. Surely he won't expect her to eat a cake. The brightly lit grass sways on the slope below the cabin. Already it's long enough for scything.

He likely won't stay very long. Gunnar would want her to make him feel welcome, offer a meal and make conversation. She's not fit for it. The thought is outlandish. What does she even know of John, but that he's a trapper who hires out his labor. She doesn't even know where he lives, or if he has a family to feed, or if he's the loner kind of Indian who treks to the port to drink his money away. Come back, Gunnar, and greet him yourself. If it's so important, you come and tend to it.

The streaming bright light on the floor feels invasive, so she gets up and crosses the room. John is walking along the beach. When he looks up at her, she closes the door.

He's still there. She can hear him from her pallet in the loft, rooting around behind the fish house. It sounds like he's going through the rakes. The lake in the bottom panes has grown slightly darker. The cat has gone. She didn't see her slip out. When she and Gunnar first were settling, they'd had two. Then at some point there was just the one. She hadn't fretted much, assuming that it was probably taken by a fox or a raptor. But she'd surely notice now if that were to happen to Katt-Katt.

There's a scraping sound up at the cabin. Good Lord, could she make it any clearer that she wants to be left in peace?

Standing in the doorway, Berit shades her eyes. The sound is definitely coming from the cabin, but she can't see what he's doing up there. She needs nothing from him.

Berit steps out into the bright day, and starts up the waving grass slope. She pauses on the hill, squinting her eyes, needing to let them adjust to the glare. The leaves of the birch trees above the cabin are spring green. A cool wind blows off the water. She feels it fresh against her face and neck, then she's batting back tears that blur her vision, liquid light blinking in her lashes.

John's crouched by the back window of the cabin, a bucket and shovel lying at his feet.

Berit crosses her arms in front of her chest. "What in heaven's name are you doing?"

"I moved some soil from the garden," John says, wiping his hands.

Berit looks at the twiggy lilac bush, and the disturbed ground where he'd planted it. "But, what ever . . ." she says, gesturing toward the bush. "That was from Gunnar. It was for my birthday."

"I know," he stands. "It was dying."

"You don't know. How could you know? It came on the boat. I didn't even know."

John picks up the shovel and the bucket. "He told me," he says, and walks past her.

When John comes around the corner of the cabin he finds Gunnar's wife weeping on the ground. It's unseemly that there are no women around to help her. He pours lake water at the base of the tree. It's the same bad soil as the government allotments.

Berit lifts her head from her arm, and looks John over anew. This man with his brown skin and dark eyes, his black hair and strange presence—this man, she understands now, holds a piece of her Gunnar.

"What else did he tell you?" Her voice quivers. "What else do you know?"

John gives her a look she can't read, but it doesn't seem particularly pleasant. He pours the rest of the bucket on the new planting, then turns and walks away from her again.

1622

Grey Rabbit adjusts her load before beginning the climb that opens onto the bald rock. The path is thin, well packed, and crossed with gnarled tree roots that offer good footholds. On her back she carries a bundle of hardwood, steadied by a strap across her forehead. Speaking to Bullhead has relieved but also frightened her. She shifts the load of wood that pulls at her neck.

Higher and higher she climbs the path, the wood pressing into her sweating back. Little Cedar is in her mind. His face—half with its smooth brown skin, and half covered with the white poultice—and the path becomes a river of him, the image of his face laying on its surface, the tree roots crisscrossing below.

Her breath comes hard through her nose, and Grey Rabbit is relieved to see the path's end ahead. She leans into the last short incline as the way opens to the long vision of the shining water. She lowers the wood to the rock and rests, her eyes roaming over the blue, and the morning sky with its thin clouds like fish bones. She lays wood and removes striking stones from her pouch.

Grey Rabbit stands at the edge of the bald rock, turning a thick bundle over in her hands. Her thoughts are of Little Cedar and the dreams of the children. Bullhead and Three Winds were confident of their remedy's ability to overpower bad medicine, if bad medicine had been cast upon her. The sun is warm and the air cool. The horizon is soft and vague. Grey Rabbit sends out her raw heart.

The big water slides and shines. The bundle made from a piece of her clothing is soft and smooth against her hands. It holds an offering of tobacco, copper, and fresh rabbit meat. Grey Rabbit speaks into the air, wrapping the bundle in words of prayer. She holds it to her chest for a moment, then throws it solemnly from the rock. The bundle falls toward the water. Dropping, dropping, it splashes through, leaving circling rings that expand with light.

The stone she'd laid in the fire is hot, and Grey Rabbit nudges it from the flames, sprinkles the dried herbs as directed, and pulls a hide over her head. Slightly swaying to the rhythm of her prayer, she takes deep breaths of the protective fumes, and lets the strong air coat her body. In the dark and the heat, she tries to push aside her fear, and create a small space for the medicine to take hold.

She prays until she can't feel the weight of the skin.

She prays until the medicine stone grows cold.

Grey Rabbit uncovers her head to the dazzling morning, the water below her sloshing with light, and the wind blowing through the tops of the pines. Her heart feels open and sore, as she stands humbled before the Great Spirit, Gichi-Manitou. The essence. The mystery surrounding her.

Her legs and her feet tingle as she stands. She stretches tall, breathes the pine-filled air, bends forward and touches the rough rock with her fingers. The sensation of heat rises with her torso, through her chest and up the back of her neck, boring finally through the crown of her head. When she stands her full height, the world goes mute and a strong silent wind blows against her face. She spreads her arms and lets it blow over her.

A white bird is racing over the water. Not a bird, but a mass of small white butterflies. When they pass overhead they take the wind with them and give her back the sounds of the morning—a piping chickadee and the water below. And for that moment she becomes the water's sparkling energy, the rock, the pines—she's indistinguishable from the air. Like sunlight. Like the expansive nature of gratitude. Grey Rabbit encompasses everything.

2000

The morning is overcast with a low hanging sky that darkens out over the islands. Nora stands on the town dock. Gulls are lined up on the harbor break wall and the Madeline Island Ferry is loading with cars. She has no reason to be in Bayfield. She'd sat at the table half the night at the motel, the window open, smoking, the TV on. When the sky grew light, she settled her bill and drove off. Nora steps carefully to the edge of the pier, where the pilings descend into the water—grey, with dark ripples running over its surface—then backs away to a more comfortable distance. She looks toward her car and the phone booth she'd parked near, intending to call someone and check in, but it's too early for Rose, and engaging Janelle so soon after an argument can sometimes set her off again.

The cars disappear, one by one, into the ferry's open white mouth. She'd heard stories about Madeline Island from Rose, from back in the days when she and Buck lived there. The reservation she'd passed just outside town is the one Buck was connected to—his mother or father, one of them was Indian. He didn't look like an Indian, though. "Findian. Half Finnish, half Indian," Rose said.

The ramp rises and the deckhands wind the rope, as the ferry backs slowly away from the landing, filling the air with the smell of diesel. The ferry turns its bow toward the gap in the break wall. It chugs through and the sound of its engines disperse, the boat shrinking as it moves into the grey, behind it, the flock of begging gulls.

Nora finds a bench and taps a cigarette from her pack. The boats moored in slips shift in the wind, their ropes growing slack and then taut. When she drops her match she sees little white things, sticks and tiny drums scattered at her feet. She bends to look closer and picks one up, to find it's a bone, fish or bird, something small. They're behind her too, now that she sees them, lying on the ground wherever the ledge keeps them from blowing into the water.

"Nice town you have here," a man says as he passes, a camera dangling from his wrist. She almost has to laugh. She's a fish out of water. She couldn't be more lost.

Cold drops of rain spot the pier's pavement and cover the water surface with dark rings. Nora lowers her head and makes for the phone booth.

"Nanny!"

"Well, Bun. What are you doing home?"

"School's out. I can't go back till fall."

It's a mystery the way Nikki has taken to school. She certainly didn't get it from her or Janelle. "Can I talk to your mom?"

"She's in the shower. Do you want me to have her call you back?"

"No." Nora toes a penny on the floor. "Actually, I'm not at home. I'm in Bayfield."

"Cool. How come? Are you going to the islands?"

"I don't think so." Rain patters on the roof of the phone booth, and needled streaks appear on the glass. "I'm just taking a little car trip."

"Nooooo. Without me? Where are you going? Are you going all the way around?"

"Around what?"

"The lake, Nanny. You can drive all the way around. We did a section on it in school, but we didn't get to go. Just read stuff and saw pictures."

"Well, that's something to consider."

"Oh wow, I want to come. We could go to the locks and everything. I've never even been to Canada. Mom, Nanny's going around the lake. No really. She's on the phone right now."

"Mom? Where are you? What's this?"

Nora can hear Nikki talking excitedly in the background. "I'm taking a vacation."

"You're kidding? And you're what? Nikki, shush now. You're driving around the lake?"

"Well, I'm just trying to decide." Nora twists the metal phone cord.

"But all by yourself?"

"I'm perfectly capable."

"Of course, Mom, it's just . . . I can't remember you ever taking a vacation."

"I was in California last year."

"That's different. You were with Grandma and Aunt Joan. What's that noise?"

"It just started raining."

Nikki's voice cuts in from the other phone. "You've got to send me postcards from everywhere, Nanny."

Nora closes the long door to her car. The flags on the boat masts are flying stiff and the water beyond the break wall is white-capped. The man with the camera dashes past, and the rain comes down a racket on the roof of her car. Everything out

the windshield—the pier, the masts, the long dark break wall—
blurs and runs together on the glass. Nora picks up her notebook and pen. "Nobody knows if you belong or not," she writes.
She's completely exhausted. Her body feels like lead. She needs
to find a room and draw the shades. Nora drives a few blocks,
wipers flapping. Edgewater Motel. Vacancy. The word blinks in
pink neon light.

She's walking along the edge of the pier when someone grabs
her from behind, trapping her arms and she can't break free. She
struggles and twists, but still they go over, sliding splashless into
the water.

"Don't worry," a voice says, "just breathe. Breathe."

"Let go. I can't swim." Her legs kick wildly.

"Relax," the voice says against her ear. "Trust me." She recognizes the voice as Frank's.

"Shhhhh." He pulls her underwater.

She elbows and kicks, but she can't get loose. He has her
squeezed in his arms as he drags her down. She kicks at his
calves and butts back with her head, until his teeth bite down
hard on her neck, shocking her into stillness.

"See," he says, and she realizes it is true. She can breathe. She
is breathing underwater. The world is thick green, with yellow
spokes of light that angle down and dissolve around them. She
turns to Frank to speak, but he shakes his head, no, his blue eyes
calm behind a snorkeling mask. Deeper and deeper they sink
through the water, the silence pressing down as the color drains.
He tightens his grip and flips her around. There, hovering overhead, is their undulating image looking back. Her stricken face,
and Frank's calm next to hers, as if reflected in wavy glass. He
tugs her back around, and they sink into darkness.

They are in a narrow slanted hallway, walking, though she has no sensation of her feet. A man in underwear and dark socks is brushing shaving cream over his jaw. He's watching a woman behind him in the mirror. She's talking, but Nora can't hear any sound from her lips. The man nods, stretches his cheek taut, shears a swath of white cream with a straightedge blade. Garter and stockings, her slip is beige. She trails her finger down his spine, smiles at him, and turns away.

An emerald-green dress is laid out at the foot of a bed, its coverlet strewn with broken glass and books. The woman pulls the dress over her head and the fabric floats down around her pearly legs. She looks straight into Nora's face, with hazel eyes, slanted, catlike.

She is swimming, but not swimming, Nora's just there in the water, her head dry in the dry air. Above her, the hills of town are dotted with spring green, and quiet houses face the lake. All the windows reflect the blue sky, and she knows that each house holds the secret. Of course, she realizes, that is why the people live there.

Nora's in bed, her eyelids heavy. She's hot, her body sweaty under the covers. Her mind slides back and forth, trying to bring all the pieces together. The man shaving. She can picture him clearly, down to his round, flat fingernails. And Frank. What the hell? Frank of all people.

It's late in the day, almost 4:00 on the clock, and Nora feels muffled and disoriented. She gets out of bed, slides the drape back, and peers into sunlight too harsh for her eyes. A kid is biking on the sidewalk across the street, and the tops of the trees are swaying in the wind. Nora shoves the window open and lets the drape fall back, blocking out the bright light. She feels the woman with the catlike eyes. Hazel. Slanted. Looking right through her. She feels her as if she were in the room. She turns on the lamp and then the TV, filling the space with laughter and color.

1902

John sits on the stone beach. He draws on his pipe. The water ripples blue. He'd like to move on and forget he ever came, forget Gunnar's wife standing over him with a gun, forget how he'd left her crying by the cabin. He sucks on his pipe and sends the smoke out, floating his feelings over the water. Gunnar's body is somewhere out there, somewhere under all that icy-cold water. There had been something true between them, which he'd thought a lot about since hearing the news of his death. They had a rare comfort with each other, even though Gunnar came from a faraway land. In thinking, he'd decided that was part of it. They were both born in one world, only to find themselves navigating another. John tamps another pinch of tobacco in his pipe and cups a match against the lake breeze.

"What happened out there?" he asks the horizon.

The lake rocks lazily.

He remembers the time he told Gunnar about having lost Alice and his youngest to tuberculosis. The conversation was striking not because Gunnar had so much to say, but because of the way he'd listened.

John catches movement out the corner of his eye, as an animal dips under the water. He waits for it to surface again. It could have been a loon or a cormorant, he didn't get a good look before it dove. The round head of an otter pops up. He follows its progress across the cove, a short wake trailing behind its head.

"Will you eat?"

Gunnar's wife stands near the small shed. She has wound her hair back and put on an apron. She gestures to him with fish in her hands. John nods and turns back to the water. She needs to go back to her people, he thinks, trying to recall if Gunnar ever mentioned any. He'll take her as far as the head of the lake.

John lets the water fill his eyes, the sliding, shifting, calming blue. He scouts for the otter, but it's gone again. Up on the hill, the cabin door shuts.

Berit sets two places at the table, which she can barely stand for the pain it causes. Two cups and saucers, two sets of silver; it's the ghost of a life. It's for Gunnar, she tells herself, making a plate of flour and meal for the fish. John knew about the lilac. She tries to picture the two of them talking, Gunnar revealing his surprise for her. Tears seep from her eyes again. She's like a pail with a weak seam.

Her hands lay the fish in the meal, turn them, making sure that the coating is even, but it is as if they are not her hands and she's watching them work from a long distance. It occurs to her that she's only serving fish. She can offer no bread because she hasn't baked, and there's nothing to take from her unplanted garden. The smell is overpowering when she lays the fish in the pan. She rushes to the door and props it open.

Berit sets a plate in front of John. The sugar bowl is on the table, and a box of dried peaches. Nothing feels or looks right. She pours him coffee and sits down at the table. She can't bear to be sitting as they are, with she in her place and John in Gunnar's. Eating her plate of fish is unimaginable.

John cuts into his food. It's good, and he's hungrier than he'd realized. His plate is nearly half empty when he notices that Gunnar's wife hasn't touched hers.

"You should eat," he says, but she stares out the window.

The music teacher. That's who she reminds him of—the straw hair, the line of her jaw. He pushes fish bones to the edge of his plate. The fire in the stove caves and crackles. She is the one who haunted him the longest, with her soft approach and her urging them to sing in the new language. And the singing would feel good to him, but afterward, he always felt bad.

Berit doesn't know what to say. Her only words have been to the cat. She nudges her plate to the side.

"Thank you for planting the lilac," she says. "I missed the smell of them in the spring. He remembered things like that." She glances at John, her eyes welling, but he's intent on eating, not looking at her.

"Katt-Katt," she says, glad for her appearance at the door. She rubs her fingers together under the table. The cat trots over and brushes against her leg. Berit sets her plate on the floor, and the cat launches in hungrily. She looks up to find John's incredulous face. He picks up his coffee cup, and strides out the door.

"Why are you even here?" says Berit, marching out of the cabin. "I didn't ask you to come. There's no one keeping you." John stands at the woodpile, cup in hand, looking up at the spring-green woods.

"That was good food you put on the floor."

"I don't need you here judging me." Berit paces back and forth. "How dare you even. You don't know." Tears stream down her cheeks. "You have no idea what this is." Her hands wave in the air.

John turns his head slowly, and she sees in his eyes something soft and penetrable. In that moment, she knows that she's absolutely wrong.

1622

"Just a few more," says Bullhead, holding a bowl in each hand.

Grey Rabbit maneuvers hot rocks under the stew, sets the antler on a mat, and takes up a spoon. Portioning food into the bowls, she makes sure that each has a piece of the deer that was Standing Bird's first kill. There are wild potatoes, new sugar for seasoning, young green ferns, and last season's dried berries. Bullhead breathes in the rich aroma. "Is the stew container going to last?"

"The bark still has a little moisture left."

"Imagine if we had the pot that doesn't burn." Bullhead laughs remembering last summer, when she'd finally made it through the crowd and touched the pot with her own hand. "Even without fire, it heated better than a rock in the sun. Walking Through says that more could come over the eastern trade routes. We'll see when we get to Bawating." Bullhead sniffs the stew again. "Regardless, you've done well with the feast. It's no easy task to prepare for so many."

Grey Rabbit lowers her eyes. A hopeful watchfulness lies between them these days as they see how the medicine takes hold. Bullhead considered the white butterflies a good omen and Grey Rabbit is grateful, yet tentative. She feels as if she's floating in a placid inlet, with the fast flashing river still near. She checks the stew pot, now beginning to burn, pours what's left into Bullhead's fresh container, then looks over the gathering.

Her husband and sons sit together with the guests, everyone having made it a point to greet Standing Bird and acknowledge his new status among them. Little Cedar sits watching his brother in awe, looking even prouder than Night Cloud, she thinks. Her son glances over and smiles, or half smiles, as the thick poultice stiffens his skin, and the pain keeps one side of his face still. Daily, he greets her without any blame, only love for the care she gives. She sees the way he hides his discomfort, barely flinching as she spreads the mixture on the wound, still seeping and raw red. It splits her like wood every time, though she hides her feelings too, and tries to be only soothing.

Bullhead approaches, more bowls in hand. "These are for us. Everyone's well fed." Grey Rabbit serves up a large portion for Bullhead, but takes only a taste for herself.

They find a place to sit behind the guests as pipes and pouches of tobacco are drawn out, and the story of the hunt is told again. Standing Bird isn't brash in its telling, but cautious, as if ordering each detail in his memory. He'd prepared his whistle with milkweed root, and she'd answered its call, doe to fawn, stepping out from behind a dense spruce. While she sniffed the air, he took aim, then let loose an arrow that found the base of her neck. The sharp flint sent her leaping, the arrow shaft breaking off against a tree. He shot another, but missed her entirely, and the arrow was lost in the woods.

He told how she ran in fear, he following her through the dark cedar grove, and beyond the place of brown water through split rocks. At one point he was certain he'd lost her, but then he picked up her blood trail on new green moss. Eventually, she'd slowed to a walk. He could hear her snapping twigs as she moved, still trying to rid herself of him. By now they were near the deep hole in the river. Heads nod around the circle, the guests tracking the tracker in their minds, knowing each landmark he describes. It was there that he realized the doe was circling, so he began to circle as well, a larger circle that slowly enclosed her, until at last he could hear her breathing and see her plainly, bloodied and exhausted.

The guests joke and tease, stand to speak in earnest. Bullhead scrapes the last stew from her bowl. She's only half listening to their words, as similar words once spoken echo in her head—the first feast she'd given for each of her sons, the first feast of her brother, when she was just a girl. And though she wasn't there, her father's first feast. The same skills learned, the same rites of passage. The same challenges presented by the land, while the people of the people of the people pass through it. And so will be the feast of Standing Bird's son someday.

By then she will have crossed to the land of the spirits. She thinks of those she'll see again. Her parents, who lived long and died in peace, and her husband, captured and murdered in a raid. There are stories equally as awe-filled as brutal. She looks up into the evening sky, where the fisher with the arrow in its tail is rising.

I see corralled logs. A giant wooden rug. Rolling slowly overhead.

And the many scattered timbers. They waterlog and sink on the long journey across the great lake.

Cedar. Red birch. Bird's eye maple. Hemlock. Red oak. The pine, and the fir.

Voices stream on the currents. Men at work in the woods. The undercutters. The swampers. The crosscut saw teams. Comes a whinnying horse. The ring of an ax. And a tree rooted for half a millennium falls.

From east to west. In fifty-odd years.

The sky opens. The winds sweep in.

I find logs in jumbles like broken-down cabins. Each marked with the timber stamps of the men who staked claim. They lay at the bottoms of pitch-black valleys. Appear as ridges beneath the silt.

This one lies on a ledge of bedrock swept clean by an underwater current. A slumbering giant. Femur of a god. A sharp flint lodged in its side.

And then his dark shape. It slips over the ledge. His pale hand trailing like a falling star.

2000

The afternoon keeps changing from grey to sunny, Nora's mood swinging along with it. She sips on her coffee-to-go, the hole in the plastic lid sharp against her lip. Going around the lake is Nikki's idea, not hers. And while it holds only a mild appeal, she didn't want to turn around and go home any more than she wanted to stay in Bayfield.

"Sorry, lady, I don't know what you're talking about." The man's condescending tone still irks her.

That morning, she'd gone back to the pier, the dream clinging like a dryer sock. Gulls cried in the morning sky as she retraced her steps, eyeing the cold water.

"Excuse me, is there a sunken ship off the pier?" she asked a man bent over his boat engine.

He looked at her like she was stupid. "Off the pier? It's shallow. Maybe fifteen feet."

"Are you sure? Really? What about farther out?"

"I guess there are schooner wrecks off the islands that people dive."

"No. This was a fancy boat, with dressed-up passengers."

"Sorry, lady." He turned his back. "I don't know what you're talking about."

Nora checks her rearview mirror. There aren't any cars, just the orange sky of Rose's painting and her old suitcase on the seat. She hasn't seen the lake for a long time, only sensed it at the end of long red dirt roads. According to the circle map she'd picked up, she is still going the right way. The map is simple, small and glossy, with nothing on it but major roads and an outline of the lake. She would have needed to buy a handful of real maps— Wisconsin, Michigan, Ontario, Minnesota—just to have all the pieces.

"In area, the largest lake in the world, holding ten percent of its fresh water," the map reads. "Maximum depth 1,333 feet." Nora lights a cigarette, her mind attempting to picture the depth. She recalls being in the lighthouse on the cliff, but that is nowhere near high enough. She pictures a thousand-foot-long freighter, then flips the ship on end in her mind, but a distance in open air is simply not the same as a drop below the water surface. It's unimaginable in the worst way.

Michigan has a different feel than the forested land of Wisconsin. There are yellow yield signs for deer and for moose, and occasionally a huddled community. Winter-battered with peeling signs for fresh pastries, they have names like Tula, Topaz, and Matchwood. None of the towns are marked on her map.

Watch for falling rock, the signs read.

It's mining country, with rugged hills and cliffs. Even the sky looks worked hard, as if all the metal below the ground had leeched up and was tarnishing the air. "Watch for blowing and drifting snow." A fat bug splats against her windshield. She's watching all right. Just plain watching.

Nora squeezes the cold metal handle of the gas nozzle, and flips the tab down so she doesn't have to hold it. She reaches through the window and lifts out the map. The gas station sits at a clearly marked juncture, and she has to choose which way to go. North up the Keweenaw Peninsula, the long arm of land that juts into the lake, or east toward Marquette, passing the whole thing by. She doesn't remember the shape of the lake appearing so much like an animal's face. A wolf, maybe, pointy and menacing, with Isle Royale for an eye and the Keweenaw forming the animal's open mouth.

"Anything else?" the man asks, stacking two packs of cigarettes next to her coffee.

"Actually," Nora sets the map on the counter, "can you tell me about these different ways to go?"

"Where do you want to end up?"

"I'm doing the circle drive."

"Then you want to go toward Ironwood." He taps his finger on the map.

"I just came from there."

"You did? That's unusual. You're going around backwards. Everyone goes the other way."

Big snow country, the sign says. She is out in the boonies, and second guessing her decision. Mass City. Winona. Toivola. She'd picked the north route up the Keweenaw so she could tell Nikki about the peninsula. But there's nothing to see, just the two-lane road flanked by pines stunted from all the snowfall. "An average of twenty feet," the man at the gas station told her. "The lake effect is extreme up here. The clouds fill up over the water and then dump their load when they hit the land." But there is no water in sight, only short trees, and the road that is taking her further from anywhere familiar.

Nikki is in her thoughts, then Ralph's lost ship photos. She tries in vain to recall a passenger boat like the one in her dream.

It's weird how dreams sometimes affect her, like strange weather inside her head.

The road unspools endlessly before her. She's in the middle of nowhere. What if she had car trouble? Nora pushes the lighter knob and opens her notebook. "Storage Room." She sets her mind to a task.

The long curve descending to the towns of Houghton-Hancock appear without hardly a warning. There are fast-food restaurants, a superstore, a car lot lined with pickup trucks—red ones, yellow, and black, all in a row like bright hard candies. Just like that, Nora's back in civilization. She feels like waving and honking her horn.

In minutes she's on a bridge above a river that separates the towns. It feels a little like a miniature Duluth/Superior—old buildings, old neon signs. Right away there are markers for the road out of town, so Nora drives into the lot of a place called Alfredo's.

"I'll have the spaghetti and a side salad with French." Nora closes the menu, feeling dazed. It was only that morning that she'd left Bayfield, though it feels like a week's time has passed.

"Anything to drink?" asks the waiter. He's small waisted and wiry, with short legs. Nora wonders if he's Alfredo.

"I'll have a glass of the red." She points to the menu.

She can feel the road in her body, the constant motion and the blur of green trees. Nora smoothes the bent cover of her notebook. There is a coffee spill on the back now, too. "No one knows if you belong or not," she reads.

She peruses the pages she'd added to while driving, making sure that the entries are legible. "Plaster arm." Someone stuck it up in the nets as a joke, but it never got taken down. "Antique railroad lantern." Remembering it had brought to mind her first trip to California. Joannie, everyone said she was crazy not to fly, but she grew up in a town crossed with railroad tracks and she always wondered what it would be like to ride out on one. By then, all the traffic was freight. Passenger service to the Twin Ports was defunct. So she rode a train west from St. Paul. Once was enough. She's flown every time since.

"You're not taking notes for the Health Department, I hope." The man puts a glass of wine on her white paper place mat.

"No. God no. I'm writing . . . it's hard to explain, really. Lists of stuff."

"Groceries? Laundry? I usually do mine on the backs of envelopes." He smiles. A smoker. She can tell by his teeth. "But hey, maybe you save yours or something. Keep them all together in a book for posterity."

"How long have you been psychic?" Nora tastes her wine. "Do you want to know what I bought at the drugstore in February?" She flips to a page and starts reciting. "One bottle of citrus fingernail-polish remover. Kleenex, pocket-size." She keeps a straight face, but the man is chuckling.

"No, really. What are you writing about?"

"They're lists. I told you. You see, I had a fire."

"Ah," he says, holding his hand up for her to stop. "I'm truly sorry to hear that. Are they the insurance lists, or the ones for yourself?"

"You know?"

He nods sympathetically. "My apartment. I lost everything but my guns and the clothes I was wearing. And just when you think you're settled, something comes at you out of the blue. Once—and this was several months after the fire—I was shaving, not thinking of anything special, when I remembered this photograph of me and my kid sister. Well, I hadn't looked at it since who knows. It was just sitting in a desk drawer with a lot of papers, but still, you see, it can't be replaced. I hope you didn't lose your photographs."

Nora feels her heart soften, and pressure well behind her eyes. She's glad for the dinging counter bell, calling him away from her table.

He passes her carrying salad plates, then clears and wipes an empty booth. Nora drops her gaze whenever he looks her way. Sit down and tell me everything, she wants to say. She imagines him drawing her a map on the place mat. "It's easy," he'd tell her, "just follow these lines." But when has anyone ever shown her what to do? She's always made do for herself. When he comes to clear her plate, she doesn't bring up the fire.

"Do you mind if I give you a little advice?" asks the waiter, holding a plate with a piece of strawberry pie.

"Absolutely." Nora straightens, grateful before he speaks.

"Forget the lists."

"What? Why do you say that?"

He smiles sadly but doesn't answer. "On me," he says, placing the pie in front of her.

1622

The sun is high and bright after three days of steady rain had cast a hush over the camp. Grey Rabbit squints against the wood smoke, lifted from her fire by the wind. The fire is warm and also the sun. It seeps into her skin and scalp as it does only when winter has truly fled. She stirs the hot pitch and adds a bit of the powder she'd pounded from burnt cedar chips. She has not dreamt of children, her dreams have been vague. She feels like a hollow log.

"Look at my deer," calls Little Cedar. He has his deer sticks under his arms and is walking four-legged in a large circle. He has more energy these days, though he's still not himself. She hopes he'll feel well enough to join in the gaming when they move to the long rapids at Bawating. The pitch bubbles. Grey Rabbit checks the bottom of the container.

"Look," calls Little Cedar again, pointing his lips to the sky. An arrow of geese is flying over, honking and clamoring, flapping their huge wings. "Look at those two, trying to catch up."

She turns around. Her son stands head back, face to the sky, one hand shielding his eye. Grey Rabbit's stomach drops. She worries for his sight constantly, for the difficulties he could meet if left with one eye.

"The geese return."

Grey Rabbit whirls.

Bullhead lowers her load of fresh birch-bark rolls. "The stand by the island in the river was ready. The trees shed their bark as quickly as young husbands dropping clothes." Laughing, she loosens the tie around the rolls.

Grey Rabbit smiles faintly, then turns to rake a hot rock toward the pitch. Bullhead searches the side of her face, noticing the dark half-moons below her eyes. The loss of laughter is not a good sign. If need be she'll arrange for a medicine man at Bawating.

2000

Nora twirls the postcard rack in the Stop and Shop in Calumet. At least the sun had come out after lunch, the light glowing through her glass float as she drove. She chooses a pink sunset over the lake, and one of a house that's so piled with snow it looks like three mattresses are stacked on the roof. Nora pays for the postcards and asks the cashier if she has any ideas about where on the Keweenaw she might go.

"Well, it depends what you're interested in. Lighthouses. Waterfalls. Ghost towns." The woman behind the counter looks at Nora over her glasses. "You're between snow season and summer, so you won't find much open. The site of the old Cliff Mine and stamp mill aren't far, and Eagle River is a popular destination. From there, 26 is a nice drive along the water."

Nora sits on a bench in the sun between an ice machine and a free air pump, looking at the pamphlets the woman gave her. A sheet with information about the copper booms and busts. A glossy pamphlet from a historical society with pictures—a parlor with a Victrola, crosscut saws, and other logging memorabilia, a cluster of roughly hewn miner's cabins, the blue water of the lake beyond.

The road winds like a serpent through blink-of-an-eye towns: Kearsarge, Allouez, Ahmeek, Cliff. There's a boarded-up church, and everything is quiet. Welcome to Copper Country, a sign reads, but there's nothing around that looks like copper. Nor do there seem to be any people.

She's alone in the bubble of her car. Nora pulls onto the shoulder and stops. She picks up the map. She's not lost. If she had a loaf of bread she'd be dropping crumbs. It's as if she were journeying backward in time, making her way up the hard spine of some creature long ago turned to stone. She holds the notebook against the steering wheel and writes, "Everything around this lake is about the past."

The plaque on the main street in Eagle River reads Founded in 1843. The town's so tiny she can drive every street in the time it takes to smoke a cigarette. Some of the buildings are nondescript and some have historic clapboard storefronts, but the only sign of life that she has seen is laundry hanging in a backyard.

The lake is down at the end of the street. She can hear its faint hiss like radio static. She drives the couple of blocks and parks on the shoulder, then walks down to the shore. It's water as far as she can see, and nothing on the horizon but long low clouds. There is no one in either direction, not a single soul along the beach. The waves fan and sink back, hissing in clear sheets over long ridges of sand.

It's empty. Eerie. The lake slides up and down. Behind her the silent town. The houses. The Victorian inn. The water hisses and goose bumps rise on her arms. She could be the last person on earth. The water rises, folds, and drains back, and she feels everything soften and slide with it, as if all the solidity were seeping away, leaving everything boneless and mutable.

Nora turns away from the lake. Her neck is warm and she feels short of breath. Even the tree that she parked beneath, the sunlight on its spring leaves, looks fragile and unreal. Vague, more like a memory of a tree. The only thing that appears to have any weight is her car, and she heads straight for it, starts the engine, and gets out of there.

1902

Berit sits on the bench at the end of the point, her skin chilled and the sky paling orange. Her blouse, she sees, is rumpled, her skirt, filthy. She's in the calm dull space after crying, where nothing exists but unanswerable questions. How can the water be orange-skinned and beautiful even while there is no second chance?

A gull sits on the water in the orange light, its white wings folded, its beauty undeniable. And she feels her innards stretch, her heart, her lungs pressing against her ribs, as both pain and beauty try to claim the space. Either she'll stretch large enough to hold both, or she'll rip in a way that will be beyond mending. Neither feels like a choice.

The sky is in its last glow, and the surface of the lake is rolling. Berit makes her way in from the point. She's rubbing the cold out of her arms and watching where she steps when something red catches her eye. She climbs down onto the slanting lower ledge, where a small birch-bark dish filled with tiny red straw-berries is placed in the rocks near the lapping water. John must have left them the other day. She bends down and fingers a berry. Some kind of Indian offering. To Gunnar, maybe. Or maybe the lake. In light of where he placed them, they're certainly not meant for her.

"You don't know," she had accused him. But he does. She saw it in his eyes. Most people must. Of course everything dies. Given that, it's beyond belief that anyone or anything functions at all. Seeds get sown. Lumber cut. Horses shoed. Children washed. She picks a red berry from the dish, turns it in her fingers, and puts in her mouth.

2000

Nora drives all the way from Eagle River to Marquette, chain-smoking with the radio on, trying to shake the sensation she felt, and questioning her mental health. She finds a motel just past town, goes straight to her room, and lies down shoes and all. The highway and the lake sound through her closed window, her body buzzing from the road. She lifts the phone onto the bed.

"Nanny, you're in Marquette? Let me get the map. Oh, you're getting close to the Shipwreck Museum. I can't wait." Nikki's excitement hums across the line. "Will you bring me a souvenir? Pleeeease?"

"You know I will, Bun." She'd agree to anything as happy as she is to be hearing Nikki's voice, connecting and grounding her to something real.

"Guess what? I already got two postcards. I never got mail before."

"Well you keep checking, 'cause there's more on the way. Tell me everything you did today."

Nora's hoping her mood won't come through with Janelle, but Janelle asks straight off whether she is okay.

"I'm fine," Nora assures her, "a little tired."

"This just isn't like you. Are you talking to anyone? Rose, or Aunt Joan?"

"Listen, you don't have to worry about me."

Nora feels the severed connection as soon as the receiver clicks down. She looks around the unfamiliar room. It's white. Still. The ceiling is water stained. Nora lifts the receiver again.

"Hi, you've reached Joan. I can't get to the phone right now . . ."

1622

It's no longer night, but not yet day. Grey Rabbit stands alone, listening. At first she'd thought her sons were awake. Then that someone was whispering outside the lodge. There are no signs of morning activity, no smoke rising, no sound of gathering wood. Still, she hears the murmuring. It seems to be coming from the big fire ring, but as she walks toward it, the sound subsides. She stands over the charred logs and ashes.

A stubby log trembles and lifts from the others. Grey Rabbit drops to a crouch. Murmuring, it inches out of the ring, dragging something flat on the ground behind it. It's a tail. It's a beaver. Murmuring. She has never heard a beaver make such a sound.

Keeping a distance, she follows its path, a dark line of turned dirt and pine needles. The animal leads her toward the river, but then it changes course and heads for Gichigami. Its murmur carries an urgent tone, and Grey Rabbit can feel the worry. Something is very wrong.

She is running, shielding her face with her arm as she pushes through branches that fling back behind her. The murmuring is everywhere, winding and winding around her head. Grey Rabbit spills out at the forest's edge, on a rock that slopes steeply to the water. Gichigami's surface is roiling and murmuring, as if a wind wider than she'd ever imagined is agitating its entire skin. The beaver's haunches roll as it moves, its tail waddling over the rock, and then its lumbering movements transform as it glides into its element.

In the lifting light, she can see their hunched shapes crossing the rocks all along the shore. She jumps as one brushes against her leg. It stops and looks at her, then scurries on.

Clouds like a village to the east flush red. In the growing light she can see what's happening. The agitated waters are filled with beaver. The dark tops of their heads and their furrowed wakes, their wide, dark tails lapping. From all directions, they stream toward to the water. The sound is anger. The beavers are leaving, swimming into the rising red sun.

Grey Rabbit drops to her knees and presses her hands over her ears. Beavers brush past her on either side. The beavers are angry. The beavers are leaving. The water churns. They are leaving, swimming into the sun.

Grey Rabbit feels a hand on her shoulder. She squints into the bright sun, at a smooth youthful face.

Standing Bird touches his mother's arm. He kneels in front of her. Her legs are cold to the touch and her staring eyes are frightening. "What happened?" he whispers. "We've been looking for you."

The boy is pulling on her arm, trying to lift her hand from her ear, but she clamps it back each time he pries it away. "The beavers," she nods urgently.

"Come, we'll go back." He holds out his hand. "Mother," he repeats, and jiggles her leg, urging her to get to her feet. She looks at him with eyes flat as a fish's, and it makes him want to run away. He reaches around her waist and pulls, but he can't budge her from the rock. He tries from the side with one arm beneath her knees, like he once saw his father do, but still, he can't. He must, but he can't.

A voice calls from the woods. Standing Bird jumps to his feet and pierces the morning air with a shrill whistle.

2000

The Shipwreck Museum is an entire compound of buildings, white with red roofs, a well-trimmed lawn, and a lighthouse standing in the center. Nora peers through the door of the building that houses the main exhibit. She has a handbag of feelings about going inside and thinking about sunken ships.

She walks across the lawn to the gift shop. Inside, she buys Nikki a purple hooded sweatshirt with *Great Lakes Shipwreck Museum* on the front, then picks out a matching cap. There are snow globes with boats trapped inside, and picture books of ships going up in flames. A penny-flattening machine stands near the door.

Nora fingers through the change in her wallet and picks out a new, nearly pink penny. She and Joannie used to lay coins on the railroad tracks, then run into the woods as the train barreled by. She'll send it just to make her laugh, with a card that reads, "How I'm spending my time." The penny falls into a shallow cup, an oval of copper embossed with the museum's emblem.

Nora smokes on the sidewalk in front of the shipwreck exhibit. She can see the dark vestibule every time the door opens, and hear snippets of the song about the *Edmund Fitzgerald*. She knew the aunt of one of those boys, and frankly, she can't stand the song.

People die on the water every year. Small boats. Large. People swept out in riptides. Lost kayaking. Hypothermia. No one with any sense disrespects Lake Superior. But it had been almost twenty-five years since the lake had taken anything near the size of the *Edmund Fitzgerald*. She was ten the year that the *Steinbrenner* and half her crew went down. Eventually one of its hatch covers washed up on Park Pointe. She remembers it as clearly as the day she saw it. It lay on the beach, a gruesome remembrance. Battered and enormous, gouged and scratched, it haunted her in the darkness of her bedroom that whole year. When the *Fitzgerald* disappeared in that November storm, people sat glued to the television over the bar, waiting for news, for the ship to come through. And when all hope was finally lost, she and a lot of people who should have known better were stunned. Somehow they'd all become comfortable, as if modern technology had grown more powerful than the lake. If she hadn't promised Nikki, she'd skip the shipwreck exhibit.

It's low lit and blue inside the building, creating the effect that the exhibit is underwater. There are glass display cases around the perimeter, and spoked steering wheels like starfish on the walls, but Nora crosses to the center of the room, where a lighthouse lens identical to the one she'd seen gleams in the wash of blue light. She walks slowly around the lens, watching rainbows form and disappear in the crystal rings. It's gorgeous. She ought to take Nikki to Split Rock. She pictures her in her little dragonfly jeans, hopping up the spiral stairs. She'd love to see her reaction to the giant crystal eye.

The display cases along the walls are filled with objects recovered from the bottom of the lake. There are blocks and bilge pumps. Watch fobs and dolls. She almost has to laugh at a ship's good luck horseshoe. A banjo. A typewriter. It's absolutely grotesque. Scissors. Binoculars. Wedding bands, books, and coins.

A fork. A ladder. An iron trap. Wooden winches. An inkwell. A silver shaving brush. Nora sees the lathered face, and the man's flat fingernails. The woman's catlike staring eyes, and she walks back out into the daylight.

Nora crosses the lawn, follows a boardwalk toward the shore, sits, and tamps a pack of cigarettes on the wood plank of a bench. A museum for shipwrecks. It's a morbid idea. Why not a car wreck museum—fill it with broken glass, maps, kids' car seats, to-go cups.

It's sunny overhead, but the lake is fogged in, leaving only the sandy shoreline visible. The fog hovers, not moving in or out, but in places lifting slightly off the water. Down the beach, a rusty bicycle is lying in the sand. She wonders if there are any boats out in the fog.

The *America*. The name just comes.

Nora slides her notebook out of the gift shop bag and pages through to find her list of Ralph's photographs of sunken ships. "The America," she writes, her pen hovering. A stream of cigarette smoke rolls against the page. The air is still, moist, and even a little warm. When she looks again, the mist has enshrouded the bicycle. And why not. The fog might as well keep coming. She's already lost. Completely adrift. If there's a foghorn somewhere it's surely skipping over her. She looks down the list of sunken ships, and in heavy block letters she adds her own name: "Nora Truneau—Gone Missing." They can put her suitcase in the museum, her map, her postcards, her glass float, she's going home.

1902

Berit sees a vague reflection of her head in the window, layered over the moonlit water. She takes another small sip from the bottle, the liquor thick, bittersweet, and smoldering in her stomach. She'd found it wrapped in an old net, saw the glint of glass when it was struck by the moonlight. It is not so much the idea of the drink—growing up on the Keweenaw there were three different groceries—but the shock that Gunnar had hid something from her.

And what else? If there's one falsity, how many more? Did he take a drink every day, hiding bottles from her when he rowed the supplies in, or had he put it up for a particular occasion? If he'd been a tippler she would have known. Certainly she would have smelled it on him. What else had she been unaware of, sitting with her comfortable assumptions? What secrets? What unshared thoughts?

She brings the bottle to her lips. It shines like ice, but burns in her throat. No. She knew him, she knew him well. Gunnar was not a deceitful man. She swirls the clear liquid against the sides of the bottle. Lord knows she'll never know the truth now.

Berit climbs down the ladder, holding her skirt hem and the bottle in one hand. It's a warm windless night, the lake dead calm, the June moon rising toward a long bank of clouds. She wedges the outhouse door open and sits. Silver light floods across their clearing, where everything's throwing long shadows: the net reel, the stack of fish boxes, Gunnar's overturned skiff. She can't bear looking at his boat. Most often, she averts her eyes when she passes. Why did Hans have to bring it back in? Berit takes another drink, and the moonlight flares through the bottom of the bottle.

Suddenly it's simple.

Berit steadies the bottle in the grass, squats, and heaves the boat over. She runs her hand along the smooth gunnel; he always took care to keep it that way, protecting his nets from catching and snagging. The grasses hiss against the hull as she drags the boat down to the cove, where it scrapes across the rocks.

An owl hoots in the woods as she works her way from bow to stern, pouring the liquor from the bottle. Down the boat's ribs. Dousing the seats. Running a line down her center seam.

The moon is halfway into the cloud bank and disappearing before her eyes. Berit strides up to the fish house to fetch a lantern. When she returns, the moon is gone, though her lantern throws a circle of light on the beach stones. Filled with purpose, she pushes the boat forward, grabs the lantern, and steps into the flat black water.

The lake is frigid around her ankles. Here, your beloved skiff, she offers. Take your liquor. Take your skiff. The cold clasps her above the knees, her heavy skirt wicking. The lake is a vise squeezing her hips. She won't be able to stay in much longer. Berit shoves the boat as hard as she can, sends the lantern crashing against the seat. It glides for a moment into the darkness, and then in a flash of bright orange, the skiff bursts into flames.

I will tell what I have learned about black water.

Black water is obsidian gone soft. A liquid image of dark space.

Where one dark realm opens to another. Opens to another.

Or maybe closes.

All manner of depth is at once obscured.

It is a dark wool coat. A black serpent's scales. Quick flash of a copper tail.

Can such a thing be anything but furtive? Concealing razor sharpness. Jut of bone. Open mouths.

Black water calls for vigilance.

Every conceivable bearing is a portal.

2000

Nora's eyes adjust slowly to the darkness. If the museum was underwater, she is now underground. The bar is made entirely of dark split logs, with moose racks mounted on the walls, and squirrels, beaver, rabbits, and mink staring down from the rafters. The place smells like burgers and cigarettes. Nora nods to the bartender as she crosses to the doorway labeled Restrooms/ Telephone.

"Hey, where are you now?" asks Rose.

"Paradise. I'm serious. That's the name of the town. I just left the Shipwreck Museum. It was absolutely grotesque. What's wrong with people?"

"You don't want me to answer that, do you?"

"What's going on there? What are you doing?"

"Watching a program."

"About?" Nora knows that Rose will tell her the whole thing, but that is fine. She just wants to hear her voice.

"The human body. This is good. . . . Did you know that the fluid in your body is the same salt-to-water ratio as the primordial sea? We're all still carrying it around. That slays me." Rose laughs, and Nora hears her lighter click.

A coffee can is in the middle of the floor, below a spot in the ceiling that apparently leaks. Nora nudges it with the toe of her shoe.

"So, get this." Rose is still cackling. "Those saline drips they give you in the hospital are basically bags of old seawater."

"I think I may head back tomorrow," Nora says.

"Are you all right? Your voice sounds funny."

"I'm fine. Oh, I have something for you. I found a painting like the one by your couch."

"You did? I've missed it. That was Buck's, you know."

"Well it's not exact, but it reminds me of yours."

"Nora, you don't sound so great. If you're not up to the trip, you should come on back. You don't always have to be the Rock of Gibraltar. No one's judging."

The bar is small with only a handful of stools. They're mostly taken, but there's one for her. "Just a beer," Nora says, setting her things on the bar. This time she'll ask about the motels. So far her rooms have been hit or miss, one with rust stains in the sink and a loose toilet seat, the next perfectly clean and for the same rate.

"The Drifter's a good deal," says the bartender. He's a big man with black hair and a drooping mustache.

"We've stayed there ourselves," the man on the next stool concurs. "Did you just come over the bridge?"

"What bridge?" The cold beer feels great on her throat.

"The Mackinaw. It's the only way up from the rest of the world."

"I'm from Wisconsin. Superior," she says.

"Oh, over there. I've never been west."

This strikes her as funny, west being Wyoming or California in her mind. Wisconsin couldn't be more in the middle. The man's seventy, maybe, with glasses and thick skin. He looks like a farmer, someone who knows weather.

"Bob O'Meara," he says. "This is my wife, Margaret. That big guy there," he lifts his beer to the bartender, "is Mike Stone, owner of this fine establishment."

There's a snowmobiling calendar behind the bar, and a boar's head wearing a baseball cap, a bunch of key rings dangling from its mouth. "I like your place. It feels well lived in."

"I can't argue that. There's been a lot of living here."

"Not too much dying, recently," Bob laughs.

"Are you passing through?" Margaret asks, looking at Nora's notebook with the postcards sticking out. She has a tremor and arthritic hands, so her beer glass shakes when she lifts it off the bar. The couple looks like bookends, in his and her versions. Nora tells them she's been going around the lake.

"By yourself, dear?" Margaret looks incredulous, her eyes widening behind thick lenses.

It hasn't been an uncommon response, second only to that she's going the wrong way.

"That's so brave."

Nora has nothing to say to that.

"Flint here went around the lake," offers Bob. "What was that, two, three years ago?"

"Yep. Ninety-seven."

"Flint?"

"Yeah, yeah," the bartender empties the ashtray. "It's the stone . . . flint. People have to amuse themselves."

"Flint, Michigan," Margaret says.

"Sam Granite," Bob cuts in.

"Looks like Rocky Shoreline to me," adds Nora.

"Oh great, you too. You'll fit right in."

A steady trickle of people are coming through the door, all to big "hellos" and "how have you beens" occupying Bob and Margaret each time.

Nora slides the postcards out of her notebook. She bought the last two that morning in Munising. One is of an old wooden lighthouse on Grand Island—as big as Manhattan, the card says. The other is from the Pictured Rocks Lakeshore, the place that Frank said she really should see. But the only way to see it was from a boat. The pictures in the brochure looked impressive though, enormous striped and sand-colored bluffs. One looked like a castle, another an Indian's head.

"Dear Bun Bun," Nora writes on a postcard. "You wouldn't believe this place. How do you think this Indian head got carved? Just from the wind and water, they said. Pretty amazing, isn't it? Next, I'm going to the Shipwreck Museum. Lots of love, from your Nanny." She's not really lying. Nikki doesn't need to know that she didn't actually take the boat tour. She addresses the card and presses a stamp in the corner.

"Are you always this busy in the afternoon?" she asks, ordering another beer.

"It's the first weekend of the season. People are up to open their summer camps."

Nora feels like she's meeting half the town, Bob and Margaret introducing her around, her mood lifting with each new encounter. There's Stan, who has the smallest eyes she's ever seen. "He's the second best fisherman in the U.P.," Bob keeps telling her, and Stan laughs each time he does.

"I'll have a vodka rocks when you've got a minute," Nora says, catching Mike's eye. "And a grilled cheese." She needs to get something in her stomach.

On her way back from the bathroom she notices the lights hanging over the line of bar stools. It's a regular string of Christmas lights, though each bulb is covered with a plastic shotgun casing—red, blue, green, yellow, pink—the shells wired over each little light.

Her grilled cheese comes in a red plastic basket, the same kind she served food in at the Schooner. It takes her aback when Mike sets it at her place.

"Isn't that what you ordered?"

"Yeah. Perfect." It makes her sad, but happy in a way, too. Not that the baskets are particularly rare. She just likes that they both use them. Used.

When Nora dials home again, Rose doesn't pick up. She wanted to let her know that she's okay, not to worry, and to tell her all about the shotgun-shell lights, and the friendly people. "Rose, listen, you'd love this bar I found," she says to the answering machine. "And I'm fine, really. Hell, it's Friday night in Paradise."

1622

"How is she?" Night Cloud bends as he enters the wigwam.

Sitting on the floor near Grey Rabbit, Bullhead turns up her hands to show emptiness.

"I think she is asleep. It's hard to tell." She moves over and pats the mat by her side.

Night Cloud kneels next to his wife's curled figure. "I thought she was getting better." His voice is as thin as a wisp of smoke. "Her eyes look like a raccoon with those dark markings."

"They don't see when they're open. I don't know where she is." Bullhead picks a pine needle from Grey Rabbit's hair. "Have you noticed anything about the beavers?"

"Why?"

"Their behavior, have you heard or seen anything? She said that the beavers are angry."

Night Cloud touches Grey Rabbit's shoulder gently. "The beavers?"

Bullhead turns up her hands again. "They were her only words."

Night Cloud looks up at a crack in the bark, where a finger of blue sky is showing through. "The beavers' numbers are strong. You've tasted the meat. Their furs were as thick as the winter was cold."

Bullhead places her hand against Night Cloud's leg to quell the fear she hears in his voice. "When we get to Bawating she'll need to be tended to. I don't know what to do for her. Has the time to move on been discussed?"

"The decision was to wait. The water surface has been murmuring all morning. We'll travel after the storm has passed." Night Cloud grazes Grey Rabbit's cheek with his fingers. He closes his eyes, and rises slowly.

"Ask about the beavers," says Bullhead.

He nods and pushes aside the door flap, sunlight spreading across the mats.

2000

Nora stands beside the locks at Sault Sainte Marie, where the International Bridge spans the water, its ironwork yellow against high stretching clouds. She has traveled clear to the end of the lake. And it does feel like an end of sorts, with the mammoth locks forming a gateway, the lake on one side and the river on the other, connecting Superior to Lakes Huron and Michigan. But lakes don't really have ends, she thinks, popping an antacid into her mouth. They just keep going around in a circle.

The ore boat's hull is a reddish-brown wall gliding slowly in front of her. It is marked with draft lines, rivets, and scrapes— a colossal rust-colored whale. Groups of people are lined along the fence and standing on the observation platform, waving to the sailors with the open-faced cheer usually mustered for firemen. The ship is the *Oglebay Norton,* and she's headed for the Twin Ports. Home.

The sailors lounge nonchalantly against the ship's rails, talking to each other, waving down to the crowd, biding time while the water level rises to match the lake. "Twenty-one feet," the brochure says. "Iron ore called the tune, and America danced." She doesn't feel at all like dancing, though that morning, she'd been determined to continue with her trip.

Everyone around her has someone else. Couples. Families. Tour groups. Friends. She walks along the fence in pace with the freighter, looking up at the sailors, hoping for a familiar face. She's pretty sure Jim Haala is still the *Norton*'s cook. She doesn't recognize anyone.

"How long till they make port?" Nora asks through the fence.

A man who's wrangling a rope as thick as his arm looks over. "Twenty-four to thirty hours, depending," he says.

From the window in the visitor's center, the International Bridge looks particularly high, and as flimsy as a roller coaster. Go or turn back, Nora can't make up her mind. She's never been indecisive. In fact, indecisive people try her patience. So she has never left the country before; why should it be a big deal? Her reflection in the large pane is transparent, and people down on the pavement are walking through her head.

Nora drifts haphazardly through the exhibits—a model of the locks, a photo display of their construction. The information is all steel and tonnage capacity. It's something—the engineering, and the enormous scale. But it's like war in her mind; it belongs to men.

A small section displays artist-drawn renderings of the area hundreds of years ago. The pictures show a long rapids and an island lined with Indian huts instead of the locks. "Bawating— water beaten to spray," she reads. The people in the drawings are dressed in skins—a group of children playing, adults at work. Large fish hang from racks like clothes left to dry. It looks serene. Idyllic. Not of this world. She skims over a plaque headed "Etienne Brule." "At the age of sixteen, Etienne Brule, came from France to Quebec. The first to leave the European outpost. He lived among the Huron, learned their language, lived their lifestyle. Captured and tortured by the Iroquois. The first to paddle four of the five Great Lakes. The first white man to reach Lake Superior."

Nora chews on a chalky antacid tablet as she peers down at the locks from the high yellow bridge. The locks look like long watery landing strips. A big lumber operation sits on the Canadian shore, and a plant with flaming smokestacks, like the refinery back home. Surprisingly, she doesn't even have to get out of the car at customs. And Sault Sainte Marie, Ontario doesn't look all that different than Sault Sainte Marie, Michigan, except for the maple leaf flag and conspicuously fewer signs trying to draw in tourists. She feels foolish. What did she expect, the trees to look different, the sky a new shade? The road she's looking for is 17—the Trans-Canada Highway according to her map—but she's lost right away, her stomach flip-flopping.

The first surprise at the gas mart is the familiar brand names in the aisles. The second is the exorbitant cost of gas and cigarettes. On top of the price, they don't carry her brand. She picks out two packs—one green, one blue—and the counter girl, who looks like any American teenager, puts them in with the rest of her things. Nora hands over a number of bills. The girl gives her an exasperated look, and points to a bank across the street.

Nora steps back into the lot, the clouds overhead breaking up and blowing. The antacids aren't helping at all; her stomach feels like a big raw hole. She should have gone back. She needs to be home. Not crossing this foreign street with its empty planters, where no one even knows her name.

The outer lobby of the bank is airless. French or English, the screen asks. It seems implausible that her card will work, but colorful bills soon cascade into the tray.

When Nora pushes the heavy glass door open, the sun is out

and lighting everything—the curb, the gas pumps, the hoods of parked cars. But the brightness only makes her feel worse, smaller and more alone. The blue day feels impenetrable, as if behind glass. She's alone. She's not attached to anything. Nora sits on the edge of a planter, her breath short, her neck sweaty.

In the car, she leans back against the headrest, eyes closed, smoking her last cigarette. She could leave her car and fly home if there's a plane. Somehow come back and get the car later.

She picks up the flimsy map. She has two options—keep going or turn around. If she did go back, what would she say to Nikki? And what kind of example would that be? What would she tell herself, for crying out loud? She looks at the map, at the northern and then the southern route. Either direction, she'll be on her way home, driving toward, not driving away anymore.

Nora walks back into the station.

"I need a real map," she says to the counter girl.

The girl snaps her gum, and reaches for the bag she's kept off to the side. "Where to?"

"Superior."

"Where's that?"

"Wisconsin. The other end of the lake."

1902

Berit places a jar of wildflowers in the center of an overturned fish box. The day's warm and calm. The lake laps. An occasional breeze stirs the long grasses. She adjusts her skirt and opens the sketchbook she'd found propped against the fish-house door the morning after John's visit. It was weeks until she had the heart to open it. She pages through the drawings she'd done in the winter—a baby spruce lined with snow, a pair of chickadees, black bears, then the unfinished spray of pussy willows. And the new things, drawn over the last week. The first, of her boot lying on the floor. The second, of the sleeping cat. The new drawings are hardly recognizable as hers with their heavy marks instead of finely hewn lines.

Berit twists the jar of wildflowers, leaving the white daisy off center. She adjusts her posture to get a better position for her leg. It used to be that she would savor starting a new drawing. Now it takes sheer will. The day is soft and hazy, so there are no shadows within the arrangement of flowers. She looks over the relative sizes of the blooms, and the shapes of the spaces between each stalk.

The tip of her lead rests on the blank sheet while her eyes drift over the striped water—tawny, white, pale blue. He's somewhere out there. She'll never hold him again, smell his head, or feel his calloused palm on her cheek. She closes her eyes, opens them on the flowers. If she can concentrate long enough to enter the drawing, she will reach the place where the rest of the world dissipates. Her gaze moves from the flowers to the paper. The stones in the bottom of the jar stretch and curve against the delineated edge of the glass, and the handful of stems criss-crossing underwater are dotted with tiny air bubbles. Her pencil moves lightly, barely touching the paper, just a curve of space marked, an angle suggested. Then another. And another.

Berit doesn't hear the *America* until she's in view, steaming southwest toward Duluth. She keeps her eyes on the paper, listening to the boat engine, fighting the urge to run into the fish house. She can picture it out there perfectly—white top, dark bottom, the big doors in its side, and the smudge of smoke trailing from its stack. She moves her pencil in time to the drubbing, darkening and darkening the edges of stems, feeling that everyone aboard is watching her. She won't look up until it has passed.

If she were on the boat, bags packed, she'd soon find herself on the town dock. And then what. Back on the hillside in her rented room that smelled like cut cedar and faintly of bleach. The room was a tiny rectangle, with yellow-rose wallpaper, and one dormer window that faced a wasteland of tree-stumped hills. She used to try and imagine the view before the hills were clear-cut. She was living there when she'd first met Gunnar.

Her pencil has lifted off the page. The smell of burning coal is coming off the lake. There's a stalk of purple harebell in the jar, wild columbine, and oxeye daisy. She'll know the boat is out of view by the change in the sound. She tries to focus, tracing a stem that dips over the mouth of the jar and then rises, but her line is too exaggerated. She never liked living in town. It was barren and noisy with the sawmill and the railroad, and the ship whistles from the working docks. But maybe it would be for the best now. She could throw herself into all the commotion, find full-time employment, rather than the piecework she'd done.

The boat's gone. Her view peacefully unbroken. The banded water. The pale sky.

The hawkweed blooms on her curvy stalk are made of hundreds of tiny blunt petals, yellow in the center circled by orange. With small radiating lines she defines their texture, her pencil jotting quick marks. The room they rented after they married was much larger and papered blue. He'd leave his hat hanging from the bedpost at night. The train rumbled their windowpane. Berit's pencil stills, hovers. She can't go back to Duluth. He would be on every corner, in every striding gait. He'd be every grey hat.

The first wave from the boat's wake angles in. It rises, curls, then hits, sweeping sideways along the shore. The hawkweed bloom. She applies herself, her pencil marks moving out from the center. There is no place she can imagine going to. The Keweenaw would feel like moving backwards, erasing the life she'd led. And the south shore's been entirely logged. Entire vistas she once loved are gone. More erasure. More disappearances. Her thoughts turn backward, then forward again, eddies in circles. She applies her lead.

Berit holds her drawing at arm's length. It's a terrible mess. The curving stem of the hawkweed looks like a dark serpent, the bloom a bursting sun in its mouth.

She lies on her side. Grotesque. Inert. Her resting place at 112 fathoms. The wheel house windows. Eyes no longer seeing. Cheek to frigid lake bottom. Like no boat I have ever known.

A tolling silence.

I make no reflection in her windows.

But I see her hold filled with a cargo of ore.

The wind shrieks, and she's taking spray. No green water on deck.

The spray, turned ice, hits the windows like gunshot. Zero visibility. Screaming wind.

Winches and kingposts thickening.

Grey beards reaching to twenty feet break over the bow and sprawl across her decks. Holding steady. Temperatures dropping. Deck ice-coated with freely roaming seas.

Forward crew members severed from aft.

Pitching and rolling dangerously.

They are shoveling like madmen at the fire doors.

Wastebaskets. Wheelbarrows. All hands fly as the rogue plunges her bow below the surface.

She dives headlong toward the lake bottom. Windows blazing yellow behind a curtain of bubbles. Icicled bow like a monster's frozen maw.

She careens through the water in a reckless plunge.

I see her coming, she approaches herself, hits silently and merges.

She lies on her side. Grotesque. Inert.

Cheek to frigid lake bottom.

Everything and all hands entombed.

1622

She is wrapped tight as a papoose in a cradleboard, lying with her arms snug against her body, the weight of a fur heavy across her chest. Bear. The smell of the fur is bear. Above Grey Rabbit there is only clear blue, framed on the edges by smoothly carved cedar. There is rich brown birch bark and dark pitch seams. She's in motion, her feet rhythmically lifting and falling, her whole body sometimes shuddering side to side. She hears water, the splash and drip of paddles. She understands that she is on Gichigami, vulnerable, her arms bound at her side. Her feet rise up and then fall again. She hears Night Cloud's voice, though not his words, they fly away on the wind. There is only the cold blue pressing down on her face.

Blue.

Blue, close, cupped over her eyes, or sometimes seeming far away. The blue is alive with subtle patterns of light, with flecks and flashes that keep her eyes busy. When she closes them, orange flowers bloom.

A dragonfly has lit on the smooth cedar, and it's watching her with bulging oval eyes. Its outstretched wings flutter on the wind. Its wings are water, held by strands of fine hair, and they're snaring the flecks of light from the blue. Stay, she asks. Don't fly away. But the dragonfly lifts and careens out of view.

The movement subsides to a gentle rocking. She hears lapping water and words of prayer. She feels the place, the all-watchful presence. They are at the base of the sacred cliff, where the stories are painted and the spirits honored in images. She can't sit up or move her arms. She can see only part of the painted turtle. Whispers echo in the caves of her ears—eager, insistent—but she doesn't understand. The water laps. A tear slips across her temple.

Again, the movement grows to a pitch and roll. Fingers of sparkling water reach over her body and fall, leaving tiny clear beads in the fur.

A white gull hovers, then slides away. A trail remains across the sky that looks as if it's been drawn with a soft white rock. Her feet rise up and drop with force, shining scales of water arching. Grey Rabbit closes her eyes, her heart beating hard. Her feet drop and the spray flies. Her eyes open when the cold water hits her face. There are three white trails crossing the sky, and a hanging gull forming another. Sweat beads at her temples. The gull veers out of sight.

The white lines weave a web above her. A white net, and she is the fish. Cold water slides into her ear, and her hands ball into tight fists. Her body rolls up and down. She feels the great horned serpent below, only thin bark and fur between them. A flick of his tail, and they will be under. A nudge from his horns and the boat crumples like a dry leaf.

Her body rides the rolling seas, her face sweating cold, her shoulders tense, her fingernails cutting half-moons in her palms.

A dragonfly lights on the smooth cedar. Its thin bent legs grip the wood. Jaw moving. Oval eyes. Its wings are made of water and light. Stay, she asks. Please, stay. The dragonfly lights in the dark fur.

2000

The highway cuts through low knuckled hills, pink and white bluffs showing through the pines. Nora fiddles with the tuner and finds some soft jazz, the announcer speaking French between the songs. The map of Ontario is folded open and lying over her notebook on the passenger seat. It's much more substantial than the circle map, showing towns, rivers, islands, and landmarks, with names like Batchawana and Point aux Mines. She lights the first of her new cigarettes. They're short, fatter, stronger, tolerable. The design of the box is elegant though, with the cigarettes sliding out from a sleeve.

Another one, Nora remarks aloud. High on an outcropping at the side of the road is a pile of stones balanced like a statue. She's been seeing them for miles. They're like markers, cairns, or directional guides, but they don't actually point anywhere. It's impossible that they're natural. No one lives in the area, it's all Provincial Park land, so someone must have climbed up, and made them.

There aren't any stations on the radio. None. The land is mountainous and the sky pristine blue, the sunlight in sheets on the high cliffs, where a thin waterfall is streaming down. Nora cranes her neck to look up through the windshield. It's like she's driving through a never-ending postcard. She wishes Nikki were along to see it. She pictures her holding the glass float to her eye, pretending that everything's underwater.

There. Water is back on her left again, dark blue and sparkling. A touchstone in the unfamiliar landscape. Yet the water isn't exactly familiar. It's hard to believe it is all the same lake.

The lake shimmers to the horizon. If she could see across the hundreds of miles, she'd probably be looking at the Twin Ports. The sun shines through the green glass float. Home. The water connects this shore to that. To Rose. It touches Janelle and Nikki's.

A place with Native pictographs is marked on the map, and Nora needs to find a restroom. She turns off the highway and follows a road that ends in a small gravel lot. As soon as she parks, she feels the quiet. She gets out of the car and stretches her back. There's no store, bathroom, or building there, just a pickup truck with two girls on the tailgate. Sisters, she thinks, when they smile at her. The kiosk has a box with brochures inside, and a map that shows a path leading down to the lake. She looks at the map and then over to the girls.

"Did you go down there?" Nora asks.

"It's amazing," says one of them. "I can't get over it. I mean, how could the paintings last hundreds of years when the Natives made their pigment from powdered rock?" The girl looks at Nora as if she might have an answer. "You've got to see it," the other one says. "The turtle is awesome." She smiles encouragingly.

Nora's footsteps seem loud on the path. She stops, listens,

peers through the woods. There are rustling noises on the forest floor. She lights a cigarette, refusing to indulge this new gutlessness that keeps coming over her.

The path descends between high rock bluffs. She must be close because she can hear rolling waves. Nora walks tentatively between the stone walls, feeling as if someone is watching her. It's mossy and cool and the air is damp. She could reach out her arms and touch both sides. All she can hear is water dripping. Her own footsteps. The slow waves of the lake. Overhead is an empty strip of blue sky. No one is on the path in either direction, yet she can't shake the feeling that she is not alone.

Nora steps onto a ledge that slants precariously into the clear water. The drone of a distant motorboat rings off the cliff as it passes. The cliff on one side, the lake on the other. Extreme Caution, the sign said. A wave rolls lazily halfway up the ledge.

Someone is watching her. She can feel it at the back of her neck. No one's around. Just the receding boat. She will absolutely not edge herself along below the cliff. It's not gutless; it's common sense. If she fell in there would be no one to help her. The brochure showed the turtle the girl mentioned and stick figures in canoes, but a few faint lines, rust red and grainy, are all that's visible from where she stands. The lake rolls. She is being watched, she's certain of it.

The cliff top is lined with pines. It's too high and sheer to tell if anyone's up there. A large crow takes to the air, and the icy lake water is around her ankle. She gasps and the wave rolls back to the lake.

1902

The sky is warm white and the water grey, the horizon line long and empty. Berit sits on the slanting rock ledge, staring off across the water, her wood bucket submerged and heavy on the rope. The air is soft and the lake sounds muted—a swash, then a quiet lapping. Berit draws in the line and the bucket rises, breaks the surface, spilling over and dripping. She hauls the bucket up the ledge. Watches the dark water rings expand. With one hand on the handle and one underneath, she slowly tips the bucket over. A clear sheet of water pours back to the lake.

The air tingles on Berit's wet cheeks. She wipes the tear streaks with her sleeve, tosses the bucket from the ledge. It's curious to her, how much she can cry, how the water springs daily from her eyes. The bucket lists on the lake surface. A raven beats the air as it crosses overhead. Berit tugs the rope and the bucket rim tilts, the water instantly claiming the space. The bucket sinks and the rope tightens. She lets the wet fibers slide though her cold hands.

The lake appears grey and opaque, but if she looks carefully at its wavering surface she can see a thousand clear eyes of water, blinking under sky-hooded lids. The rope goes slack. The bucket sits on the lake bed. When she leans forward the lake holds her face. The dark circle of the bucket below. The stone ship is in her mind. As a child she'd spent many an afternoon there. One long leap from land to the craggy boulder, where she'd lay studying her face in the water, the rocks below, maybe a fish, the sky and the clouds around her head. Or else she'd sit scout, her eyes keen, searching for a smudge on the horizon that might become a sail, the possibility of a mast. She'd take herself to her stone ship when she was angry at her parents. Take herself there when she was sad, knowing that when she stared at the water, its beauty would eventually soothe her and her feelings would dissolve into calm.

Hand over hand, Berit draws in the rope, and the bucket rises toward the surface. When she gets hold of the handle she tips it over, pours it back to the lake in a long thick arc. A scavenging gull lands nearby, paddles back and forth as it turns its white head. The empty bucket lands in the water with a splash. All her life, most everything has come and gone by the water—ships filled with provisions, new settlers with their trunks. Always the possibility of something she desired—confections, glue, a new hair ribbon, pencils. And ships left, their holds filled with copper or fish. The old schoolteacher, waving good-bye from the deck.

Gunnar. He came and left by the water.

Berit pulls the rope up a distance. The taut fibers wet and rough. Then lets it slide bit by bit through her hands, the bucket dropping back down to the lake bed. The white-grey horizon holds little promise. She can't imagine any object aboard a ship that could spark an interest, touch a desire. Even the lake's ability to soothe her has waned. It's simply too small for the enormity of her feelings.

She should make herself some food, split more wood. Berit hauls in the rope and lifts the bucket from the water. It's queer how she moves through her days—one foot following the next, one breath, one drawing, one stitch.

Berit balances the bucket on the ledge, the spilled water darkening the grey rock, and cups a handful to her mouth. Again and again she scoops and sips. Thirsty. She hadn't realized how thirsty. She lifts the bucket to her lips and gulps, the icy water spilling down her neck. No matter, it is one thing she won't run out of. She has been drinking the lake her entire life, could drink it forever and not make a dent.

Berit lowers the bucket as the thought surfaces. Could it be so base? Simply primal? Is it raw instinct that causes her to gaze at the water? Merely her body as it recognizes the promise of its own continuing?

If she stopped drinking the lake, she'd be dead within weeks.

2000

The bay is a wide horseshoe, enormous, with sheer cliffs on one side. And the lake is royal blue, filled with little coins of light that scatter constantly, rearranging themselves. Nora positions her shoe to dry in the sun. Only some of the images are recognizable inside the pictograph brochure—an odd looking lynx, a deer, bears, a long wavy snake with horns. Other figures are abstract, just circles with dots, lines.

Good grief. That water about gave her a heart attack. She digs for the pretzels in the gas-mart bag. Down by the shore, a couple boys are playing catch. She hears the lazy thwap of the ball hitting in the mitt.

Thwap. The water surface jumps with light. Thwap. Something white, maybe a gull, is crossing in front of the huge cliffs. She follows it for a while, but it's hard to say what it is. It's just a small spot of white drifting across the dark rock.

Nora yawns and rubs her eyes. Splotches of light float behind her lids. She feels like she's been riding a fiercely painted horse, up and down, on an emotional carousel—from the spineless way she felt at the gas mart to the pristine beauty of the drive, and then from the eerie pictograph place to this perfectly calm sunny beach. She'd always thought of herself as the painted sleigh type, moving evenly along while other people rode the horses. And each extreme is vivid and consuming, so where is her true self in that?

Nora closes her eyes, her face to the sun. Thwap. If she had a lawn chair, she'd sleep for a week. Thwap. The warmth seeps into her skin. Her cheeks. Thwap. Her eyelids. Her neck.

She's working alone and the bar is busy. She's holding a pint glass under the tap. When she pulls it, foam sputters out. The storeroom is five blocks away and she simply doesn't have the time; two new tables just walked in, and she has burgers on the grill. She rushes down the sidewalk, has to wait to cross the street. She's pushing the keg on a dolly, across a dry lake bed. It's hot, and sandy fish are lying around; they aren't dead, but they don't move. The dolly maneuvers easily around discarded cans and ropes of seaweed. The distance seems endless. She has to get back. Finally, she pushes through the door. The crowd has doubled. She hooks up the keg. There isn't any glassware behind the bar.

The afternoon has grown sullen and drizzly, the road having taken a long swing inland. Nora takes her foot off the gas to let the logging truck gain distance again and give herself a break from the wood chips bouncing back. Her neck is sore from the way she'd slept sitting up. It's disturbing to think she'd napped in public, not knowing what had been going on around her.

She passes whole hillsides filled with dead trees, birch and spindly balsam, bald rock showing through. She yawns and looks down at the map. Napping has made her disoriented, and she probably shouldn't be driving. She cracks the window for air, but flecks of water come in.

It's been raining hard enough for lights and steady wipers. She's going to have to stop soon. Nora spots another of the rock figures above the road. They've grown comforting, little guides to show her the way. She lifts the map to check on her options for stopping. It shows a few towns after the road finally swings back to the lake.

She sets the map down and then grabs it up again. Her notebook isn't on the seat. Nora veers onto the shoulder, rocks sliding under her tires. It's not on the floor. It's not wedged against the car door. It has to be in the gas-mart bag. She reaches back and drags the bag over the seat. The pretzels are there, her half-eaten sandwich, a can of Coke. No way. Impossible. Rain pelts the roof of her car. She stretches her arm beneath the seats.

Nora gets on her knees and leans into the back, pops her suitcase open and rifles around. She tilts Rose's painting to look behind it, but she can already see the notebook where she left it. Hours back. On the bench. At the horseshoe bay.

She can't drive back, not all that distance, and in the rain this late with nowhere to stay. She pictures the notebook lying open on the bench, all the pages soaked and wavy, the ink blurred.

1622

It's dark. Grey Rabbit can hear the rushing water, and then the entreating words of prayer. She can feel the words; they touch her like sunlight. She feels them as she feels the ground beneath her body, as she smells the thick sweetness of burning tobacco. A face below a short crest of feathers floats in and out of view. A face as creased as an old hickory nut. And faded eyes, one smaller than the other. A long thin mouth intoning. Grey Rabbit's eyelids flutter shut.

A rattle is shaking, small pebbles to wood. The sound comes from one side and then the other, comes from two directions at once. And a song. A reedy cracking voice. Words punctuated by the shaking rattle. A song to spirit, from the thin mouth, asking for her health and long life. Grey Rabbit feels heat rise to her face, feels the shifting air as the rattle moves over her. The rattle and the song. The words and the heat.

With gentle hands, her head is turned to the side, and she feels a sharp cut at her temple. She flinches with each small incision to her skin. Then a smooth round rim is laid against her head. There's a sucking sound, as the circle of skin pulls.

The prayer song mingles with new smells, broken root and

herbs, and she hears the sound of mixing. Wood scraping against wood. Something soft moves over her cuts, and a warm wet sensation seeps into her temple.

Her head is being lifted and turned the other way.

From the lightless depths I hear birds. There is the first to sound. The following others. A squawk and cackle that moves throat to throat.

Open beaks and necks exerting. I see the call pass through the forest. A westward wave. Cresting overhead. Cleaving at the eastern rim of the lake.

I see the night water, silky against the shore. The grains of sand beneath the black air grow discernable in the faint shift.

And the eye of the Great Lake turns toward the sun.

In the final hush. The surface of the water greys. The solid mass of the woods begins to separate. Bough from trunk. Log from forest floor.

Then comes the sun's slivered edge. Sandy rays. To copper. Rising carnelian. Iron red.

Yet here. At the lake basin's western edge.

The forest is still cushioned in night.

I watch a crow in a dead birch. The lake wind riffles its feathers.

While on the cobble beach below, the waves unfurl in the rhythmic dark.

The crow senses the advancing call. It composes its wings. Claws the soft wood.

It cocks its sleek head to the east.

The night stars still reflected in the bead of its eye.

2000

The motel is called the Innland Sea, a huge statue of a voyageur standing out front. "It's all non-smoking," the man tells Nora, "but there are chairs on the veranda, if you must." She doesn't care, not about anything. She's absolutely sick about the notebook.

Nora unwraps a glass from its thin white paper, fills it with ice and cracks the bottle she'd picked up on her way into town. She sits on the edge of the bed with the remote, trying to find the news so she can see about the weather, but the only station that comes in clearly is from Detroit. When they get to the weather forecast with the map of the States, Canada is just a blue blank across the top.

The "veranda" is the walkway fronting the rooms, lined with white plastic chairs and coffee-can ashtrays. Nora sits smoking, water dripping from the eave, looking at the voyageur's backside and the red-headed paddle he holds like a staff. The rain has stopped, and in the distance are clouds with fiery gold edges hanging over a thin strip of lake. She can buy another notebook easily enough, it's the recreating of all the lists. Unbelievable. She heaves out a stream of smoke.

The door to the room next door clicks open, and a big round woman steps out. She's carrying a blanket and a grocery bag. *"Bon soir,"* she says, setting down her bag.

"Hi," Nora musters, but doesn't look over.

"Hi, all right." The woman settles into a chair, and fusses a blanket over her legs.

The clouds turn slowly from gold to orange, then temper to a dark rose.

"Red sky at night," the woman says, her English sounding perfectly normal.

"Let's hope the driving will be as good as the sailing."

"The weather changes all the time around here. I meant to make it to Wawa, but I can't drive in the rain."

The woman's face is moony and thin skinned, her grey-blond hair tied in a knot on her head. Nora drains her drink, then goes inside for the bottle.

"Hors d'oeuvre?" the woman asks, reaching over with a tray of crackers covered with spread. "I make the mix myself. Good port is the key to the flavor. I'm Paulette," she says, nudging the tray closer, "but most call me Tinker, so feel free."

"Nora." She takes a cracker from the tray and leaves it balancing on the arm of the chair while she picks ice from the bucket at her feet. "Do you want a drink?" she asks.

"Thanks dear, I have everything I need." The woman pats the brown bag by her leg.

Everything you need in a brown bag. What does she need—a plan, a life? The notebook's her only need that would fit in a bag.

The sunset is over. Their cigarettes glow. Nora shuffles the ice at the bottom of her glass, shining and dark in the low light. She appreciates that the woman isn't a talker, the kind who barges right in if you open the door a crack.

"Another?" The woman reaches over with the tray.

"Thanks, Pauline. They're good."

"It's Paulette, but like I said, you can call me Tinker."

"How did you get Tinker from Paulette?" Nora splashes more vodka in her glass.

"People have called me that forever. It could be because I'm a whiz at fixing things. Clocks, radios, anything mechanical. It's hard to remember how it started, though."

Nora tries to picture the woman's pudgy hands working a small screwdriver, or placing tiny springs.

"And you? *Mon Dieu.*" Tinker shades her eyes as the lights along the veranda switch on.

"Oh, I'm not very mechanical."

"I'd fix this with a BB gun." Tinker points to the bare bulb over her head.

Nora stands and unscrews the bulb.

"Good girl." Tinker smiles. "Maybe he'd like your help, too." She points to the giant voyageur, now lit up from a ring of spots in the ground.

"Nice sash," says Nora.

"Pretty nice legs."

Nora chokes on a swallow and a laugh.

"My great, great," Tinker says, twirling her hand. "Who knows how many greats, was a voyageur. Of course, I never knew him. My son did the research. He filled four contracts with the fur company before getting killed at Fort William."

"What happened?" Nora pictures an Indian raid.

"He died in a brawl over a game of checkers."

"You've got to be kidding."

"That's what George says." She holds the tray out again. "This place is filled with hard-to-believe stories." Her gaze floats off past the voyageur. "A lot of strange things happen."

Nora sips her drink and nods, thinking it's hard for her to tell what's strange from what's normal anymore.

"Today when I was driving there was an island in the lake. It had a dreamy look, with a collar of cloud around it. But then," she smoothes her blanket, "it disappeared."

"I've heard stories like that from sailors. It's some kind of weather phenomenon."

"Some say weather, others say it's an optical illusion. I wouldn't put a name on it. Would you care for a peanut butter cup?" Tinker pours some out on the tray and leans over. "There's a crack in the lake where boats disappear," she says quietly, before settling back into her chair.

"I've heard that one, too." Nora lights a cigarette and throws the match into the coffee can. "But really," she says, blowing out smoke, "How can a lake have a crack? Water doesn't crack. It's water."

"If you say so." Tinker pops a candy in her mouth. "What about ice?"

"Boats don't sail on ice."

"True, true, but nonetheless."

Nora watches the end of Tinker's cigarette flare orange and then fade. The rest of her is a silhouette.

"Where was it you said you were from?" she asks.

"Superior, Wisconsin. It's on the other side. But I'm thinking of moving to California." Nora exhales a stream of smoke. She's never said it out loud. She likes the sound of it.

"All right, well, you've come quite a distance. Haven't you seen anything strange?"

"No, not really. Not seen." Nora ashes in the can. "Unless you count what I've seen in my sleep."

"This water does that. It gets into your head. Tell me."

Nora shrugs.

"Please, I'd like to hear."

"My dreams?"

Tinker nods encouragingly.

Nora feels stupid describing how Frank pulled her underwater, but Tinker doesn't laugh or judge. The woman in the emerald-green dress stared at her with those weird catlike eyes. Then Nora finds herself talking about how she'd felt on the Keweenaw, standing alone looking down through the water, and that even the tree was a ghost of itself. Something was watching her down at the pictographs—maybe just that bird, but she swears to God she felt it. The litany seems long as she strings it together.

"Uh-huh. Uh-huh," is all Tinker says.

"So what is it?" Nora asks.

"Well, dear, it just is." Tinker chuckles and reaches deep into her bag.

Nora waits. She tops her drink, sure that she must have more to say about it.

"You'll be seeing Thunder Bay then." Tinker pops open a can of soda. "Give my regards to the giant."

"What?"

"The Sleeping Giant. You can't miss him, he's lying right there in the water. You'll hear a lot of differing versions about how Nana'b'oozoo was turned to stone. The point to remember is that he's only asleep. One has to wonder about his dreams."

"Nana who?"

"Oh, you'll meet him for yourself. He's Ojibwe. Half human, half manitou, so to speak."

"What is that word, manitou? There's a river named that on the way to my daughter's."

Tinker takes a long drink of soda, then covers her mouth and burps quietly. "There are a lot of ways to think about it. One could say spirit. Or mystery, or God."

"Good grief, I thought it was a deer."

"Could be a deer."

Nora cocks her head, but doesn't ask for an explanation. "I guess the Indians used to live all around here," she says, recalling the drawings of the village she'd seen at the locks.

"Used to? That's a funny comment. Haven't you noticed they're still here?"

Tinker sets down her can and wags her finger toward the voyageur. "I'll tell you, it really bothers me the way that statue's lit up. It's light pollution. The night is supposed to be dark." She pours more peanut butter cups on the tray. "Have you seen the UFOs?" she whispers.

"UFOs?" Nora rolls her eyes. "You're not serious, are you?"

"Uh-huh," Tinker nods. "Absolutely."

1902

Berit reaches to the back of her head and feels for a knot of hair. The sound of the scissors blades meeting is succinct, and a clump falls down her back to the ground. The morning is filled with the sounds of summer—the white-throated sparrows calling back and forth, and the persistent hollow knock of a woodpecker.

Berit looks for its bobbing head, sees a jay pass like a blue ribbon through the trees. She slides her hand over her head, feeling for the next knot. Pale tufts lie on the ground around the chair, and long strands taken by the breeze hang in the tall grasses around the fish house. There is satisfaction in the cutting, in feeling the abrupt ends of her hair, and the sun on her newly bared neck.

Up at the cabin, Berit finds mouse droppings on the table, and all along the kitchen shelf. She flicks one off the bar of soap. There is something else, too, she can sense it, maybe a bird or a squirrel in the roof beams. She takes clothes from the box she'd shoved under the bed, and leaves the animal to its new home.

The lake mirrors the wide sky, except for the dark skittering patches where it's grazed by a zigzag breeze. She unbuttons her blouse and lets it fall, feeling both the warm sun and the cold lake air on her skin. It's difficult to stand shoeless on the beach;

the rocks dig into the soles of her feet. She unfastens her skirt and steps out, leaving her undergarments in a heap, feeling achingly vulnerable in the elements—the warm and the cool touching her everywhere. She's not been in the lake since Gunnar disappeared.

The water is icy cold, even with the surface water blown toward shore. Still, she has experienced much colder. She steps gingerly along the rocky bottom, gets in past her knees, pauses, winces.

She hesitates, but not because of the cold. What if she were to find him now, her hand brushing against something under-water? It's silly. The lake bottom is clearly visible. The water swirls where her legs disturb it, the sunlight rippling, the cold starting to grab. He'd be her Gunnar. He'd be a monster.

She squats and stands. Good Lord. She braves in to her waist, takes a full breath and dives under. Berit rises with a yelp, turns immediately, and scrambles to shore. Shaking, she rubs her body down with soap.

Her fears are a schoolgirl's, and yet they are not. Being in the water connects her to him. She walks in waist-deep, clench-ing her fists as the soap floats milky from her skin. The second time is always easier. Just go ahead now. She takes a breath and dives.

Berit stands in the sun on the slanting rock ledge. Her skin is still taut with cold, her nipples tight, her body hair risen, though she feels only a vague numbness, and the water from her hair dripping down her spine. She dabs at herself with her old blouse, and steps into clean undergarments and a skirt. Her hair feels strange as she combs her fingers through it, its stubbiness and lesser weight.

She finishes dressing and climbs to a dry rock where she sits, legs drawn up under her skirt, feeling the lake chill set in as her half-numb skin slowly comes back to life. She drops a round birch leaf into the shallows. Submerged yet still floating, it casts a shadow over the stones. The leaf drifts over a waxy orange agate, it grows dark in the shadow, then light again.

2000

There's pounding on the door, and pounding at her temples.

"Housekeeping."

Nora lifts her head from the pillow. It's almost noon. She must not have taken aspirin before bed. She doesn't remember. She feels like hell.

"Housekeeping."

"Yeah. Okay. Give me a minute."

When Nora hands her key to the man at the desk, he looks her up and down accusingly. "Do you know anything about my lights out there?" He points. "The lights. The ones around my statue. Somebody tampered with them during the night."

Nora walks slowly around the giant voyageur. Sure enough, the spotlights are disassembled, their glass covers lying in the grass. The man's watching her from the window, and she's doing her best to look concerned, but she has to turn away from him when an image of Tinker on her knees, armed with a screwdriver, pops into her head. It's possible she'd been in on it too. Part of her night is a flat blank.

The icy fizz of Coke is heavenly on her throat, and she alternates between the cold pop and the warm coffee. Nora slides her plate to the side to make room for the new notebook she's bought.

"Pool Room," she writes at the top of a page. "Main Bar." "Storage Room." Surprisingly, she's able to jot quite a few things beneath each heading.

"What Next?" She adds more cream to her coffee. "California," she writes. The word sits on the page, the big *C* and the rest rolling out after. She could start over someplace new. In California, she wouldn't have to deal with winter. No freezing cold. No dirty grey snow. No scraping ice from the windshield of her car. The last time she'd traveled to California in the winter, she'd gone from clench-fisted, skin-freezing cold to lounging in the sun on Joannie's patio, marveling at the gorgeous bright pink flowers of that huge plant—bougan . . . something—that grows up her house. People leave the northern climates as they age for a good reason. "No winter," she writes under California. "Pink plant." Joannie would put her up in the guest room until she got settled.

"Can I take your plate, ma'am?"

"Just a bump to warm it, thanks."

But California would mean being far from Nikki.

The day out the window is too bright for her eyes. Nora swallows another pair of aspirin. She's been drinking a lot more since the fire. Or differently, at least. Used to be she'd pour one toward the end of the night, and then one, maybe two, to wind down during closing. Not this all or nothing routine.

The clock on the restaurant wall reads past one o'clock. If she hauls, it's possible she could make it back to the States today.

The lake is brilliant blue and shining, the sky cloudless. It's blue over blue. But her car is sluggish on the roller-coaster terrain, the high rock bluffs and steep drops to the water. Nora cracks the windows to let in fresh air. She'd been driving, she couldn't say for how long, without being behind the wheel. Her eyes saw the road obviously enough to stay on it, but her head was in a different place entirely. She was thinking about how scared she'd been when the wave got her foot at the pictographs, and how she'd hightailed it back to her car, thinking about Frank and searching for agates, and the deserted town on the Keweenaw. It's crazy. She'd left home just over a week ago, planning to spend a little time at Janelle's, and now here she is in Canada, driving around the never-ending lake.

She crests a hill and the view is panoramic, then she's down in a gorge with a waterfall. How is she going to explain what she's been through? And aside from Rose, who would she even want to tell? She'd always felt that her life was full of people, but since the fire it doesn't seem true. Seeing old customers out of context is different—say, in the grocery store, with a spouse or a kid in tow. Even with the regulars she'd known for years, there had always been the bar between them.

The lake shines between a hopscotch of islands, and the road continuously climbs and falls, curving one direction and then back, her glass float swinging like the pendulum of a clock. She passes a rock statue on a ledge over the road. She should have asked Tinker about them. She'd probably know who made them, and why. She sees Tinker sitting in the dark, the blanket tucked over her heavy thighs. Nodding her head—"Uh-huh, uh-huh." She liked her. Tinker was good company. Rose will get a kick out of that night's story.

Nora turns off to find a restroom. The sign on the shoulder reads First Nation. She stops at a small store just beyond a bridge, where two Indian women are fishing. She'd never thought about Canada having reservations, if in fact this is one. Minnesota and Wisconsin, she knew about those. She saw them in Michigan, too.

A furry fly buzzes around Nora's head as she makes her way

back to the car. Leaning aganst it, she cracks a can of cold Coke. The man behind the counter was Indian too. The women on the bridge laugh as one reels in a small wriggling fish. She's thinking about how little she knows of Canada, that her mind is no better than the TV weather map, when the woman with the fish turns around and gives her an annoyed "Take a picture . . ." look. Nora turns away, embarrassed. She hadn't realized she was staring. The fly won't stop harassing her, and it's too large to want to swat with her hand, so she gets in the car and quickly closes the door. She is a voyeur, she supposes. How else can it be when you pass through a place where other people spend their lives.

1622

The water of the long rapids swirls, parting around boulders and sliding over ledges, flitting like tiny white butterflies in the shallows. Grey Rabbit no longer hears the fast water, though its sound is constant throughout day and night. She only notices its absence when she ventures to the woods. Nor does she smell the smoking whitefish in the air, as each day they're split and dried over the fires, to be stored for the next turn of winter.

She feels quiet and numbed, her thoughts drift like mist.

"That's good," she says to Night Cloud again, as he helps her tighten the thongs of her tanning frame.

"Are you sure you want to keep working here alone?" He looks back over his shoulder at her.

She'd set up downstream, in a clearing near the water, instead of in the tall pines behind the long bay where all the other women are working. She wants to work beside them, she feels the need, but still she knows she is not ready. She touches her fingertips to the small scabs at her temple. "It's better that I work here," she says quietly. She sees the disappointment in the shift of his shoulders. "I'll move back once I finish this hide."

Night Cloud works in a circle, tightening the thongs around the splayed skin. He doesn't care about the teasing he'll meet with for helping her with women's work. He was scared that he was going to lose her, felt helpless as an overturned beetle. Now that she's getting stronger, he is determined to assist her in any way he can. He has never felt so close to her. He thinks of how they sleep now each night, like two cedars grown together, her back warm down the length of his chest as she holds on to his arm or his hand.

"Are you sure you feel well enough?" he asks, tightening the last of the thongs.

Grey Rabbit kneels next to him and bounces her finger off the hide. "It's good for me to work."

"Do you want me to send Little Cedar?"

"No, let him play. He needs to."

"He's well," Night Cloud assures her again. "The wound is healing, and his vision is good."

Grey Rabbit nods, her eyes lowered. "The scar looks terrible, like a crayfish on his cheek."

Night Cloud squeezes her shoulder and stands. In the long cove upstream, the men are sitting in the shade. "There is talk of sending a war party to avenge Always Day."

Grey Rabbit looks up with interest. "Has anyone stepped forward?"

"Five will go."

The scraping is hard on Grey Rabbit's back, but she'd rather feel her body ache than be left to her mind's lulling numbness. From her spot, she can see up to the cove, and beyond it to the island and the tail of the rapids, where the older boys shoot down in canoes, whooping and hollering and showing off, their near-empty boats skittering over the water. She watches for Standing Bird among them, but she hasn't seen him all day. She was told that he was the one who found her the morning she disappeared from camp, but she has no memory of it.

She wipes the coarse hair from the edge of her scraper. Slowly, small pieces of memory have returned—Bullhead's cool hands hovering over her, the whisper of concerned voices. The hard remembering comes only as a sensation in her body, a slow-growing heaviness that spreads through her chest, weighting her arms with a feeling of helplessness.

Grey Rabbit fingers the new medicine bag at her neck. She can feel the small piece of copper inside, hard among the roots and herbs. In the long cove, her people are gathered. Soon she will take her place among them. Soon she will feel her own worth again.

1902

John's hand rests on the straight-backed chair, pale hair at his feet like an animal kill. There's no sign that anything has changed around the homestead, nothing packed or sorted, no sign that anyone has come.

Gunnar's wife is sitting on the rock ledge, still, as if she were part of the stone. She's cared for the lilac at least; its twiggy branches have dark green leaves. He couldn't keep the images from his last visit at bay—the hollow look in her eyes as she held him at gunpoint, her dirt-streaked cheek as she poured his coffee. In the end, he felt he owed it to Gunnar to see her safely off the shore. Still, he had hoped that someone else would take care of it, and that he'd arrive to find the place deserted.

John's not sure if she looks better or worse. She's loose in her clothes, her hair is cut jagged, and without the dirt she looks yet frailer. He recalls her small breasts and her pale pink nipples as she scrambled naked from the water. "I've come to take you away from here," he announces, mounting the ledge behind her. She doesn't answer or turn around, just continues staring into the lake. A squirrel natters defensively. John looks down at her dripping wet head, then over to the approaching boat. "How long do you need to get your things ready?"

"What?" Berit finally acknowledges him. "I can't. I'm not."

Her head whips around at the sound of oars and the bow of a skiff appears around the point. Nellie is staring at her wide eyed, mouth agape. Hans turns the boat and stills it with a stroke.

"Is everything all right here, Mrs. Kleiven? Captain Shepard said you were still on the shore."

He is speaking to her, but looking over her head. John, above her, stands arms crossed, his gaze somewhere out on the water. Everything all right? She is as confused by the question as by all the people.

"What happened here?" Hans asks sharply.

"Poor dear," Nellie mutters, fingering her hair.

Berit puts her hand to her head, feels her short hair, and then bursts into laughter.

"Oh, my," says Nellie, aghast.

John finally speaks. "I'm taking her to Duluth."

Berit doesn't know which is funnier, Nellie's face, Hans with his hackles up, John talking to the water, or the notion that anyone is concerned about her hair. Oh, Good Lord, she laughs even louder, realizing that they think John did it. She slaps her hand against the rock. She can't stop laughing. She's being rude, she knows.

Berit's unsteady walking barefoot over the stones, which strikes her as funny, too, as does the crow standing in the grass, a clump of her hair hanging from its beak. Out on the point, they're all talking together, John gesturing down the shore. The crow flies past with the strands of her hair.

"Go away, all of you," she calls out, and their heads swivel in unison. "Fly on," she yells, flapping her arms. Let them think she's gone daft.

John approaches Gunnar's wife reluctantly. She sits on the beach raking her fingers through the stones. He should have agreed to let them handle things, but he was so incensed at the man's in-sinuations that he simply wanted them to leave. "Are you well enough to travel?" he asks, standing over her.

"What do you mean, well?" She caws and juts her head to-ward him, watching the surprise in his eyes. She laughs and con-tinues picking through the stones. The ones on top are smooth and dry, but as she digs down they grow smaller and wet.

John sits, draws out his tobacco.

"He's out there somewhere," says Berit.

John nods.

"I haven't lost my senses. I'm fine."

Thoughts of the dead man in Gunnar's net come to mind, and John questions Gunnar's choice to leave the body there. He lights his pipe and shakes out the match. Water spirits are not to be taken lightly.

"I only want people to leave me be." Berit fans her hand through the stones. "Is that so difficult to understand?"

"How will you live? You don't fish." John blows pipe smoke toward the sky. "You don't even have a boat."

"I had it. I didn't want it."

Her profile is thin boned. Her hair wisps up, yellow in the light. "Had what?"

"Gunnar's skiff. Hans found it and towed it over. It's out there," she lifts her face to the lake. "I returned it to him. Don't ask me to explain."

John watches her rake her thin fingers through the rocks. He understands sending Gunnar his boat. But not her. He doesn't understand her.

Berit pushes away another layer of stones, the tiny wet ones sticking to her fingers. She picks a shiny red cylinder from among them.

"Look at this." She holds out her hand.

John's eyebrows lift and he picks it from her palm.

"It's a trading bead," he says, and flicks it into the cove.

I see sunlight hit the water surface. It bends back at its radiant angles of incidence.

Everything joins in the reflecting sun.

Rock to wading child. Canoe to bird in flight.

These receiving waters show the blue spectrum of the atmosphere. Or become a semblance of whatever floats above it.

The airy ricochet is shimmer and dazzle. It gives structure to what the darkness leaves vague.

It calls up color.

Articulates shape.

There is so much at play in this house of bent light. The lake holds each image. Moves in rivers of likeness.

I watch a rock ledge. It reflects on the water.

And its round splotch of lichen. The palest grey green.

Twins.

Forming two eyes.

One of water, one stone.

2000

Nora rests on a bench at a scenic overlook, high on a cliff above the water. Her skin feels alive and vulnerable in the air after being in the closed car for so long. She blows on her coffee-to-go, but it's still too hot, so she sets the lid beside her on the bench. Young parents are laying out a picnic nearby, while their two girls laugh and chase each other, around and around a historic plaque. She's at the top of the world, the water ranging forever, its surface filled with sparkling yellow light.

"*Venez ici,*" the father calls to his girls, a sandwich held in each of his outstretched hands. The two run over, but when they reach for their food he lifts his hands high over their heads. The girls jump up. They grab at his thighs. Nora can't understand their French, though their laughter doesn't need translation. The girls giggle and squeal. The light bounces on the water.

Janelle when little would laugh so hard that sometimes she'd simply fall down—on the floor, on the sidewalk, it didn't matter. The steam from the coffee is warm and wet on her face. When was the last time she heard Janelle really cut loose and laugh? She wishes they had a better relationship. She has to learn not to react when Janelle aims for her soft spots. She has to learn to hold her tongue.

The girls run past laughing, sandwiches in hand. Down below, the wind blows dark streaks across the water. What's hardest is watching her hover over Nikki, trying to control her every experience. Kids need room to make their own mistakes. Nora feels a pang of guilt. She probably gave Janelle too much room. She'd made plenty of mistakes parenting. But all you want in the end is for your children to be happy. Nora stares at the light and the water.

The giggling girls run past again and the light on the water jumps, jiggles, and spreads. The sparkling water fills Nora's eyes. Nikki's in her mind. Bright. Skipping stones. The sparkling water titters. It jumps. The air is filled with the jangle of laughing and shimmering light. Then her thoughts dissolve and she feels the light slowly collide with the laughter, merge, become one, indistinguishable. She is seeing laughter. The lake is laughter.

A wind picks up the lid to her coffee cup and sends it skittering across the ground. Nora jumps up and follows, but she's not fast enough. By the time she reaches the guardrail the lid has sailed off the cliff. Nora peers down the sheer rock wall. A kayak is in the water below, tiny, like a toy. The light on the lake jiggles and spreads, the girls are still laughing, but the sensation has passed. When she looks at the lake, it's only water and light.

The thick gold sunlight is mixed with shadows that make the forested hills seem to vibrate. Nora turns down her visor. She has passed a lot of things that she should've stopped for. Nikki would have been interested in the amethyst mines.

The lake is back again, a big swath of it visible. Always, it seems to change color and mood. It disappears for miles, and then opens up. According to the map, if she could see across the lake she'd be looking at Michigan. She pictures the lighthouse at the Shipwreck Museum. Mike Stone pouring taps for the O'Mearas. It's weird how memory freezes time and place, as if the O'Mearas are still sitting at the bar, as if she's sitting next to them, too, or in her blue car on the other shore, driving the opposite direction. Nora finds an aspirin in her purse, and washes it down with the dregs of cold coffee. It's still thirty-eight miles to Thunder Bay. Thunder Bay is going to have to be the end of the line.

There are strip malls, car washes, and grain elevators, the familiar smell of pulpwood in the air. The sign reads Population 113,000. Nora chooses blindly from a string of motels on the street paralleling the working harbor. She lugs her suitcase up the open stairway and opens the door to number 18. She doesn't even bother to check out the room, just leaves her clothes in a pile on the bathroom floor, and takes a long hot shower, still seeing the road.

A plastic letter holder on the table is stuffed with pamphlets. Nora calls for pizza delivery and slides open the heavy drapes. Her view is crisscrossed with power lines. There's a lumberyard across the road, the lake beyond, and lying in the lavender water, the prone body of the sleeping giant. There's not a shred of trying to imagine it. It's enormous, lying face up. Oval head, arms crossed over its chest, the long thick length of its torso and legs. Nora can't take her eyes off the giant as the water darkens purple and the day slowly fades.

1622

There are frogs trilling in the night air, their rhythmic chorus encircling the wigwam, pulsing through the bark walls. Night Cloud and Grey Rabbit lie in the dark, the boys asleep, Bullhead snoring softly.

"Have you gone to see Stony Ground's blanket?" whispers Night Cloud.

"Not up close, but one can see it from everywhere. It's as red as a chokecherry from end to end. Bullhead says it's rough like dry moss."

"He boasts that it's warm, yet light across his shoulders. And he claims to have seen the Huron's white-faced man."

Grey Rabbit ducks her head and giggles.

"Shhhhh." Night Cloud touches her lips. "It's rumored that he will travel west."

"Is it true that like the white squirrel, his eyes are red?"

"Ha," laughs Night Cloud.

"Shhhhh," she giggles.

The frogs chirp and croak.

"Look." Night Cloud rises to his elbow.

Grey Rabbit rolls over. Out the open door flap there are beams of green light rippling across the night sky. "The ancestors dancing in the land of the spirits."

Night Cloud sighs and pulls Grey Rabbit closer. Thinking of his father. Gone so suddenly. And the raw hole that took his place. Already, he has passed his father in years.

Grey Rabbit nestles into Night Cloud. Beams of light shift in the sky. His hand is softly stroking her leg. His thumb now tracing the contour of her hip bone. A bright streak of light sways back and forth. His breath is warm at the edge of her ear, as his fingers stroke her side, tentative, asking.

She's willing, her body responding as it used to, her breath quickening as his hand rides her skin. She rocks her hips back against him, his hand circling softly at her belly, his mouth now against her neck. She rolls toward him, her heart soft, remembering their private world of mouths and rhythm.

It's been so long. So long. Her fingers reach into his hair. The chorus of frogs chirp and croak. The sky above his head shimmers green through the smoke hole, and once again they choose each other.

2000

Nora wakes bolt upright in bed and runs her hand over the lamp until she finds the hard round switch. TV. Bureau. Luggage stand. Thunder Bay. She has no idea what woke her. The room is still, the door's chain lock in place.

She turns off the lamp and pulls up the covers, but her eyes remain wide open. The clock reads 1:45. She considers a slice of cold pizza. The open box lies on the table, and behind it the sky out the window is flickering. Fire. Nora snaps on the lamp and is out of bed, shoving her arms into her coat. She throws open the door to her room.

The entire sky is moving with bits of light. She leans over the balcony rail, her heart beating rapidly as she scans the rooftops for flames. In every direction the sky is tumultuous, but there is no fire. It's northern lights that fill the sky, and not just a hovering glow, or a few shimmering curtains to the north. Everything is green and wild, breaking and scattering overhead.

Nora hears the click of a lighter in the parking lot. Someone is smoking by the office door. It surprises her to hear the small sound with all the commotion going on. But then she realizes it's absolutely quiet. Everything is coming through her eyes, not her ears.

The sleeping giant lies in the lake. Flat oval head, arms over its chest, the long thick length of its body and its feet. Above it, the green lights shimmer and undulate, beams flare bright and then disappear. The curtain of light above the sleeping giant jumps. Spears of green light stretch and shoot, appear and disappear faster than she can track, rippling like runs of piano keys.

Nora pulls a chair up to the rail and feels for cigarettes in her coat pocket. She regards the giant's long dark profile as she smokes. It seems to be watching the sky, too. No, she decides. The giant looks to be presiding.

The person down below has their head thrown back. Nora follows their gaze to a ring of light spinning at the top of the sky. The light circles, then suddenly breaks apart. The lights dash and twirl around the rim of the sky, then rush together, reforming the circle. Nora's cigarette falls from her hand. The lights scatter, sway, and pulsate. The circle breaks apart again. When Nora looks back to the lake, she half expects to meet the giant standing, its head towering into the green sky, black water to its knees. Tinker says hi, she nearly whispers.

1622

The day is hot, humid, and still, with bugs droning and pesky flies. Grey Rabbit dips her finger in a bowl of hot water, where she has a buck's brain soaking. Around her are the familiar sounds of women tanning, the rasp of the scraping bones, low voices, punctured by small bursts of laughter.

Grey Rabbit has kept mostly quiet, not because she has nothing to say, but because, for now, she enjoys simply listening. The smell of the brain is acrid and unpleasant as she works it to a paste between her fingers. At least it gives her arms a rest. They are sore from the scraping and her thighs ache, too. She wonders for a moment and then smiles, thinking of Night Cloud.

Grey Rabbit scoops a handful of paste onto the hide and rubs it in vigorous circles, trying to saturate the skin evenly. The flies harass her and land on the fresh paste, and she wishes for a wind to keep them down.

"Aieee, this heat, even in the shade." Bullhead lowers herself to the hot dry ground and waves a reed fan at her neck. "I know the heat is good for the squash. But on days like this I see the gift of snow."

Grey Rabbit stiffens. Her hands stop moving on the hide.

"What is it? What did I say?"

Grey Rabbit picks brain from her fingers, reluctant to speak.

"A dream," she whispers. "It wasn't like the others," she adds quickly. "There weren't any children, I've not dreamt of children, it just gave me that feeling of heaviness."

"Can you tell me?"

Grey Rabbit squats on her haunches, holding her pasty hands in the air. She's sweating everywhere beneath her robe, her back and belly, behind her knees. With her forearm, she shoos a fly from her head. "I just remembered it."

"What did you see."

"There was snow. And I was underneath it, tunneling with the voles and the rabbits. They showed me how to move and how to keep watch for the swooping shadows of hunting birds. Then I felt the weight . . ." She slowly closes her fist, the paste squeezing between her fingers.

Bullhead starts fanning again. "I've made arrangements with one who interprets. She is willing, when you feel ready."

"I am ready." Grey Rabbit bends to her work. "When I'm finished I'll clean up and approach her myself."

The heat has only grown thicker, and in the small cove the air bends and waves. Grey Rabbit walks to the water, holding her pasty hands from her body. Her people are gathered up the shore where smoke from the drying fires hangs in the air. The women work and the men sit in the shade while dogs chase a group of children who turn and twist like a flock of birds. Little Cedar is there among them; she can pick him out even at a distance by his funny jumping gait.

The water in the small cove is so still that it looks like it's layered with ice, just the barest skin stretched over the surface. She slips off her moccasins and steps in. A crow calls from high in a tree. The cold around her calves is good, and the feel of the sand giving way beneath her feet. It's luscious to plunge her arms in the still clear water, to swirl them in the cold while bits of brain float away.

The crow calls again and again. She finds it at the pointed top of a pine. It caws and opens its black wings against the sky.

Grey Rabbit stands unmoving.

In her dream she'd heard crows cawing, huge numbers of them, as she'd tunneled and the snow drifts claimed the land.

Grey Rabbit wades deeper, tosses water over her hair and face. Her reflection breaks into bits of color and scatters across the water surface.

She hears them first and then she looks up, blinking bright water from her eyes as the high bows of the Huron canoes quietly traverse the flat water before her. There are three boats, and in the last sits a man with pale skin. His face is scarred, his cheeks covered with spidery brown hair.

The white-face pauses his paddle midstroke. He looks in her direction, nods as he glides past.

Grey Rabbit feels the dream heaviness come over her. It expands and spreads like wide wings in her chest. The crow caws. The boat wakes cleave the water.

Grey Rabbit turns and splashes back to shore. His eyes were not red, but the blue of a winter sky. She rushes along the shoreline, after the canoes that fast approach the long cove.

Already the men have moved from the trees and are standing tall along the beach. Her mind spins. The dream heaviness drops through her legs, forcing her urgent steps to a halt.

The three canoes draw in their paddles. They drift in slowly. Show no aggression.

The men line the beach.

The canoes hover in the bay.

It's silent but for the rushing water of the rapids.

The crow caws from the tree once again.

Grey Rabbit drops to her knees, water dripping down her neck and arms, drops falling from her fingertips. She can see Night Cloud and Standing Bird among the men, their shoulders upright in identical posture. The pale man rises to his feet. He speaks loudly in the Huron tongue, words of greeting and friendship ring through the cove.

Her thoughts flicker, twist, and lift. Ungraspable. Ungraspable as smoke. The men on the beach relax their posture, and the women and children come out of the trees, stifling laughter and fingering their hairless cheeks.

The white-faced man picks up his paddle. The boats land. And he steps ashore.

2000

The motel parking lot has largely cleared out by the time Nora drags her suitcase down the stairs. She shoves it into the backseat, shuts the door and slides behind the wheel. The sleeping giant now looks to be resting. Serene under the blue morning sky. According to the map, she could make it all the way home, but she doesn't feel compelled to race the way she did the day before. In fact, she feels like slowing down, almost a bit disappointed when she looks back over her route, and all the territory she'd sped through. Her report to Nikki is going to be swiss cheese.

She peruses the brochures she took from the room. One has the sleeping giant on it, and a tale about Nana'b'oozoo turning to stone. The other is for Old Fort William. Its cover shows people dressed up like voyageurs, Indians dancing, white clapboard buildings.

Nora cleans up the floor of the car, gathering stuff into a plastic bag—snack food wrappers, empty cigarette boxes. There is more in the back—an empty pop can, a piece of cellophane clinging to Rose's painting. She pours the last of an old coffee-to-go on the ground. She is going to do something before leaving Canada.

Fort Williams is huge, at least a couple dozen buildings, each having a designated purpose and each inhabited by people in costume who pretend to be living two hundred years ago. Indian Shop, Counting House, Hospital, Ammunition, Liquor Storage—it goes on and on. Nora stands behind a group of children who are listening to one of the actors. He's dressed in old-style pants and a balloon-sleeved shirt, his hand resting on a giant wooden contraption as he explains how the voyageurs' packs were loaded with pelts laid skin to skin, and fur to fur. "This press is used to compact the furs, optimizing the limited space and making the packs easier to handle."

The sun is warm and sounds drift through the air—bleating sheep, someone hammering metal. Nora doesn't join any particular group; she just wanders around, listening in.

Off the main square lies a low wooden barrack. It's dim inside after the bright sunlight, quiet, and the air feels preserved, thin and dry like pressed flowers. The floor sounds hollow under Nora's feet as she walks down the aisle between rows of cots, surveying the artifacts—a smoking pipe and pouch, a fragile-looking book. "Hey," she says, her own voice breaking the quiet, when she sees the opposing chairs and the tree stump, a grid of checkerboard squares burned into its top. Maybe Tinker's "great, great . . ."—she sees Tinker twirling her hand—had died in that very room. She touches her finger to one of the burnt squares, but it doesn't come off ashy.

"Have you gotten separated from your group?"

"Holy . . ." Nora starts. "You scared me, geez."

A young man in costume stands in the open door. "You should be scared, a woman wandering the fort unescorted. Many of the lads here are not to be trusted."

He's feigning an accent, but she can't tell what it is supposed to be.

"I'd be happy to show you around myself. Have you visited the Great Hall?"

Nora declines, but he is insistent. She looks him over, his woolen cap and his sash. "Thanks, but I'm just leaving."

The smell of baking bread wafts across the grounds, and a group of actors are square-dancing, clapping, and calling out in theatrical voices. It doesn't look like a bad life, at least in its make-believe form, with the sun shining on the white buildings and the warm yeasty smell in the air. But then, she figures as she leaves the walled fort, it's hardly the dead of winter, without heat, electricity, or running water.

The shuttle to the visitor center is not due for ten minutes, so she follows the path away from the gate. It leads her to a small clearing and a sign that reads "Native Encampment." A fire burns in an open pit below an iron cooking pot, though there isn't anyone around. On the ground lies a halfwoven mat made of reeds. She pokes her head into one of the birch-bark structures, surprised by how large and cozy it seems.

Inside, the air smells of ash and cedar. It's calm and quiet, but there's no place to sit. Baskets and wooden implements hang from the walls, along with tied bundles of dried plants. She guesses she's not supposed to touch anything, but she can't resist touching the tawny birch-bark wall, or holding the hanging white hat in her hands. The fur is soft and luxurious between her fingers. A circle of stones forms a fire ring on the floor. Straight overhead is a circle of blue sky. The northern lights spin in her mind.

Nora emerges into the daylight to find a girl pouring water into the pot. She's wearing an old threadbare dress, a scarf wrapped around her head. "Pronounce it over, would you, please?" she asks a man who's sitting on a log.

"You're learning fast. Don't get frustrated. Ojibwe is not an easy language."

"Excuse me. I'm sorry," Nora says, feeling as if she's been caught trespassing. The girl startles. The man removes his glasses.

The girl clears her throat and composes herself. *"Boozhoo. Welcome."* The man looks down the path past Nora, then says something to the girl in Indian.

"My daughter will demonstrate weaving a mat. There should be a group along any minute." He tamps tobacco into a pipe. "Feel free to look around, and if you have any questions. . . ."

"Actually, I do have a question. Did you see the northern lights last night?" Nora looks from the girl to the man.

"I didn't," he says.

"It was unbelievable. The entire sky was covered. They were everywhere, and then spinning in a circle," she points straight overhead. "They'd spin and break apart and come back together."

The air fills with the sounds of chattering children, an adult's herding voice rising above them. The girl turns to the man with a questioning look. He gestures toward the children as they swarm into the clearing. They gather around her. "Boozhoo. Welcome," she says.

Nora walks back up the path. She's disappointed; she thought they would have something to say. The circle thing was so strange. And the sleeping giant lying out there in the water. It seemed like something Indians would know about. But then, of course they were only actors, not real Indians. Well, no. They were real Indians. She's not exactly sure what she means.

Nora wanders around in the gift shop, not seeing much that attracts her until she comes across a small birch-bark canoe. It's perfect. The bark is white on the outside and satiny brown inside, lined with seams of black pitch. And though it's over a foot long, it's light as nothing in her hand. Nikki could store her hair ties in it, or maybe her agates. That would be pretty.

Nora holds her cigarette to the crack in the window and lets the ash fly off behind the car. She opens her notebook to the "What

Next?" page, and sets it beside her on the seat. She's only twenty-five miles from the border. The land out her windshield is different from anything she's seen so far. It's farmland, though there are flat-topped buttes rising up like in the old Western movies, but they're not brown and dusty, they're green with trees. She hasn't seen a rock sculpture since she left Thunder Bay. "What Next?" Under the heading are three entries: "California," "No winter," "Pink plant."

"What Next?" The page is irritating. Nora stubs out her cigarette. Life doesn't work that way. More often that not, it simply happens. Janelle wasn't exactly planned. And she never expected to be a bar owner; the bar came with Ralph. She never had a big plan for herself, never envisioned anything in particular. Unless her little-girl fantasies count—princess, nurse, playing bride. There was a phase, she must have been eight, when she'd stop at the bakery on her way home from school. She'd stand at the window and watch the woman squeeze colored frosting from a cone-shaped bag. She'd make ribbon designs and flower petals, write out Happy Birthday and people's names perfectly.

When she was little, she drew pictures of cakes. She didn't want to bake them; it was the decorating. Nora reaches for the notebook on the seat. She writes "ck. dec." in tiny letters, so at least there's something new on the page.

The lake is on her left as soon as she crosses the border. She can feel its airy coldness even when the view's obscured. The Pigeon River. Hat Point—it's reservation land. She passes a casino sign advertising a powwow.

Rivers cascade from the hills to the lake, spring-high and rushing beneath the bridges. The Hollow Rock River. The Reservation. The Flute Reed. Twenty-five miles to Grand Marais. Twenty-five miles and she's back in known territory. The Brule. Nora lets her speed lag.

I hear the beat of the primordial ocean. The submerged volca-
noes building on themselves. The seas that bring the new islands
down. There is the tumult of earthquakes. Underwater landslides.
Laying new strata. Building new landmass.

Rock and sky form a barren arc. Turn of day, the sun's heat
falls unchallenged. Turn of night, the rock is a frigid plain.

Held in these waters is the wrenching echo of the mid-
continental land tearing. The lightning bolt rift spews plumes of
liquid rock. There are burning fountains in the sky. Scalding heat.
Acrid fumes.

The glowing lava plains turn flood basalt in air. Layer upon
layer of molten rock. The weight compresses the rift's axis. Heaves
the edges of the plain toward the sky.

Rain and wind. Persistent erosion. Bring the new landmass
down. The sunken rift fills with rock and sediment. Piling to a
depth of miles.

The grinding glaciers creep down from the north. It's the
blunt smell of ice that lifts from these waters. The glaciers gouge
debris from the sunken rift. Take the wieldable rock on retreat-
ing tongues. In their wake they leave this lake basin. Its northern
rim still rebounding from the weight. In their wake. This billion-
year-old cradle of rock.

1902

The predawn birds have stopped their cacophony, but Berit's windowpanes are still dark over dark, reflecting her face in the lantern light. "I was in the skiff and there was nothing," she scribbles, her letters tiny at the top of the page. "I couldn't see land. My hands were blistered from rowing, but every direction I attempted was the same. There was nothing. No birds. No clouds. No land." She pauses the tip of the pencil below the words, but she doesn't know how to draw it. She makes a straight horizon line, but the feeling is entirely wrong; it's flat and singular, not encompassing. She draws herself as a dot in the center of a circle. It's better; it captures her sense of turning.

"The boat started to vibrate," she writes. She could feel it in her feet through the bottom of the boat. She makes a quick sketch of the skiff in the water, lines circling out from its hull. "There was something happening below the surface," she continues, "a rumbling, but I was afraid to look over the side. Suddenly, I was walking in a dark forest, though I knew it was day because thin spokes of light were coming through the canopy." She draws heavy tree trunks and fills the space between them, then rubs in the angled lines of light with an eraser.

Out the window, the sky through the upper panes has lightened. There was something else about the forest. Something she always knew, or felt. The pale oval of her face in the glass stares back. She has no idea how to draw them. Her pencil hovers over the page. The first one she saw was a glimmer between the tree trunks. She applies her pencil again. I followed it as it darted and crouched. It was human in form though small as a child, and shimmering as if it were made of copper. She sketches its shape passing through the trees, but can't represent its shimmering.

She was on a cliff and they were dancing below. She'd had to shield her eyes from the brightness. She sketches the shape of the movement, twirling and sinuous. The pink light from their bodies spun and flashed against the cliffs.

She looks over the page, knowing there's something missing, but not knowing what it is.

2000

Everything on the shelves is made of glass, and lit from the sunlight coming through the windows—red, yellow, purple. Tumblers and bowls. Nora's eyes fill with the glowing colors. Green platters. Orange and pink plates. She lifts a vase with scrolled yellow handles. The name, P. Eck-something, is etched in the bottom, and a sticker reads $110.

When she'd entered the office, a buzzer went off, but nobody has come to the door behind the counter. A blue plate dabbed with yellow catches her eye. She's holding it to the light when the door finally opens and a man wiping his face with a handkerchief walks in. He's forty maybe, brown hair, bearded, wedding ring.

"Sorry," he says, "I heard the door, but I had to finish up what I was doing."

"It's gorgeous in here," says Nora, setting the plate back on the shelf.

"Thanks. That's a new one. Just made last week. What can I do for you?"

"I'm looking for a room."

"Well, what we have is a couple of cabins. A two-bedroom, and a smaller one-room."

"Cabins?" She's not so sure. "Do they have plumbing?"

"Oh, yeah. Bathrooms, showers, fully equipped kitchenettes."

Behind the counter, a shelf holds a small stock of food. She wouldn't mind cooking something for herself. "Does your pancake mix use only water, or would I have to buy eggs?"

"Water," he says, lifting a box down.

"And syrup?"

"The best. It's from our neighbor's grove up the road. I helped them tap the trees this year." He stands a small bottle on the counter.

The two cabins are separated by a tall, leafy hedge. Hers looks the older of the two, but inside it's not dingy or smelly, it's just a little dark. Nora dumps her stuff on the bed and parts the thin curtain on the window, where a bush crowds against the glass. In the living area, there are sliding glass doors that lead to a deck facing the water. She unlatches the door, pushes it open, and the sound of the lake sweeps in.

Nora settles in one of the deck chairs and taps a cigarette from her pack, happy to be back to her old brand. It's only two o'clock, the sky huge and cloudless, the horizon a straight sharp line. She takes the box of color from the bag at her feet. It's not exactly her shade, but it's close. She'd stopped at the drugstore in Grand Marais, hesitant about what to do next—stop at Janelle's or go straight home—when it occurred to her that she didn't want to do either. She needed a day to get back to herself.

Nora lounges on the deck with her hair in a towel, feeling the kind of rejuvenated that only comes from standing under running water. Her skin is still damp, her head wet and clean. Patrick—his last name was Eckdahl, he'd said—is sitting beside the big open door of the building down below her cabin. He waves and she waves back.

When she digs in her purse for a nail file, her fingers touch something hard. She pulls out a cream-colored rock. She can't imagine why she's carrying it around until she turns it over. It's the fossil she'd found with Frank. Bits of tobacco are stuck in its ridges. "Once there was an ocean," he'd said.

The expanse of water is vast and blue. She shakes her purse and fishes with her fingers. Sure enough, she still has the agate. She holds it up to the sun and looks at its banding. The lake washes against the shore. A family of ducks is in the cove, swimming with their heads below the surface.

The sun is warm and pleasant on Nora's face as she strolls around the property, holding her fingers apart to keep her wet nails from smudging.

"Cabin okay?" Patrick asks when she walks past the big open door.

"It's fine."

"Yeah, that one's our favorite. It's the oldest, the original building. We think it has the most character."

Nora checks her nails, then lets her fingers fall naturally.

"I'm going to work a bit more before I call it a day. Have you ever seen glassblowing?" He flashes her a welcoming grin. "Come on in and check it out."

There are two large ovens and it's hot in the building. "Just pull that chair over by the door," says Patrick, dipping a rod longer than a pool cue into the mouth of one of the ovens. All she can see inside is white heat. When he draws it out there's a mass on the end that's so filled with light it looks like a piece of the sun. His fingers, thick and as dirty as a mechanic's, turn the rod around and around.

"Why do you have to keep turning it?"

"People often wonder about that," he says, stilling the rod. "It's really all about . . ."

"Look out." Nora points to the glob, which is oozing to the floor like honey and landing in thin squiggly lines.

". . . Centrifugal force." He lifts the cooling squiggles from the floor with the orange-hot end.

"You did that on purpose."

He laughs and puts the whole thing back in the oven. "No problem, you just start over."

"What are you going to make?" she asks, as he removes the rod from the oven again and rolls it against a smooth flat surface. He nods but says nothing, then sits down on a bench, lifts the rod to his mouth, and blows. The bright glob expands with his breath, filling like a small balloon. Then he's up and over to the other oven, where he slides one end in and sets the other in a brace, turning, turning, his fingers like spiders.

"Sorry," he says. "I'm making a footed bowl. They were my best sellers last year." She can see right into the glowing orange oven. It's a heat beyond flames, it's pure light. He lets the balloon droop like a marshmallow about to fall off a stick, but then has it turning again.

"I never thought about glass like this. It's so soft and oozy," says Nora.

"Glass is a liquid." He grins, glancing over.

"Oh, come on."

"True. And not just in this oozy, as you call it, state. Goblets, windows—even after it's cooled, all glass is still a liquid."

"You're not serious."

"Already I have a credibility problem? Did you ever notice the waves in really old windowpanes? Well, they're like that because the window is liquid. It's just extremely slow moving."

Nora raises her eyebrows and looks at her nails. She doesn't believe him for a second.

He sits in a chair and lays the rod across the armrests, then rolls it back and forth while shaping the glob with a paddle. As it cools it darkens and shines. Then he's up at a table that holds shallow trays of color—blues, reds, pinks, and greens—some are filled with powder and some with small chips of glass. He touches the glob—Nora can't see anything like a bowl—into them like he's dipping an ice cream into sprinkles.

He moves from the oven to the table, to the chair, to the oven. Nora's waiting for the thing to break, the way he keeps swinging it around. He cuts the taffylike glass with a scissors, pulls it with tongs, heats it, and then dips it, moving rhythmically around his workshop.

When he barely misses the table again, Nora realizes that he's not about to break the glass. He knows exactly where it is. He knows the rod's reach precisely, how many steps and when to turn. She's familiar with the dance. She can do her own version. It's the late rush after the bars close in Minnesota, and all the people who want to keep their night going flock over the high bridge to Wisconsin. Some nights her crowd doubled in ten minutes. It's all timing, the taps and the pours. It's knowing the back-bar and everything on it, and how long a reach, and what's where in the longboy, and whether you can make it to the register and back.

"Thanks a lot," she says from the door, fanning herself as if the heat's too much.

Nora climbs the sloped path to her cabin, feeling the Schooner so strongly she could be standing behind the bar. The cabin is still. The curtains hang. A dish towel is draped over the faucet and a box of stick matches lies on the counter. The sound of the lake washes through the room.

She picks up her notebook and starts for the deck, but her deck chairs are already in the cabin's shadow. Below, the water and the arms of the cove are still sunlit, and there are more chairs on the end of the point.

1902

The surf is high and breaking against the shore. Berit is at the kitchen table she'd hauled down to the flat spot outside the fish house. A glow on the horizon marks the coming sun. The sunrise, she notices, has been shifting, little by little, back toward the point. Daily, she's been working on the woodpile, both for the supply and for the satisfaction of the chop, as the logs cleave and knock to the ground. She runs her finger over the inside of her thumb, where a popped blister left an oval of pink skin.

The sun appears, first the rim, followed by the glowing orange orb, lifting steadily, widening and brightening, until it reaches its fat halfway and spills in a line across the water. It's beautiful. The new breeze stirs the grasses around her. The sun lifts, the ball narrowing again. For just a breath it balances perfectly on the lake.

The orange light grazes the trees on the point, and the backs of the lifting waves where a gull sits peaceably. She turns. The cabin windows glint orange. And there's John sitting in the tall grass.

Berit rises to build her morning fire. When she glances up the slope, John is standing so she motions for him to come down to the table.

"You could have slept in the cabin. The nights are getting cold."

John shakes his head.

"Why not?"

"Cabins are dirty and full of bad air."

The morning sun is now yellow on the windows. "I suppose you're right," she says, taking no offense.

John watches her strike a match and hold it inside the tent of logs. The kindling ignites and crackles. "You haven't packed anything?"

She shrugs off his question and lifts the kettle lid to see how much coffee is left.

John brushes a seedpod from the table planks. He assesses her shoulders as she walks into the fish house; at least she's not grown any thinner. She reappears with a stool, and the cat trailing along behind her. "You can't stay here alone," he says, but she walks away again as if he hadn't spoken, this time returning with a cup and a bowl.

Berit sits on the stool and watches the surf. It advances in lines that break high on the boat slide, throwing up spray and cool air.

"What about provisions?" he persists.

"I'm fine."

"You're thin."

Berit levels the fire with a stick. "The shed's full of food, you're welcome to help yourself. And I have a gun. I can hunt." She balances the kettle on top of two logs.

John looks past her into the morning, smelling the smoke and the fresh lake wind. He understands now why Gunnar called her stubborn.

Filling his cup, and then the bowl for herself, Berit places the kettle on the flat rock in the fire ring. She smoothes her skirt and sits on the stool. John takes a sip, makes a face, and puts his cup back on the table. "There's sugar up there," she tilts her head toward the cabin and the birch slope where the leaves have begun to yellow. She wraps her hands around her warm bowl.

Coming down the path with the sugar bowl in his hand, John strikes her as both amusing and sad.

"Did you see the northern lights last night?" she asks.

John stirs sugar into his coffee. "The ancestors dancing."

"What did you say?"

"The ancestors. Dancing in the land of the spirits."

Berit's face floats on the dark surface of her coffee. She takes a sip and holds the bowl at her chin, remembering the night's flickering sky. "That's a lovely thought," she says, then turns her attention back to the water.

John watches Berit watch the lake, her eyes seeming to drink it in, ingest it as if it were nourishment. She must have the strength of a plant, he thinks, consisting entirely of sinewy fibers. "Don't you have people? Where are your people?"

She shrugs. "It doesn't matter. I can't go back yet." The water is blue except in the curl of each wave, where it rises soft green before rolling over.

"What about winter?"

"I'll move back to the cabin for the better stove, but something else lives there now. I don't know what."

"Listen," John says, looking to the sky. "Nothing survives all on its own. I need to take you away from here."

A wave lifts, revealing the soft green ribbon. "You need," she says. "Your need. Well, now that's something else." Berit sets down her bowl.

She stands and pokes the fire with the stick, lifts the lid of the kettle, and pours the last in his cup. "He cared a lot for you," she says softly, and John lowers his eyes to the table planks. Berit leaves the empty kettle on her stool, and walks down to the cove without turning back. She's not ready to leave the homestead, yet. She'll make plans for herself come spring.

John watches her cross the rocky beach, her skirt blowing in the wind, her lame gait, her short pale hair winging. She climbs over the slanting rock ledges, pauses and peers down at the thimbleberries he'd left.

She stands with her back to him facing the water—the wind flapping the arms of her blouse, a dragonfly knitting the air above her head—and he knows that's how he'll remember her.

2000

Nora walks out on the ledges of rock and settles in one of the high-backed chairs. The sun is warm, the lake air cool. The lake and the sky are two shades of blue. The water lifts against the ledge, sinks back and glugs, rolls over itself smooth and curling. There are half-burnt logs on the ledge below. She sees the charred walls of the Schooner, and the hole through the roof.

"What Next?" She forces herself to look over the page—"ck. dec." it says in tiny letters. She can't believe she wrote that down. She draws a rectangle around the words and inks them out entirely. Nikki's in her thoughts, and then the little canoe. The lake rushes and rolls back. She thinks about glass being cut with scissors, the drawer in the back bar that stuck all the time, and her figurehead Josephine. She pictures her burning.

The sun shines yellow on the water. Nora squints, and tries to hear the Canadian girls giggling in her mind. She had seen laughter, felt the sparkling. Nothing happens. The water doesn't turn.

"What next?" She's sick to death of the question. She could move to California. Maybe she should. Maybe it would help things with Janelle if there were that much more space between them. In truth, her time with Nikki is mostly on the phone.

The cars up on the road blow by like wind.

"For crying out loud. What should I do?" She flings her question out into the lake, the weight of it heavy and raw.

The water lifts and rolls. The light slides and sparkles.

Should she move and be with Joannie, leaving Nikki behind? What would she lose? What would she gain? The lake doesn't answer. The water shifts and shimmers and sloshes, moving both toward her and away.

The cars blow by.

A bird sings in the trees.

"Gorgeous day," says Patrick, rounding the point in a wide wooden rowboat. "Climb on in. I'll take you for a ride."

"No. I don't think so, but thanks."

"Oh, come on. You don't have to do anything, just sit and I'll ferry you around."

"I'm not much of a water person."

"Look," says Patrick, standing up in the boat. He spreads his legs and rocks it back and forth. "This thing is more solid than that honkin' car of yours."

"People die out there."

"I'm not going out, only following the shore. I want to catch a little sun before it's gone. You're going to be in the shade in about ten minutes."

Nora turns. The shadows have almost reached her chair, but the water around the boat is still sparkling.

"There's nothing to be afraid of. Get in." He gives her his big grin again. "If you don't like it I'll drop you off over there." He points across the cove, and lifts a hand to help her into the boat.

Nora sits on the bench seat, grasping it with both hands. She peers down over the side. There are boulders and ledges and black shadows in the cracks, and a jittery reflection of her head on the surface.

Patrick leans forward and back as he works the oars through the water. Nora feels the strength of the stroke, the glide followed by a short lull. The oars squeak and clunk. It's exhilarating. Her stomach rolls. She focuses on the land, the cabins on the slope, Patrick's workshop down below, solid and unmoving as they slide past.

"How are you doing?" Patrick asks.

Nora gestures with her head to the rock ledge where he'd promised to drop her.

"Okay. No problem." He angles the boat, takes another stroke, but then lets the boat hover. "Check that out," he points his oar through the water. Nora peers over the side at what looks like a gigantic broken ladder.

"What is it?"

"The remains of an old boat slide." He grins. "They were used to haul small boats in and out. I've come across a couple of them along the shore."

The shadow of the rowboat lies over the sunken logs, and the ducks are back, she can see their bright feet. "I can't do this," Nora says.

In three strokes he has the rowboat sidled up against the ledge rock. "Sorry. I hope you liked the glassblowing, anyway."

Nora pictures the glowing orange glob, feeling a lot better with the warm stone beneath her hand. "Yeah. I had no idea."

"I love what I do. The color, the light, the way glass is worked. Even how temperamental it is."

"There aren't many people who can say that. Really, you're a very lucky man." The boat bumps gently against the ledge each time the lake lifts.

"Well, I used to think so," he says, his eyes softening. "I thought I had it all." He smiles, but it's not his big grin.

Nora can feel the water under her feet. And really, she'd like to get out of the boat, but she knows what's coming. She's seen it a hundred times. The half-smile, not really a smile at all. The downcast eyes. The sudden quiet.

Patrick stares out at the water as he speaks. "Some people aren't cut out for these winters. My wife, Ginny, she thought she'd love it up here. And at first it seemed like she did. But then . . ." He shrugs, his gaze shifting to the ribs of the boat.

Nora grips the ledge rock with her forearm, leaving him room to talk.

"She's been down in Minneapolis since November. Just a trial sort of thing. I thought she'd be back in May. That's what we'd talked about, anyway. Well, it's June and so far . . ." He shrugs again and looks out across the water.

Nora doesn't have a drink to pour for him, or a single word of advice. "I hope things work out for you," she says. "You've got real talent. You make beautiful things."

"Thanks for saying so." His eyes are still soft. He stands and helps her out of the boat. "Anyone ever tell you you're a good listener?"

The lake is loud even through the sliding doors, and something keeps rattling, causing Nora to start and peer over the newspaper into the room. The sky out every window is dark. She'd be more comfortable in a motel. A cabin has the feel of someone else's home. And there's no TV, only books in an old bookcase. Nora turns her attention back to the page.

The rattling starts up again. She should have asked Patrick if there were bears. The dim haze from frying pancakes hangs in the air. The sound is coming from the kitchen corner, as if the teakettle were shaking against the burner.

Nora lays the paper on the bed. Her imagination is going to cut loose if she doesn't figure out what's making the noise. But of course, when she gets to the stove the rattling has stopped, and the kettle is just sitting there. She stands with her arms folded, waiting.

At the sliding glass doors, she cups her hands around her eyes. No northern lights, but she'll never forget them, never forget that sleeping giant. The wind has kicked up and the lake's whipping against the rocks, throwing spray and slamming around, and there's a bright star or maybe it's a planet shinning low on the horizon. Her breath fogs against the glass.

The windows are lit in the workshop below, which is comforting though she can't see anyone. The rattling resumes. Nora walks quietly toward the stove. The teakettle is sitting on the burner, not moving in the least. The sound is in the wall or the roof, just a vent flap or something, clattering in the wind.

Nora turns off the lamp by the bed. In the dark, the lake seems to drum even louder. The bush out the window throws a shadow on the wall. Her heart jumps when the rattling starts again, even though she knows it's nothing. She closes her eyes and pulls a pillow over her head.

She can hear the rhythmic waves of the lake, and she knows if she can get there she'll find the way out. She is lost in a maze of hallways made of snow. The corridors cross through, turn one way and then another. She has been walking in the snow halls for miles. She pauses at an intersection to listen for the water, so she will know which way to turn. Her hand rests on a snow wall, neither cold nor wet to the touch. She can't find the way out. She walks down another corridor and listens. But now all she can hear is the tapping.

Tapping. Someone is tapping on the windowpane. Nora rolls over, her eyes half-open. The lake sloshes through the room. A shadow is waving against the wall. It looks like a dog's head or maybe a wolf, its long mouth hanging open. As the tapping sub-sides, the head slows to a nod. Its eye is a sharp narrow slit. The stove rattles, and the head swings and rears back. And then there are two, entangled, circling. Shadows leaping up the wall. Switching. Rearing. Shadow and moonlight.

Nora watches below heavy lids.

Light is liquid, she thinks. Remember. Light is liquid.

There is a crack in the lake where boats disappear. A bearing below the water's unmappable surface. Where splintered wood and twisted steel hulls lay scattered along the frigid lake bed.

There is a crack in the lake. A hushed dwelling. Here in the darkness. A cold furrowed lair. Where a great horned serpent lies unblinking.

There is a crack in the lake. Alive. Trembling. Where rock tears from rock. The waters lap like flame.

There is a crack in the lake. It has no name. Deep within Superior's keep. Its teeth are astral. Its beauty terrifies. And all things eventually come.

There. At the thin line of the precipice.

He turns his marble face.

And waits.

Crossing the water current's sizzling edge.

I am the harmonic thrum.

The echo.

The tinkle of the long-time shimmering.

2000

The lake is slate grey and moody, and the sky the same color, hovering low. Yield for deer, the sign reads, the yellow of it glowing as it shudders in the wind. Nora had woken that morning feeling strange, small and quiet, as if she were holding something fragile.

The hills are a mixture of light green and dark, and the lines of the ridges slant toward the lake, where a freighter is so far in the distance that it's hard to tell if it's even moving.

The Poplar River slides under the bridge. Nora ashes out the crack in the window. She's not sure what she wants to do, stop in at Janelle's or go on home. It would be nice to give Nikki her things; she's always so delighted with presents. But she doesn't feel like seeing anyone. She could call them when she gets home, make arrangements for another time, after she's unpacked and settled.

The Onion River. Janelle's place is coming up after the next guardrail.

She puts her blinker on, thinking about hugging Nikki.

Halfway down the drive she can see there's no car.

Nora parks anyway, gets out, and rings the bell. The small

yellow rambler is quiet. She can hear the lake on the other side of the house, hitting against the low bluff. There was something about the lake in her dream. Dirty dishes lie on the table near the picture window, and her postcards are taped to the window frame. Dancing Indians. A lighthouse. The big locks at the Soo. Coats, an umbrella, and Nikki's little red knapsack are hanging on the pegs in the hall. She should have called. It's her own fault. She tries the door and finds it unlocked.

Nora arranges Nikki's gifts on the table, but then changes her mind and arranges them on her bed—the shipwreck sweatshirt laid out and the hat on the pillow, the sleeve holding the birch-bark canoe. It'll be a fun surprise for her when she gets home. Out the window the lake is rough, and gulls are sitting in the dark rippled water. Nora walks back to the car.

The long door of the car squeaks open. Nora shoves her suitcase to the side and slides the painting out of the back seat. It's scratched in the corner from the metal edge of her suitcase. She has grown fond of the painting—the orange sky, the gulls, the little boat off in the distance. Nora rubs her finger across the scratch.

She'll have to explain things to Rose, try to make her understand.

Nora carries the bulky painting inside, slides Janelle's chair from the table, and leaves the present propped in her place.

The Temperance River spills over ledges of rock. She'll need to make a budget for herself, she's been spending without keeping track. The last thing she needs is to chip away at the insurance money. She passes the sign for Nikki's agate beach.

The clouds have pulled apart from each other, and cracks of blue sky show through the grey, brightening strips of the hillsides and patches of the lake. The Caribou River is brown and rushing. The Manitou.

Little Marais. An old man stands on the shoulder of the road, a big yellow dog at his feet. The man opens his mailbox. He waves as she passes.

News is on the radio, but Nora's mind won't follow. She turns the volume down to have the quiet low sound. Tettegouche. Palisade Head. The taconite plant at Silver Bay. Beaver Bay. She's low on gas.

Split Rock Lighthouse. Nora sips her coffee-to-go. She'll bring Nikki there the next time she visits. She remembers Nikki at her agate beach, nestled out on the rock ledge, her little shoulders square to the lake, content to sit and watch the water. "This is my special spot," she'd said. Nora opens her notebook to the page marked "What Next?" and crosses out California.

At Gooseberry Falls there are people all over—walking out on the flat rocks, standing at the river's edge, families and kids throwing stones in the water. She can hear the river when she crosses the bridge.

The road is banded in sun and shade. Her car filling with light and then dimming. Castle Danger. Crow Creek. The car brightens and abruptly goes dark as she enters the tunnel through Lafayette Bluff. At the end of the tunnel is an oval of light, and she drives right out into it.

Nora jiggles a cigarette up from her pack. She hasn't figured anything out; she should be arriving home with a plan, or at least some good ideas. She has no stock to check, no orders to fill. She enters the mouth of the Silver Creek Cliff Tunnel—no runs to the bank, no payroll to get out, no books to keep, nobody to serve. Her car emerges back into daylight. She imagines the spot where her bar used to stand—an old foundation, a lot filled with weeds.

Nora idles at the light in Two Harbors, the flags at the gas station flapping in the wind. There's a display of chain-saw art, bears and eagles, and a sandwich board advertising wild rice. She blows out a long stream of smoke that sways the glass float hanging from her rearview. It has made the whole trip with her. Somebody like Patrick must have made it. She lifts the float with her fingertips, finding a knob on the bottom that she hadn't noticed before, where it was attached to the rod. She pictures him blowing as the orange glob expanded, and wonders if the breath of whoever made the float is still rolling around inside.

The treetops along the shoreline of the scenic highway are blowing. And a rock island in the lake looks white for all the gulls on it. She passes small resorts with their tiny square cabins and their signs saying Vacancy, and Yes, Open. A freighter is heading toward the Twin Ports, though she can't tell if it's the same one she saw earlier. She wonders who's out there and how they're feeling, whether they're glad or sorry to be reaching port.

Knife River. The water tumbles down. She passes the smoked-fish house with its jumble of stuff. Everything is closing down toward home.

The French River. A man stands fishing.

Water runs to the lake from the fog-hung marshlands, where rotting stalks and sediment brown the water and moose lower their heads to drink, their massive racks like the roots of fallen trees.

And from creeks that meander through the shaded forest floor, with slow glassy water and matted leaves, where small birds flit from bank to bank, their brief shadows darkening the moss.

It joins the lake from rivers that fall over rock, crash in sheets, rise in spray.

And from those that wind through sandy red clay, their shoals grooved with the imprints of hooves, which harden and crack and curl like bark, until rain or rising water smooth the surface again.

Water circles from sea to sky and back. It lifts through tree roots, releases through leaves, and all the animals make their way. To the water, always changing, always wholly receptive.

2000

Nora pulls into a small gravel lot, turns off the engine, and gets out. The hood of her car is warm and ticking, the wind blowing cold off the lake. There were shadows on the wall in the middle of the night, and something important that she meant to remember.

Below her the lake sways like an empty swing. She can feel it in her stomach every time it drops away. The endless horizon isn't there anymore; the Wisconsin shoreline is on the other side, and she can see the buildings and the grain elevators of home.

It looks the same, but it feels different. Smaller, all stuck down in a tiny little corner of something she'd discovered to be unbelievably big. Maybe she'll take Nikki around next summer. She'd do it more slowly, do it right. It's there at the edge of her mind. It was something about light and animals and water. The wind blows dark streaks across the grey lake, and then the gravel lot floods with sun.

Nora passes the lift bridge, and then the Lake Avenue exit, the aquarium, the pulp mill, and West Twenty-First, before veering off onto the bridge to Wisconsin. She is all eyes and watching from a delicate kept place, both grateful to be there and uncertain all the same. There's the freight yard lined with boxcars from the DMN&R, and the Goodwill with cars in the parking lot. Then she's up climbing over the grey water of the bay, where buoys mark the shipping lanes, and barren mountains of coal and lime are mounded at industrial slips.

Wind forces her car and the glass float swings. She looks across the watery horizon. When the bridge lets her down onto Hammond Avenue she will end the circle, she will have driven clear around. But then circles, they don't have ends.

The air thins as sun hits the grain elevators, spreads over the water in shivering slivers. It fills her car and falls across the dash, catching the agate she'd only just put there. It glows red and orange and banded with white. Nikki will be amazed to see it. It was in the gravel lot when she'd ground out her cigarette. A big, red, translucent rock, lying at the toe of her shoe. All she had to do was pick it up.

Author's Note

The Ojibwe language is comprised of many dialects. Sounds, spelling, and grammar vary from place to place. I would like to acknowledge that for the purpose of consistency between stories in the text, I chose to use word spellings from more than one dialect.

This work was gratefully funded in part by two Arrowhead Regional Arts Council Individual Artist Fellowhip Grants (in 2004 and 2007), funded through an appropriation from the McKnight Foundation.

Acknowledgments

The writing of this book involved a great deal of research. I am inspired by and indebted to all the fieldworkers and the authors of fiction and nonfiction whose works helped to inform this book.

My gratitude to the many people—knowledgeable researchers, sailors, patient and amused scientists, program personnel, collection tenders, and librarians—who accepted office visits and phone calls at: The University of Minnesota Duluth's American Indian Resource Center, Minnesota Sea Grant, The Lake Superior Maritime Visitor Center, U.S. Army Corps of Engineers, The Minnesota Historical Society, The University of Wisconsin Superior's Archives, The North Shore Commercial Fishing Museum, The Blue Heron Research Vessel, and The Large Lakes Observatory.

I would also like to acknowledge the dedicated and often unsung staff that keep stories alive at historical sites, parks, lighthouses, heritage centers, small museums, information centers, and tourist destinations all around Lake Superior.

My deep appreciation to those who took the time to guide me through their worlds: glassblower Anton James (Jim) Vojacek at Oulu Glass; Blaine Fenstad, son of a son of a fisherman, who kindly allowed me into his home; and to Steve Dahl who fishes the big water off Knife River today, and who took me along as he picked his nets one cold and beautiful morning.

Many places contributed to the writing of this book by

providing crucial time and space to work. My gratitude to: The Anderson Center for Interdisciplinary Study, The Blacklock Nature Sanctuary, The Oberholtzer Foundation, Joan Drury and her little white cabin on the shore, Norcroft, The Virginia Center for the Creative Arts, and in particular, The Ragdale Foundation for its long and unwavering support.

Thank you to The Arrowhead Regional Arts Council for supplying financial support through Career Opportunity and Artist Fellowship Grants.

I'm grateful to Kurt Herke and Jane Levinson, their flexibility, good nature and support made everything run smoother. To the kind people at the Gunflint Tavern who kept me company during many long writing stints; to Claire Kirch, for the schooling; and to Emilie Buchwald, bright light and pathfinder.

I'd like to acknowledge the marvelous staff at Milkweed Editions. My sincere thank-you to each of them for their efforts on the novel's behalf. And to Daniel Slager, who championed this book from the start, understood its essence, and worked to make it better.

I'd like to thank the many people who read drafts of the book over the years, including Deb Eagle, Sheryl Eagle, and the women who gathered at their table to discuss the manuscript and in particular the Ojibwe storyline; Jeanne Farrar, Duke Klassen, Leslie Johnson, Larry Laverk, Kathy Lewis, Jane Lund, Pat Rhoades, Mary Rockcastle, Blaise Taylor, and Alice Templeton.

This book would not have been written without my family and friends. My grateful heart for your constant support as encouragers, readers, bent ears, and merrymakers—you are the backbone of everything.

To my longtime mentor and friend Pat Francisco, for every step along the way.

To Ken Bloom, air and bedrock.

DANIELLE SOSIN is the author of *Garden Primitives,* a collection of stories published by Coffee House Press, 2000. Her stories have been chosen for National Public Radio's *Selected Shorts: A Celebration of the Short Story,* and for Iowa Public Radio's *Live from Prairie Lights.* Her work has also appeared in the *Alaska Quarterly Review.* Sosin is the recipient of a Loft Mentor Series Award, a Minnesota State Arts Board Fellowship, and two Arrowhead Regional Arts Council Individual Artist Fellowship Grants. She lives in Duluth, Minnesota.

More Fiction from Milkweed Editions

The Milkweed National Fiction Prize is awarded annually by the editors at Milkweed Editions. Previous recipients of the Milkweed National Fiction Prize include:

Orion You Came and You Took All My Marbles
Kira Henehan
(2010)

Driftless
David Rhodes
(2008)

The Farther Shore
Matthew Eck
(2007)

Visigoth
Gary Amdahl
(2006)

Crossing Bully Creek
Margaret Erhart
(2005)

Ordinary Wolves
Seth Kantner
(2004)

For more information, please visit www.milkweed.org, or contact us directly at (800) 520-6455.

Milkweed Editions

Founded as a nonprofit organization in 1980, Milkweed Editions is an independent publisher. Our mission is to identify, nurture and publish transformative literature, and build an engaged community around it.

Join Us

In addition to revenue generated by the sales of books we publish, Milkweed Editions depends on the generosity of institutions and individuals like you. In an increasingly consolidated and bottom-line-driven publishing world, your support allows us to select and publish books on the basis of their literary quality and transformative potential. Please visit our Web site (www.milkweed.org) or contact us at (800) 520-6455 to learn more.

Milkweed Editions, a nonprofit publisher, gratefully acknowledges sustaining support from Amazon.com; Emilie and Henry Buchwald; the Bush Foundation; the Patrick and Aimee Butler Foundation; Timothy and Tara Clark; the Dougherty Family Foundation; Friesens; the General Mills Foundation; John and Joanne Gordon; Ellen Grace; William and Jeanne Grandy; the Jerome Foundation; the Lerner Foundation; Sanders and Tasha Marvin; the McKnight Foundation; Mid-Continent Engineering; the Minnesota State Arts Board, through an appropriation by the Minnesota State Legislature and a grant from the National Endowment for the Arts; Kelly Morrison and John Willoughby; the National Endowment for the Arts; the Navarre Corporation; Ann and Doug Ness; Jörg and Angie Pierach; the Carl and Eloise Pohlad Family Foundation; the RBC Foundation USA; the Target Foundation; the Travelers Foundation; Moira and John Turner; and Edward and Jenny Wahl.

Interior design by Rachel Holscher
Typeset in Warnock Pro
by BookMobile Design and Publishing Services
Printed on acid-free 100% post consumer waste paper
by Friesens Corporation

ENVIRONMENTAL BENEFITS STATEMENT

Milkweed Editions saved the following resources by printing the pages of this book on chlorine free paper made with 100% post-consumer waste.

TREES	WATER	SOLID WASTE	GREENHOUSE GASES
54	24,701	1,500	5,129
FULLY GROWN	GALLONS	POUNDS	POUNDS

Calculations based on research by Environmental Defense and the Paper Task Force.
Manufactured at Friesens Corporation